MORE PRAISE FOR HERE AND GONE

"**A gripping slice of dusty desert dread that plays brilliantly on every parent's nightmare.** A first-class thriller."

> —JOHN CONNOLLY, #1 internationally bestselling author of the Charlie Parker thrillers

"**Holy hell. Talk about a rip-roaring page-turner.** Readers, I dare you to try'n put this book down once you hit that twist at the end of Chapter 5. Once I reached that epinephrine shot, the rest of my night was *Here and Gone*."

> —GREGG HURWITZ, *New York Times* bestselling author of *You're Next* and *Orphan X*

"***Here and Gone* is a pretty fair description of what happens to the real world when you pick up this book, it's that good.** It doesn't put a foot wrong and, like a classic song, manages to progress at the perfect pace and also in a way that manages to be both surprising and inevitable. Not a word is wasted and it plays on the page like a great movie. **I read it in the first week of January and knew immediately that it was already one of my thrillers of the year. Hell, it might just be one of my thrillers of any year. Buy it. Read it. Just don't make any plans before you open that first page.**"

> —SIMON TOYNE, bestselling author of the Sanctus trilogy

"A nerve-shreddingly tense thriller that had me biting my nails and yelling at the bad guys. **One of the most gripping novels I've ever read.**"

> —MARK EDWARDS, author of *The Magpies*

HERE
AND GONE

HERE
AND GONE

A NOVEL

HAYLEN BECK

CROWN
NEW YORK

Copyright © 2017 by Haylen Beck

Published in the United States by Crown, an imprint of the Crown Publishing Group, a division of Penguin Random House LLC, New York.
crownpublishing.com

CROWN is a registered trademark and the Crown colophon is a trademark of Penguin Random House LLC.

Originally published in the UK by Harvill Secker, an imprint of the Random House Group Limited, London.

Library of Congress Cataloging-in-Publication data is available upon request.

ISBN 978-0-451-49957-8
Ebook ISBN 978-0-451-49959-2

Printed in the United States of America

Book design by Lauren Dong
Title page photograph: MCCAIG/iStock
Jacket design by Ervin Serrano
Jacket photograph: Lost Highway/Moment/Getty Images

10 9 8 7 6 5 4 3 2 1

First American Edition

For my children

HERE
AND GONE

CHAPTER 1

THE ROAD SWAYED LEFT THEN RIGHT, THE RHYTHM OF IT MAK-
ing Audra Kinney's eyelids grow heavier as each mile marker
passed. She had given up counting them; it only made the journey slower. Her knuckles complained as she flexed her fingers on the
wheel, palms greasy with sweat.

Thank God she'd had the eight-year-old station wagon's AC ser-
viced earlier in the year. New York summers might be hot, but not
like this. Not like Arizona-hot. It's a dry heat, people said. Yeah, dry
like the face of the sun, she thought. Even at five-thirty in the evening, even as the vents blew air cold enough to make goose pimples
on her forearms, if she put her fingers to the window, her hand would
recoil as if from a boiling kettle.

"Mom, I'm hungry," Sean said from the backseat. That mewl-
ing voice that said he was tired and grumpy and liable to get difficult. Louise dozed beside him in her booster chair, her mouth open,
blonde sweat-damp hair stuck to her forehead. She held Gogo in her
lap, the ragged remains of the stuffed bunny she'd had since she was
a baby.

Sean was a good boy. Everyone who knew him said so. But it had
never been so clear as these last few days. So much had been asked
of him, and he had endured. She looked at him in the mirror. His father's sharp features and fair hair, but his mother's long limbs. They
had lengthened in recent months, reminding her that her son, now almost eleven, was approaching puberty. He had complained little since
they left New York, considering, and he had been a help with his little
sister. If not for him, Audra might have lost her sanity out here.

Lost her sanity?

There was nothing sane about this.

"There's a town a few miles up ahead," Audra said. "We can get something to eat. Maybe they'll have a place we can stay."

"I hope they do," Sean said. "I don't want to sleep in the car again."

"Me neither."

As if on cue, that pain between her shoulder blades, like the muscles back there coming unstitched. Like she was coming apart, and the stuffing would soon billow out of her seams.

"How you doing for water back there?" she asked, looking at him in the rearview mirror. She saw him glance down, heard water slosh in a plastic bottle.

"I got a little left. Louise drank hers already."

"All right. We'll get some more when we stop."

Sean returned his attention to the world passing his window. Rocky hills covered in scrub sloping away from the road, cacti standing sentry, arms reaching skyward like surrendering soldiers. Above them, a sheet of deep blue, faint smears of white, a yellowing as the sun traveled west to the horizon. Beautiful country, in its way. Audra would have drunk it in, savored the landscape, had things been different.

If she hadn't had to run.

But she didn't really have to run, not truly. She could have waited to let events take their course, but the waiting had been torture, the seconds upon minutes upon hours of just not knowing. So she had packed everything and run. Like a coward, Patrick would say. He'd always said she was weak. Even if he said he loved her with his next breath.

Audra remembered a moment, in their bed, her husband's chest against her back, his hand cupping her breast. Patrick saying he loved her. In spite of everything, he loved her. As if she didn't deserve his love, not a woman like her. His tongue always the gentle blade with which to stab at her, so gentle she wouldn't know she'd been cut until long after, when she would lie awake with his words still rolling in her mind. Rolling like stones in a glass jar, rattling like—

"Mom!"

Her head jerked up and she saw the truck coming at them, lights flashing. She pulled the wheel to the right, back onto her own side of the road, and the truck passed, the driver giving her a dirty look. Audra shook her head, blinked away the grimy dryness from her eyes, breathed in hard through her nose.

Not that close. But still too close. She cursed under her breath.

"You all right?" she asked.

"Yeah," Sean said, his voice coming from deep in his throat, the way it did when he didn't want her to know he was scared. "Maybe we should pull over soon."

Louise spoke now, her words thick with sleep. "What happened?"

"Nothing," Sean said. "Go back to sleep."

"But I'm not sleepy," she said. Then she gave a cough, a rattle beneath it. She'd been doing that since early this morning, the cough becoming more persistent through the day.

Audra watched her daughter in the mirror. Louise getting sick was the last thing she needed. She'd always been more prone to ill-ness than her brother, was small for her age, and skinny. She hugged Gogo, her head rocked back, and her eyes closed again.

The car rose onto an expanse of flat land, desert stretching out all around, mountains to the north. Were they the San Francisco Peaks? Or the Superstitions? Audra didn't know, she'd have to check a map to remind herself of the geography. It didn't matter. All that mattered right this second was the small general store off the road up ahead.

"Mom, look."

"Yeah, I see it."

"Can we pull in?"

"Yeah."

Maybe they'd have coffee. One good strong cup would get her through the next few miles. Audra turned the blinker on to signal a right turn, eased onto the side road, then left across a cattle grid and onto the sandy expanse of forecourt. The sign above the store read GROCERIES AND ENGRAVING, red block lettering on a white board. The low building was constructed of wood, a porch with benches running along its length, the windows dark, points of artificial light barely visible beyond the dusty glass.

Too late, she realized the only car parked in front was a police cruiser. State highway patrol or county sheriff, she couldn't tell from here.

"Shit," she said.

"You said a curse, Mom."

"I know. Sorry."

Audra slowed the station wagon, its tires crunching grit and stones. Should she turn around, get back on the road? No. The sheriff or patrolman or whoever sat in that car, he'd have noticed her by now. Turning around would arouse suspicion. The cop would start paying attention.

She pulled the car up in front of the store, as far away from the cruiser as she could manage without looking like she was keeping her distance. The engine rattled as it died, and she pressed the key to her lips as she thought. Get out, get what you need. Nothing wrong with that. I'm just someone who needed a coffee, maybe a couple of sodas, some potato chips.

For the last few days Audra had been aware of every law-enforcement vehicle she saw. Would they be looking for her? Common sense told her no, they almost certainly weren't. It wasn't like she was a fugitive, was it? But still, that small and terrified part of her brain wouldn't let go of the fear, wouldn't quit telling her they were watching, searching for her. Hunting her, even.

But if they were looking for anyone, it'd be the kids.

"Wait here with Louise," she said.

"But I want to come too," Sean said.

"I need you to look after your sister. Don't argue."

"Aw, man."

"Good boy."

She lifted her purse from the passenger seat, her sunglasses from the cup holder. Heat screamed in as she opened the driver's door. She climbed out as quickly as she could, closed the door to keep the cool air in, the hot air out. Her cheeks and forearms took the force of the sun, her pale freckled skin unaccustomed to the sheer ferocity of it. She had used the little sunscreen she had for the kids; she would take the burn and save the money.

Audra allowed herself a brief study of the cruiser as she slipped on her shades: one person in the driver's seat, male or female, she couldn't tell. The insignia read: ELDER COUNTY SHERIFF'S DEPARTMENT. She turned in a circle, stretched her limbs as she did so, saw the hills that climbed above and behind the store, the quiet road, the tumbling rolls of desert scrub on the other side. As she completed the circle, she took one more look at the sheriff's car. The driver took a drink of something, appeared to be paying her no attention.

She stepped onto the concrete porch, walked toward the door, felt the wash of cool air as she opened it. Despite the chill, stale odors rode the current out into the heat. Inside, the dimness forced her to lift her shades onto her forehead, though she would rather have kept them on. Better to risk being remembered for buying water than for tripping over boxes, she thought.

An elderly lady with dyed black hair sat behind the counter at the far end of the store, a pen in one hand, a puzzle book in the other. She did not look up from it to acknowledge the customer's presence, which suited Audra well enough.

A cooler full of water and soda hummed against the wall. Audra took three bottles of water and a Coke.

"Excuse me," she called to the elderly woman.

Without lifting her head, the woman said, "Mm-hm?"

"You got a coffee machine?"

"No, ma'am." The woman pointed her pen to the west. "Silver Water, about five miles that way, they got a diner. Their coffee's pretty good."

Audra approached the counter. "Okay. Just these, then."

As she placed the four plastic bottles on the counter, Audra noticed the glass cabinet mounted on the wall. A dozen pistols of different shapes and sizes, revolvers, semi-automatics, at least as far as she could tell. She'd lived on the East Coast all her life, and even knowing Arizona was gun country, she still found the sight of the weapons startling. A soda and a gun, please, she thought, and the idea almost made her laugh out loud.

The woman rang up the drinks, and Audra dug inside her purse, fearing for a moment that she had run out of cash. There, she found a ten folded inside a drugstore receipt, and handed it over, waited for her change.

"Thank you," she said, lifting the bottles.

"Mm-hm."

The woman had hardly glanced at her through the whole exchange, and Audra was glad of it. Maybe she would remember a tall auburn-haired lady, if anyone asked. Maybe she wouldn't. Audra went to the door and out into the wall of heat. Sean watched her from the back of the station wagon, Louise still dozing beside him. She turned her head toward the cruiser.

It had gone.

A dark stain on the ground where the cop had poured his drink out, the ghosts of tires on the grit. She shaded her eyes with her hand, looked around, saw no sign of the car. The relief that followed shocked her; she hadn't realized how nervous the cruiser's presence had made her.

No matter. Get on the road, get to the town the woman mentioned, find somewhere to rest for the night.

Audra went to the rear car door, Louise's side, and opened it. She crouched down, handed a bottle of water over to Sean, then gave her daughter a gentle shake. Louise groaned and kicked her legs.

"Wake up, sweetie."

Louise rubbed her eyes, blinked at her mother. "What?"

Audra unscrewed the cap, held the bottle to Louise's lips.

"Don't wanna," Louise said, her voice a croaking whine.

Audra pressed the bottle to Louise's mouth. "Don't wanna, but you're gonna."

She tipped the bottle, and water trickled between Louise's lips. Louise let go of Gogo, took the bottle from Audra's hand, and swallowed in a series of gulps.

"See?" Audra said. She looked over to Sean. "You drink up too."

Sean did as he was told, and Audra got into the driver's seat. She reversed away from the store, turned, and drove back to the cattle grid and the road beyond. No traffic, she didn't have to wait at the intersection. The car's engine rumbled as the convenience store shrank in the rearview mirror.

The children remained quiet, only the sound of swallowing and satisfied exhalations. Audra held the bottle of Coke between her thighs as she unscrewed the cap, then she took a long swallow, the cold fizz burning her tongue and throat. Sean and Louise guffawed when she burped, and she turned to grin at them.

"Good one, Mom," Sean said.

"Yeah, that was a good one," Louise said.

"I aims to please," Audra said, looking back to the road ahead.

No sign yet of the town. Five miles, the woman had said, and Audra had counted two markers, so awhile to go still. But not far. Audra imagined a motel, a nice clean one, with a shower—oh God, a shower—or, even better, a bath. She indulged in a fantasy of a motel room with cable, where she could let the kids watch cartoons while she wallowed in a tub full of warm water and bubbles, letting the grime and the sweat and the weight of it all just wash away.

Another mile marker, and she said, "Not far now, maybe another two miles, all right?"

"Good," Sean said.

Louise's hands shot up and she let out a quiet, "Yay."

Audra smiled once more, already feeling the water on her skin.

Then her gaze passed the mirror, and she saw the sheriff's cruiser following behind.

CHAPTER 2

A SENSATION LIKE COLD HANDS GRIPPING HER SHOULDERS, her heart knocking hard.

"Don't panic," she said.

Sean leaned forward. "What?"

"Nothing. Sit back, make sure your seat belt's done up right."

Don't panic. He might not be following you. Just watch your speed. Don't give him a reason to stop you. Audra alternated her attention between the speedometer and the road ahead, the needle hovering around fifty-five as she drove through another series of bends.

The cruiser maintained its distance, maybe fifty yards, neither gaining nor falling back. It lingered there, following. Yes, it was definitely following. Audra swallowed, shifted her hands on the wheel, fresh sweat prickling on her back.

Take it easy, she told herself. Don't panic. They're not looking for you.

The road straightened once more, passed beneath rows of cables strung between the pylons on either side. The surface seemed to grow rougher as she traveled, her station wagon juddering. The mountains on the horizon again. She focused on them, a point on which to concentrate her mind.

Ignore the cop. Just look ahead.

But the cruiser swelled in the mirror, the sheriff's car drawing close. She could see the driver now, a broad head, broader shoulders, thick fingers on the wheel.

He wants to pass, she thought. Go ahead and pass.

But he didn't pass.

Another mile marker, and a sign that said: SILVER WATER NEXT RIGHT.

"I'll turn off," Audra said. "I'll turn off and he'll keep going."

Sean said, "What?"

"Nothing. Drink your water."

Up ahead, the turn.

She reached for the stalk to signal, but before her fingers could touch it, she heard a single electronic WHOOP! In the mirror she saw the flickering lights, blue and red.

"No," Audra said.

Sean craned his neck to see out the back window. "Mom, that's the police."

"Yeah," Audra said.

"Are they pulling us over?"

"I think so."

Another WHOOP! and the cruiser pulled out and accelerated until it was level with the station wagon. The passenger window rolled down, and the driver pointed to the roadside.

Audra nodded, signaled, and pulled onto the verge, kicking up dirt and debris. The cruiser slowed and pulled in behind her. Both cars halted, shrouded in dust so that Audra could barely see the other, apart from its lights still spinning and flashing.

Louise stirred again. "What's happening?"

"The police pulled us over," Sean said.

"Are we in trouble?" she asked.

"No," Audra said, with too much force to be convincing. "Nobody's in trouble. I'm sure it's nothing. Just sit tight, let Mommy handle it."

She watched the mirror as the dust cleared. The cruiser's door opened, and the cop climbed out. He paused there, adjusted his belt, the pistol grip jutting from its holster, then reached back into the car for his hat. A middle-aged man, maybe fifty, fifty-five. Dark hair turning salt-and-pepper. Solid build, but not fat, thick forearms. The sort of man who might have played football in his younger days. His eyes hidden behind mirror shades, he lowered the wide-brimmed hat onto his head, the same beige as his uniform. He put a hand to the butt of his pistol and approached the driver's side.

"Shit," Audra whispered. All the way from New York, sticking to county roads when she could, avoiding highways, and she had not been stopped once. So close to California, and now this. She gripped the wheel tight, to hide the shakes.

The cop paused at Louise's window, dipped his head to peer in at the children. Then he came to Audra's window, tapped it, moved his hand in a circular motion, telling her to wind it down. She reached for the button on the door, held it as the window whirred and groaned.

"Evening, ma'am," he said. "Do me a favor and shut the engine off, please."

Be casual, Audra thought as she turned the key in the ignition to the off position. Everything's going to be all right. Just stay calm.

"Evening," she said. "Is something the matter, Officer?"

The nametag above his badge read SHERIFF R. WHITESIDE.

"License and registration, please," he said, his eyes still hidden behind the shades.

"In the glove compartment," she said, pointing.

He nodded. She kept her hands slow as she reached across, popped the catch, a bundle of maps and litter threatening to spill into the footwell. A few moments digging and she had the documents. He studied them, his face expressionless, while she returned her hands to the wheel.

"Audra Kinney?"

"That's right," she said.

"Mrs., Miss, or Ms.?" he asked.

"Mrs., I guess."

"You guess?"

"I'm separated. Not divorced yet."

"I see," he said, handing the documents back. "You're a long way from home."

She took them, held them in her lap. "Road trip," she said. "We're going to visit friends in California."

"Uh-huh," he said. "Everything all right, Mrs. Kinney?"

"Yes, I'm fine."

He put his hand on the car roof, leaned down a little, spoke in a low drawl that came from far back in his throat. "Just you seem a little nervous there. Any particular reason for that?"

"No," she said, knowing the lie was clear on her face. "I just get nervous when I'm stopped by the police."

"Happen often, does it?"

"No. I just mean anytime I *have* been stopped, I get—"

"I expect you'll want to know why I pulled you over today."

"Yes, I mean, I don't think I—"

"The reason I pulled you over is the car's overloaded."

"Overloaded?"

"She's bearing down on the rear axle. Why don't you step on out and take a look?"

Before Audra could reply, the sheriff opened the door and stood back. She sat still, the documents still held in her lap, looking up at him.

"I asked you to step out of the vehicle, ma'am."

Audra set the license and registration on the passenger seat and unfastened her seat belt.

"Mom?"

She turned to Sean and said, "It's all right. I just need to speak with the officer. I'll be right here. Okay?"

Sean nodded, then turned his attention back to the sheriff. Audra climbed out, the sun fierce hot on her skin once more.

The sheriff pointed as he walked to the back of the car. "Look, see? You ain't got enough clearance between the tire and the top of the wheel arch."

He put his hands on the roof and pushed down, rocking the station wagon on its suspension. "Look at that. The roads around here aren't too good, no money to fix them. You hit a pothole too hard and you're in a world of trouble. I seen people lose control over something like this, they shred a tire, break the axle, or Lord knows what, and they wind up upside down in a ditch or hit an oncoming truck. It ain't pretty, let me tell you. I can't let you drive like that."

A shivery relief broke in Audra; this sheriff didn't know who she was, wasn't looking for her. But it was tempered by his insistence on stopping her. She needed to keep moving, but not at the risk of getting on the wrong side of this man.

"I've only got a little way to go," she said, pointing to the turn up ahead. "I'm heading to Silver Water for the night. I can get rid of some stuff there."

"Silver Water?" he asked. "You staying at Mrs. Gerber's guesthouse?"

"I hadn't decided yet."

The sheriff shook his head. "Either way, still more than a mile to Silver Water, narrow road, lot of switchbacks. A lot could happen between here and there. Tell you what . . . grab your keys and step back here, off the road."

"If I could just keep going a little further, I'll be—"

"Ma'am, I'm trying to be helpful here. Now just grab those keys like I asked you and come on back here."

Audra reached into the car, around the steering wheel, and took the keys from the ignition.

"Mom, what's happening?" Sean asked. "What does he want?"

"It's all right," Audra said. "We'll get it figured out in a minute. Just you stay put and keep an eye on your sister. Can you do that for me?"

Sean twined his fingers. "Yes, Mom."

"Good boy," she said, and gave him a wink.

She brought the keys back to the sheriff—Whiteside, wasn't it?—and handed them over.

"Step onto the shoulder for me," he said, pointing to the dirt at the side of the road. "Don't want you getting hit by something."

She did as she was told, Sean and Louise twisting in their seats to watch through the back window.

Whiteside reached for the trunk release. "Let's see what we got back here."

Was he allowed to do that? Just open her trunk and look inside? Audra put a hand over her mouth, kept her silence as he surveyed the packed boxes, bags of clothes, two baskets full of toys.

"Tell you what I can do for you," he said, standing back, hands on his hips. "I'll move some of this stuff over to my car, just to lighten the load, follow you into Silver Water—I'd say Mrs. Gerber will be glad of the custom—and then you can figure out what to do. You're going to have to leave some stuff behind, I'll tell you that right now. There's a Goodwill store, I'm sure they'll help you out. This here is about the poorest patch of land in the state, and the Goodwill store is about the only one left in business. Anyway, let's see what you got."

Whiteside leaned in and hauled a box to the lip of the trunk. Folded blankets and sheets on top. All bedding and towels underneath, Audra remembered. She had packed the kids' favorite covers and pillowcases: *Star Wars* for Sean, *Doc McStuffins* for Louise. She saw the bright pastel shades as the sheriff dug down into the box.

It crossed her mind then to ask why he was looking inside the box, and she opened her mouth to do so, but he spoke first.

"Ma'am, what's this?"

He stood upright, his left hand still inside the box, a stack of sheets and blankets held back. Audra stood still for a moment, her mind unable to connect his question to a logical answer.

"Blankets and stuff," she said.

He pointed inside the box with his right hand. "And this?"

Fear flicked on like a light. She thought she had been frightened before, but no, that had been simple worry. But this, now, was fear. Something was going terribly wrong here, and she could not grasp what it was.

"I don't know what you mean," she said, unable to keep a tremor from creeping into her voice.

"Maybe you should come take a look," he said.

Audra took slow steps toward him, her sneakers crunching on sand and grit. She leaned in, looked down into the dim innards of the box. A shape there that she couldn't quite make sense of.

"I don't know what that is," she said.

Whiteside slipped his right hand down inside, gripped whatever it was by its edge, and drew it out into the hard light.

"Care to take a guess?" he asked.

No question what it was. A good-sized baggie half full of dried green leaves.

She shook her head and said, "That's not mine."

"I'd say that looks a lot like marijuana. Wouldn't you?"

The cold fear in Audra's breast spread to her arms and thighs like ice water soaking through her clothes. Numb at the center of her. Yes, she knew what it was. But she hadn't used in years. She'd been completely straight for the last two. Not even a beer.

"It's not mine," she said.

"You sure about that?"

"Yes, I'm sure," she said, but a small part of her thought, there was a time, wasn't there? Could I have stashed it and forgotten it lay among the sheets? Couldn't have. Could I?

"Then you care to tell me how this wound up in the trunk of your car?"

"I don't know," she said, and she wondered, could it be? Could it?

No. Absolutely not. She hadn't smoked anything since before her marriage, and she had moved apartments three times. No way the bag could have followed her here, no matter how careless she was.

Heat in her eyes, tears threatening, her hands beginning to shake. But she had to keep control. For the kids, she thought. Don't let them see you lose it. She wiped a palm across her cheek, sniffed hard.

Whiteside held the bag up to the light, gave it a shake. "Well, we're going to have a talk about who owns this. I tell you, though, I think this is a touch more than could be considered for personal use. So it's going to be a long and serious talk."

Audra's knees weakened, and she put a hand on the lip of the trunk to steady herself.

"Sir, I swear to God, that's not mine and I don't know where it came from."

And that was the truth, wasn't it?

"Like I said, ma'am, we're going to have a talk about that." Whiteside set the baggie on top of the blankets and reached for the cuffs on his belt. "But right now, I'm placing you under arrest."

CHAPTER 3

"WHAT?"

Audra's legs threatened to give way. Had she not been leaning against the car, she would have collapsed to the ground.

"Mom?" Sean had undone his seat belt and was leaning over the backseat, his eyes wide. "Mom, what's happening?"

Louise stared back too, fear on her face. Tears made hot tracks down Audra's cheeks. She sniffed again and wiped them away.

"This can't be," she said.

Whiteside's features remained blank. "Ma'am, I need you to come with me to my car."

Audra shook her head. "But . . . but my children."

He stepped closer, lowered his voice. "For their sake, let's keep this civil, now. You just do like I say and this whole thing's going to go a lot easier for you and them. Now come on."

Whiteside reached for her arm and she allowed him to guide her away from the back of her station wagon to the front of his cruiser.

"Mom? Mom!"

"Tell him it's all right," Whiteside said.

Audra looked back to her car. "It's all right, Sean. Look after your sister. We'll get this straightened out in a few minutes."

They reached the cruiser, and he said, "Empty your pockets onto the hood there."

Audra dug into the pockets of her jeans, made a pile of tissues and loose change on the hood. Whiteside tossed the bag of marijuana on top.

"That's it? Now turn your pockets inside out."

She did so, and he turned her by the arm so she had her back to him.

"Hands behind your back."

Audra heard the snick-click of metal, felt his hard fingers on her wrist.

"You have the right to remain silent. Anything you say will be used against you in a court of law. You have the right to an attorney during interrogation; if you cannot afford an attorney, one will be appointed to you. Do you understand?"

As cool metal wrapped around each of her wrists, the back door of the station wagon opened. Sean spilled out, landed on his hands and knees on the dirt.

"Mom, what's happening?" he called as he scrambled to his feet.

From inside the car, Louise's frightened cries, rising.

"Everything's all right," Audra said, but Sean kept coming.

"Do you understand?" Whiteside asked again.

Sean, running now, said, "Hey, let my mom go."

"Sean, just get back—"

Whiteside jerked and twisted the cuffs, shooting pain into Audra's wrists and shoulders. She cried out, and Sean skidded to a halt.

"Do you understand your rights?" Whiteside asked once more, his mouth at her ear.

"Yes," she said, the word squeezed between her teeth, the steel biting into her skin.

"Then say it. Say, yes, I understand."

"Yes, I understand."

"Thank you." He turned to Sean. "Best get back in the car now, son. We'll get this all settled in a minute or two."

Sean raised himself to his full height, tall for his age, but he looked so tiny there on the side of the road.

"Let my mom go."

"I can't do that, son. Now go on back to the car." He jerked the cuffs again, spoke into her ear. "Tell him."

Audra hissed at the pain.

"Tell him, or this is going to get complicated."

"Sean, go back to the car," she said, fighting to keep the fear from her voice. "Listen, your sister's crying. You need to go and take care of her. Go on, be a good boy for me."

He pointed at Whiteside. "Don't you hurt her," he said, then he turned and walked back to the station wagon, glancing back over his shoulder as he went.

"Brave boy," Whiteside said. "Now, you got anything sharp on you? Anything that might cut me when I search you?"

Audra shook her head. "No, nothing. Wait, what, search me?"

"That's right," Whiteside said as he hunkered down behind her. He wrapped his big hands around her ankle and squeezed, moving the fabric of her jeans against his palms.

"You can't do that," she said. "Can you? A woman officer should do it."

"I can search you, and that's what I'm doing. You don't get special treatment just for being a woman. Was a time I could have called on the Silver Water PD for a female officer, just as a courtesy to you, not because I'm obliged to—I'm not—but not anymore. Mayor closed the PD three years ago. Town couldn't afford it anymore."

His hands worked their way up her calf and thigh, squeezing, exploring. Then he pressed the back of one hand up between her thighs, into her crotch, only for a moment, but enough to close her eyes and sour her stomach. Then across her buttocks, into the hip pockets, and down the other leg, before his forefingers probed down into her sneakers. Then he stood, hands brushing down her sweat-soaked back, around the front, across her stomach, skimming the outline of her breasts, up to her shoulders, down her arms.

It wasn't until he was done that Audra realized she had been holding her breath. Now she released it in one long, quivering exhalation.

Then she heard the crying coming from her car, higher and higher, nearing hysterical. "My children," she said.

"Don't worry about them," Whiteside said, and he guided her to the back of his cruiser. He opened the passenger-side door. "Watch your head."

He placed a hand on top of her scalp, pressed down, guided her inside.

"Feet," he said.

Audra wondered what he meant for a moment before she understood, then she lifted her feet into the cruiser. He slammed the door shut, and the world seemed suddenly hushed.

"Oh God," she said, and she could hold back the tears no longer. "Oh God."

Panic rattled inside her mind, inside her chest, promising to drive out all reason if she did not get it under control. She forced herself to breathe in deep through her nose, hold it, breathe out through her mouth, the tip of her tongue pressed to the back of her teeth. The relaxation exercise she'd learned when she was getting clean. Focus on the now, find something with your eyes, concentrate on that until the world levels off.

Through the cage that separated the cruiser's backseat from the front, she saw a two-inch tear in the seam of the leather-upholstered headrest. She stared at that, breathing, in, hold, out, in, hold, out.

In her peripheral vision, she saw Whiteside move to the back of the cruiser, then heard the trunk open and close again. He went to the front, lifted the baggie full of marijuana from the hood, dropped it into a brown envelope, did the same with the scraps of tissue and change she'd taken from her pockets. She returned her gaze to the tear in the headrest, refocused on her breathing. The passenger door opened, and Whiteside tossed the two envelopes onto the seat before bending down to peer in at her.

"You got family nearby?"

"No," Audra said.

"Anyone can come pick up the kids for you?"

"I have a friend," she said. "In California. San Diego."

"Well, that don't help us much right now, does it? What about their father? Where's he at?"

"New York. We're not together anymore."

Whiteside exhaled through pursed lips, disappeared in thought for a few moments, and then nodded, a decision made. He reached for the radio handset on the dashboard.

"Collins, you out there?" He remained still for a moment, his head cocked, listening. "Collins, where are you?"

A crackle, then a woman's voice. "I'm out on the Gisela Road, sir. What do you need?"

"I'm on the County Road, right by the Silver Water turnoff," he said. "I just made an arrest for possession. I got two kids in the suspect's car, so I'm going to need you to take care of them, all right? And see if you can get hold of Emmet. I need a tow out here."

Silence for a few seconds before Whiteside spoke again.

"Collins?"

"Yeah."

"You think you can get hold of Emmet for me?"

Another pause, and Whiteside moistened his lips.

"Collins? Yes or no?"

"Will do," the woman said. "Give me five, ten minutes."

Whiteside thanked her and put the handset back into its cradle. He looked back to Audra and said, "All right. Now we just sit tight and wait awhile."

Through the open door, Audra heard Louise's wailing, cutting through the simmering panic in her mind.

"Listen," she said. "My children are crying. I can't leave them there."

He sighed, then said, "All right. I'll go see to them."

"Wait, can I—"

The door slammed closed, rocking the car on its suspension. As she watched him stroll toward her station wagon, Audra said a silent prayer.

CHAPTER 4

SEAN WATCHED THROUGH THE OPEN TRUNK HATCH AS THE BIG man approached. Louise squealed, clutching Gogo tight. The bundle of stuffing and pink rag that had once been a rabbit still had two eyes, but barely.

"Shut up," Sean said. "Mom said everything's going to be all right. So just be quiet, okay?"

No good. She kept crying, even louder when the big policeman slammed the trunk closed. He came around to Sean's door and opened it, hunkered down there so he was eye level with both of them.

"You kids doing all right here?"

"What's happening?" Sean asked.

The policeman wiped a hand across his mouth. "Well, I can't lie to you, son. Your mom's in a little bit of trouble."

"But she didn't do anything."

Sheriff Whiteside—Sean read his nametag—took off his mirrored sunglasses, showing his gray eyes. And something there frightened Sean to the very core of him, scared him so bad it made his bladder ache and itch for release.

"Well, see, that's the thing," Whiteside said. "She had something in the trunk there that she shouldn't have. Something illegal. Now I have to take her into town, so we can have a talk about it. But I promise you, everything's going to be all right."

"What did she have?" Sean asked.

The sheriff gave a weak smile. "Something she shouldn't. That's all. Everything's going to be all right."

Now Whiteside let his gaze travel around the car, crawling over

Sean and Louise, and Sean could almost feel the eyes on him, picking over his skin. The sheriff raised himself a little so he could get a better look at Louise, studied the length of her from her head all the way down her body, her legs, to her feet. He nodded, and his tongue appeared between his lips, wet them, and retreated.

"Everything's going to be all right," he said again. "Now here's what's going to happen. Like I said, I need to take your mom into town and have a talk with her, but I can't leave you out here all alone. So my colleague, Deputy Collins, is going to come out here and take you somewhere safe to look after you."

Louise gave a high whine. "Are we going to jail?"

Whiteside smiled, but the look that frightened Sean lingered in his eyes. "No, sweetheart. You're not going to jail. Deputy Collins is going to take you to a safe place."

"Where?" Sean asked.

"A safe place. You don't need to worry about it. Everything's going to be all right."

"Can I take Gogo?" Louise asked.

"Sure you can, sweetheart. Deputy Collins will be here in just a minute, and everything will be all right."

"You keep saying that."

Whiteside looked at Sean, his smile fading. "What?"

Then Sean realized what bothered him about the sheriff's eyes.

"You keep saying everything's going to be all right. But you look scared."

Whiteside blinked, and his smile hardened. "I'm not scared, son. I just want both of you to know you're safe. Deputy Collins is going to take good care of you. Your mom and me, we'll have this figured out in no time, and you can all go home. Hey, you didn't tell me your names."

Sean closed his mouth.

Whiteside looked to Louise, whose wailing had subsided to hitches and sniffles. "What's your name, sweetheart?"

"Louise."

"And what's your brother's name?"

"Sean."

"Good names," Whiteside said, smiling big enough to show his teeth. "Where you from?"

"New York," Louise said.

"New York," he echoed. "That right? Well, you're a long way from home."

"We're moving to California," Louise said.

"Shut up," Sean said. "We don't have to tell him anything."

Whiteside gave a single laugh. "The young lady can talk to me if she wants to."

Sean turned to him, gave him a hard stare. "I saw it on TV. We don't have to tell you anything at all."

The sheriff turned back to Louise. "Your big brother's a smart boy. I think he's going to be a lawyer some day, what do you think?"

Louise hugged Gogo tight. "Don't know."

"Well, we're just talking, passing the time, right? Like people do. And I just wanted to make sure you kids were all right. You both got water there?"

Louise lifted her bottle, showed him. Sean stared straight ahead.

"Well, drink up. It's hot out here. Don't want you getting dehydrated."

Louise took a long swallow. Sean did not.

A rumble from somewhere outside, and the sheriff looked along the road.

"Here she comes," he said, standing upright.

Sean peered around the front seat's headrest, through the windshield. Another cruiser approached, slowed, and turned. It reversed along the shoulder until its rear fender was a few feet from the station wagon's front. A younger woman in a uniform like Whiteside's climbed out. She had blonde hair pinned back, a firm jaw like a boy's, narrow at the hips.

Deputy Collins passed across the front of the car, joined Whiteside by the door.

"This is Sean and Louise," he said. "They're a little upset, but I told them you'd take good care of them. Isn't that right?"

"That's right," she said as she crouched down. "Hi, Sean. Hi, Louise. I'm Deputy Collins, and I'm going to look after you. Just for a little while until we get all this settled. Don't worry. Everything's going to be all right."

Sean felt a cold finger on his heart when he saw her blue eyes; despite her smile and her soft voice, she looked even more scared than the sheriff.

"Now you guys come on with me."

"Where are you taking us?" Sean asked.

"Somewhere safe," Collins said.

"But where?"

"Somewhere safe. Maybe you could help Louise with her seat belt."

Sean went to answer, to tell her no, they weren't going anywhere, but Louise said, "I can do it myself. The man said I could take Gogo."

"Sure you can," Collins said.

Before Sean could stop her, Louise was out of her booster seat, clambering across him, taking Collins' hand. As the deputy helped her down, Sean stayed put.

Collins reached her free hand out to him. "Come on."

Sean crossed his arms. "I don't think I should."

"Sean, you don't have a choice," she said. "You have to come with me."

"No."

Whiteside bent down, spoke in a low voice. "Son, like the deputy told you, you don't have a choice in this. If I have to, I'll put you under arrest, put handcuffs on you, and carry you to the deputy's car. Or you can just get on out and walk to it. What's it going to be?"

"You can't arrest me," Sean said.

The sheriff leaned in close, the fear in his eyes edging into anger. "You absolutely sure of that, son?"

Sean swallowed and said, "Okay."

He climbed out, and Whiteside put a heavy hand on his shoulder, guided him toward the cruiser, Collins holding Louise's hand as she led the way. Collins opened the rear door of her car and helped Louise inside.

"Scoot on over, honey," Collins said. She held a hand out for Sean. Sean turned to look back at the sheriff's car, tried to see his mother through the windshield. All he could make out was a vague shape that might or might not have been her. Whiteside's thick fingers tightened on his shoulder, kept him moving toward Collins.

"In you go," Collins said, a hand under his arm, maneuvering him into the car. "Do me a favor and help put your sister's seat belt on, all right?"

Sean paused when he saw the car's rear seat covered in a sheet of clear plastic, taped in place, covering the bench, the seatback, the footwells, the headrests. Collins put a hand to the small of his back, pushed him fully inside.

The door closed behind him, and he peered out through the dusty glass as the two police officers talked, their heads close together. Collins nodded at whatever Whiteside told her, then the sheriff turned and walked back toward his own vehicle. Collins stood still for a time, a hand over her mouth, staring at nothing. Sean had a moment to wonder what thoughts held her there, before she walked around the car, opened the driver's door, and lowered herself inside.

As she turned the key in the ignition, she looked back at Sean and said, "I asked you to help your sister with her seat belt. Can you do that for me?"

Without taking his eyes off Collins, Sean pulled the belt across Louise, fastened it, then did his own.

"Thank you," the deputy said.

Collins put the car in drive and pulled out from the shoulder, accelerating away from the station wagon in which they had traveled across the country. The turn for Silver Water came closer, and Sean waited for her to brake and turn the wheel.

She did not. Instead, she picked up more speed as she passed the exit. Sean turned his head, watched the sign and the turn fall away behind them. The terror that had been squirming in his belly since the sheriff pulled them over now climbed up into his chest and into his throat. The tears came, hot and shocking, spilling from his cheeks onto his T-shirt. He tried to hold them back, but couldn't. Nor could he keep the whine trapped in his mouth.

Collins glanced back at him. "Don't worry," she said. "Everything's going to be all right."

Somehow, the fact that she saw him cry like a baby made it worse, piling shame on top of the fear, and he cried all the harder. He cried for his mom and for home and the time they had together before they had to leave.

Louise reached across the seat, her small hand taking his. "Don't cry," she said. "Everything's going to be all right. They told us."

But Sean knew they lied.

CHAPTER 5

AUDRA SAW THE OTHER CRUISER PULL AWAY, BLURRED BY HER tears. She had watched her children being taken from the station wagon and brought to the deputy's car, saw Sean's glances back at her, wept when they disappeared from view. Now Sheriff Whiteside ambled back, his shades on, thumbs hooked into his belt, like there wasn't a thing wrong with the world. As if her children hadn't just been driven away by a stranger.

A stranger, maybe, but a policewoman. Whatever trouble Audra might be in, the policewoman would take care of the kids. They would be safe.

"They'll be safe," Audra said aloud, her voice ringing hollow in the car. She closed her eyes and said it again, like a wish she desperately wanted to come true.

Whiteside opened the driver's door and lowered himself in, his weight rocking the car. He closed the door, slipped his key into the ignition, and started the engine. The fans whooshed into life, pushing warm air around the interior.

She saw the reflection of his sunglasses in the rearview mirror, and she knew he was watching her, like a bee trapped in a jar. She sniffed hard, swallowed, blinked the tears away.

"Tow won't be long," he said. "Then we'll be on our way."

"That policewoman—"

"Deputy Collins," he said.

"The deputy, where is she taking my children?"

"To a safe place."

Audra leaned forward. "Where?"

"A safe place," he said. "You got other things to worry about right now."

She inhaled, exhaled, felt hysteria rise, held it back. "I want to know where my children are," she said.

Whiteside sat still and silent for a few seconds before he said, "Best be quiet now."

"Please, just tell—"

He removed his sunglasses, turned in his seat to face her. "I said, be quiet."

Audra knew that look, and it chilled her heart. That melding of hate and anger in his eyes. The same look her father had worn when he'd had a bellyful of liquor and needed to hurt someone, usually her or her little brother.

"I'm sorry," she said in a voice so low it wasn't even a whisper.

Like a little girl of eight again, hoping "sorry" would keep her father's belt around his waist, not swinging from his fist. She couldn't hold his stare, dropped her gaze to her lap.

"All right, then," he said, and he turned back to the desert beyond his windshield.

Quiet now, just the rumble of the idling engine, and Audra was swamped with a feeling of unreality, as if all of this was a fever dream, that she was a witness to someone else's nightmare.

But really, hadn't the last eighteen months been like that?

Since she had fled from Patrick, taking Sean and Louise with her, it had been day after week after month of worry. The specter of her husband always looming beyond her vision; the knowledge of him, of what he wanted to take from her, hanging like a constant veil across her mind.

As soon as Patrick knew he had lost her, that she would no longer subject herself to him, he had been circling, seeking the one thing he knew could destroy her. He didn't love their children, just like he had never loved Audra. They were possessions to him, like a car, or a good watch. A symbol to everyone around him, saying, look at me, I am succeeding, I am living a life like real people do. Audra had realized too late that she and the children were simply pieces of the façade he had built around himself to create the illusion of a decent man.

When she had finally broken free, the embarrassment caused a rage in him that had not faded since. And he had so many dirty strings to pull. The alcohol, the prescription drugs, the cocaine, all of it. Even though he had nurtured those weaknesses in her as ways to keep her tame—an enabler, the counselor had called him—he now used those as weapons to pry her children away. He had shown the proof to the lawyers, to the judge, and then Children's Services had come calling, interviewed her in the small Brooklyn apartment she had moved to. Such spiteful, hurtful questions.

The last interview had broken her. The concerned man and woman, their kind voices, asking was it true what they'd been told, and wouldn't the children be better off with their father, even for a few weeks until she got herself straight?

"I am straight," she had said. "I've been straight for nearly two years."

And it was the truth. She wouldn't have had the strength to leave her husband, taking the children, if she hadn't got herself clean first. The eighteen months since then had been a struggle, certainly, but she hadn't once fallen back into the habits that almost killed her. She had made a life for herself and the kids, got a steady waitressing job in a coffee shop. It didn't pay much, but she had a little money put away that she'd taken from her and Patrick's joint account before she left. She had even started painting again.

But the concerned man and woman hadn't seemed to care about any of that. They had looked at each other, pity on their faces, and Audra had asked them to please leave.

And the man and woman had said, "We'd rather it didn't have to go to court. It's always better to settle things between the parents."

So Audra had screamed at them to get the hell out of her home and never come back.

She spent the rest of the day in a state of frenzied agitation, shaking, craving something, anything to smooth the edges of her fear. In the end she called Mel, the only friend she'd kept since college, and Mel had said, come out, come to San Diego, just for a few days, we've got room.

Audra began packing the moment she hung up the phone. It started as just enough clothes for her and the kids to last the few days, then she wondered about toys, and if they would want their favorite bedding, so the bags became boxes, and she knew she couldn't fly, it would have to be the aging station wagon she had bought last year, and then it wasn't going to be a few days, it was going to be forever.

She didn't stop to think about what she was doing until she was halfway across New Jersey. Four days ago, morning, she had pulled onto the shoulder of the highway, beset by a panic that seemed to explode from somewhere inside her. While Sean asked over and over why she had stopped, Audra sat there, hands on the wheel, chest heaving as she fought for breath.

It was Sean who calmed her down. He undid his seat belt, climbed through into the passenger seat, and held her hand while he talked to her in a warm and smooth voice. Within a few minutes, she had gotten herself under control, and Sean sat with her as they figured out what to do, where they were going, and how they were going to get there.

Smaller roads, she had decided. She didn't know what would happen when Children's Services realized she had gone and taken the kids with her, but it was possible they would alert the police and they would be looking for her and the station wagon. So it had been narrow twisting paths to here, countless small towns along the way. And no trouble with the police. Until now.

"Here we go," Whiteside said, pulling Audra from her thoughts.

Up ahead, a tow truck exited the Silver Water Road and steered toward them. It slowed a few yards away, and the driver set about turning it until its bed faced Audra's car, a warning beep as it reversed. The driver, a scrawny man in stained blue overalls, jumped down from the cab. Whiteside climbed out of the cruiser and met him at the rear of the truck.

Audra watched as the two men spoke, the driver holding out a docket book for Whiteside to sign, before tearing off the top copy and handing it over. Then the driver took a good long look back at her, and she felt like an ape in a zoo exhibit, an irrational anger at his intrusion making her want to spit at him.

As the driver went about his work, attaching a winch line to the front of her car, Whiteside came back to the cruiser. He didn't speak as he lowered himself inside and put the car in drive. He waved to the tow-truck driver as he passed. The driver took the opportunity to have another look at Audra, and his attention made her turn her face away.

Whiteside took the turn onto the Silver Water exit fast, and Audra had to plant her feet wide apart on the floor to keep from tipping over. The road twisted as it climbed through the hills and soon her thighs ached with the effort of staying upright. The shallow incline seemed to rise for an age, slopes of brown on either side spotted by the green of the prickly pears and the coarse bushes.

The sheriff remained silent as he drove, occasionally glancing back at her in the mirror, his eyes hidden by the shades once more. Every time he looked she opened her mouth to speak, to ask again for her children, but each time he looked away before she found her voice.

They'll be all right, she told herself over and over. The deputy has them. Whatever happens to me, they'll be fine. This is all a terrible mistake, and once it's settled, we'll be on the road again.

Unless, of course, they discovered she had run from Children's Services. Then surely they would send her and the kids back to New York to face the consequences. If that was the worst of all things, then okay. At least Sean and Louise would be safe until Mel could come get them.

Oh God, Mel. Audra had called her from the road, said they were on their way, and Mel had answered with silence. And Audra knew that the offer to have her as a guest in San Diego had been made in kindness, but without expectation of it being accepted. So be it. If Mel didn't want them, Audra had enough money left to pay for a week in a cheap hotel. She would figure something out.

One last sweeping bend as the car crested the rise, and a deep basin came into view, a flat bed of land like the bottom of a pan. At its center, a sprawl of buildings. Orange and red scarred the foothills on the far side, unnatural shapes dug out of the landscape below the mountains. Whiteside steered the car down the series of switchbacks, and Audra leaned against the door to keep from being thrown onto her side. Through the window, she saw the first dwellings, prefab shacks and double-wides, among the twisted scrawny trees below. Chain-link fences around the properties. Some had satellite dishes on the roofs. Pickup trucks parked next to a few, others with tires propped against the walls, car parts piled up in the yards.

The sun-bleached asphalt turned to compacted dirt as the road straightened, and the car juddered and rattled. Now they passed the houses Audra had seen from the hillside, and the disrepair became clearer. Some of the owners had done their best to cheer the buildings with bright paint and wind chimes, particularly those with For Sale signs staked in the yards, but she could sense the desperation through the glass.

She knew poor when she saw it because she was only a generation removed herself. Her mother's parents hadn't lived in the desert glare, rather the gray skies of rural Pennsylvania, but their dying steel town had the same ragged edges. On the occasions they traveled there from New York, she had played on a rusted swing set in the garden as her mother visited with them, her grandfather years out of work, their last days looming bleak before them.

Audra wondered why this place got the name Silver Water. Must be a river or a lake nearby, she thought. Communities in a desert must have gathered around a source of water. And what kept them here? Who would choose to make their lives in such a hard place where the sun could strip the skin from your back?

The houses on either side of the road grew more concentrated, but still hardly enough to make a street. Among the prefabs, a few more permanent dwellings made of wood, the paint blistering and peeling on the walls. An elderly man in shorts and a vest paused from checking his mailbox to raise a forefinger in greeting to the sheriff.

Whiteside returned the gesture, his forefinger lifted for a moment from the steering wheel. The old man eyed Audra as they passed, his eyes narrowing.

An auto repair shop, long since closed down, its signage faded. More houses, aligned along the roadside now, some tidier than others. The road smoothed and widened, and a sidewalk joined its path toward the town. A church, so brilliant white it hurt Audra's eyes to look at it. She averted her gaze, out through the front windshield, and saw single- and two-story buildings stretch ahead for perhaps half a mile, and she realized the main street lay on the other side of the wooden bridge they approached.

She looked over the railing as they crossed, expecting to see a flowing river. Instead she saw a dry bed, no more than a muddy stream creeping along the middle. The water, silver or not, from which this town had taken its name had withered away to almost nothing. Dying, like the town itself. Through the clamor in her mind, she felt a small sadness for this place and its people.

Dark windows along the main street where stores had once done business. To Let and For Sale signs cracked and faded above many. A general store, a Goodwill place, and a diner were all that still traded. A few side streets crawled away, and from the brief glimpses she caught, they were every bit as desolate. Eventually, at the far end, Whiteside pulled into a lot beside a low cinder block building with the words ELDER COUNTY SHERIFF'S OFFICE in dark letters on a white board. The lot had room for maybe a dozen vehicles, but Whiteside's was the only one here.

Where was Deputy Collins' car?

Whiteside shut off the engine, sat still and quiet for a moment, his hands on the wheel. Then he told Audra to wait, and he climbed out. He went to a shallow concrete ramp, enclosed by a railing, that led to a metal door in the side of the building, found a key from the chain on his belt, and opened it, before returning to the car. His fingers gripped Audra's arm tight as he helped her out and guided her toward the building, a few seconds of blasting heat before the relative cool of the office.

It took a few moments for her eyes to adjust to the dimness in here, the weak fluorescent lights flickering above her head. A small open-plan office, four desks, one with a computer terminal that looked at least a decade old. The other desks appeared to have not been used in years. The desks were separated from the front of the space by a wooden rail with a gate that was bolted shut. A stale smell of disuse hung about the place, a dampness to the air despite the heat outside.

Whiteside kicked a chair out from the desk and backed Audra up to it until she had no choice but to sit down. He took a seat and switched on the computer. It clicked and whirred as it booted up, sounding like an engine that didn't like cold mornings.

"Where did the deputy take my children?" Audra asked.

Whiteside hit a few keys to log on. "We'll discuss that in a while."

"Sir, I don't want to be difficult, I really don't, but I need to know my children are safe."

"Like I said, ma'am, we'll discuss that in a while. Now let's get this done. The sooner we get this all straightened out, the sooner I can let you go. Now, full name."

Audra cooperated through the process of details—her name, date of birth, place of residence—and even when he undid the handcuffs, so he could press her fingertips into an inkpad.

"We do things old-fashioned around here," he said, his tone warming. "None of that digital nonsense. We don't have the funds to upgrade. Used to be I had a half dozen deputies and an under-sheriff to assist with this kind of thing. Them, and a police department, such as it was. Now there's just me and Collins left to keep this town in order, and Sally Grames, who does admin three mornings a week. Not that we see much trouble. You might be the first person to come through here in a year that wasn't a drunk and disorderly."

Whiteside held out a dispenser full of moist wipes, and Audra plucked one from the top, then another, and set about cleaning the black from her fingers.

"Now, listen," he said. "This needn't be a whole big deal. I guess if I don't put the cuffs back on, you'll be civil. Am I right?"

Audra nodded.

"Good. Now, I got some checks to do, make sure there's no

warrants hanging over you, but I doubt there will be. Like I said, the amount of marijuana you had—"

"It's not mine," Audra said.

"So you say, but the amount I found in your car might, to some people, seem like more than for personal use. But if you're civil with me, I guess I can be flexible about that. Maybe call it possession, and forget about intent to supply. So, all things being equal, I expect Judge Miller will give you a small fine and a few stern words. Now, Judge Miller usually holds court on a Wednesday morning over in the town hall, but I'm going to give her a call, see if she'll come over and hold a special session in the morning for an arraignment. That way, you'll only have to spend the one night here."

Audra went to protest, but he held up a hand to silence her.

"Let me finish, now. I'm going to have to put you in a cell overnight, no matter what. But if you're cooperative with me, as soon as I got you settled in, I'll make that call to Judge Miller. But if you're not, if you give me trouble, I'll be happy to let you wait a day or two longer. So you think you can be good? Not cause a fuss?"

"Yes, sir," Audra said.

"All right, then," he said, standing. He walked to a door in the rear of the office marked CUSTODY, sorting through the keys on his chain, then stopped and turned. "You coming?"

Audra got to her feet and followed him. He unlocked the door, reached inside to switch on another row of fluorescent lights. Holding the door, he stepped aside to let her pass. Inside stood a small desk, its veneer surface chipped and stained, a coffee mug with an assortment of pens on top of it. Beyond, a row of three cells, barred squares with concrete floors, two thin cots in each, and toilets and washbasins screened by low brick walls.

She stopped, the fear that had been bubbling in her beginning to rise up. Her shoulders rose and fell with her quickening breaths, a dizzy wave washing over her.

Whiteside stepped around her, went to the farthest cell to the left, and unlocked the door. Metal-on-metal squealed as he slid it across. He turned to look at her, an expression of concern on his jowly face.

"Honestly," he said, "it's not that bad. It's cool, the bunks aren't too uncomfortable, you'll have privacy when you need it. One night, that's all. I just need you to take off your shoes and your belt, put them on the desk there."

Audra stared into the empty air inside the cell as tremors worked through her body and limbs, her feet glued to the concrete floor.

He reached a hand out to her. "Come on, now, quicker you get in there and get settled, the quicker we can get all this straightened out."

She unbuckled her belt, slipped it from her jeans, kicked off her sneakers, then placed them all on the desk. Her sock soles whispered on the vinyl tiles as she walked to the cell and through the door. She heard that squeal again, and turned in time to see the door slide closed. Whiteside turned a key in the lock.

Audra approached the bars, put her hands on them. She looked Whiteside in the eye, inches away, on the other side.

"Please," she said, unable to keep the quiver from her voice. "I've done everything you said. I've been cooperative. Please tell me where my children are."

Whiteside held her gaze.

"What children?" he asked.

CHAPTER 6

SEAN WATCHED DUST PLUMES THROUGH THE WINDOW AS DEP-
uty Collins pulled off the road onto an unmarked dirt track.
Without thinking, he reached over and took Louise's hand in
his, her fingers warm and sweaty. His stomach roiled inside him as
the car swayed from side to side, the track winding up through the
hills.

It felt like they'd been driving for ages. Sean figured the town
they'd been driving to with Mom had been only one or two miles
from where they'd stopped, going by the road signs, but they'd driven
far more than that now. He was sure of it.

The gnawing worry had not left him since they'd set off, even if
he'd managed to stop crying like a baby. A safe place, the deputy had
said when he asked where they were going. He asked so many times
she told him to shut up, goddamn it, just be quiet back there. Louise
hadn't said a word, simply held tight to Gogo and looked out the window, like they were going on a day trip.

The dirt track had faded and narrowed until Sean wasn't sure if
it was a track at all. The car shook and rattled and jerked, bouncing him and his sister on the seat. Eventually the ground leveled off
and they approached a small ruin of a shack, its roof caved in, the
remains of its walls blackened and charred by a long-ago fire. Beside it, what Sean guessed to be a carport of some kind, a simple
wooden frame with a corrugated-iron roof. A van stood in the shade
beneath it.

Deputy Collins pulled the cruiser in beside the van, and the interior became suddenly dark. She opened her door, climbed out, and

came to Louise's door. A wash of heat as she opened it and leaned down.

"Come on," she said, reaching in to undo Louise's seat belt.

Before Sean could stop her, Louise pulled her hand away from his and let Collins lift her out. Collins leaned down once more.

"You too," she said.

"I don't want to," Sean said.

Collins adjusted her grip on Louise's hand. "I've got your sister," she said.

Sean felt the sweat on his back turn cold. He reached for the seat-belt release, let the belt retract. He hesitated, then slid across the seat and out of the car.

"Here," Collins said as she put Louise's hand in Sean's. "Stay right there."

She shut the cruiser's door, then walked to the back of the van, fishing in her pants pocket for a key. The van looked in almost as poor condition as the shack, its beige paintwork dappled with rust. Its rear doors creaked as Collins opened them. She stepped back, showed them the dark throat of it.

"Get in," she said.

Louise stepped forward, but Sean pulled her back.

"No," he said.

Collins pointed into the dark. "Come on, now."

Sean shook his head. "No."

"Don't be difficult," she said, her face hardening.

"We're not getting in," Sean said.

Collins took a step toward them, then hunkered down, her knees to her chest, balancing on the balls of her feet. She spoke to Louise. "Honey, your brother is being silly. Now, you need to get inside out of this heat. If you don't, your mom's going to be in even bigger trouble than she is now. She might have to go to a jail for a long time."

"That's a lie," Sean said.

"Louise, sweetheart, you don't want your mommy to be in worse trouble, do you? You don't want her to go to jail, right?"

Louise shook her head.

"Well, then, let's—"

As Collins reached out for his sister, her balance shifted, and Sean chose that moment to throw his hand out at her, pushing her shoulder. Not hard, but enough. Collins' eyes widened in surprise, and her arms spun in the air as she tried to stop what would surely happen next.

Sean didn't wait to see her topple onto her back. Instead he turned and ran, dragging Louise behind him. She squealed and stumbled, almost went down, but his momentum kept her moving. He followed the tire tracks, thinking, get to the road, flag down a car. Whatever happens, run, run as fast as you can.

"Gogo!"

He spared a glance over his shoulder, saw the remains of the pink rabbit bounce in the dirt. Beyond him, Collins getting to her feet, fury on her face.

"We'll come back for him," he said, jerking Louise's hand. "We'll come back, I promise."

He kept going, churning his legs harder, his sister flailing after him. Somewhere behind he heard Collins yell at them to stop, god-damn it, stop right there. Dirt and grit slipped under his shoes as he took the slope, leaping down the steeper parts, his back jarring each time he landed, Louise somehow staying with him, staying upright.

"Stop!" Collins' voice echoed between the steep slopes all around. "For Christ's sake, stop!"

Sean ignored her, his mind focused on the road somewhere down there through the hills at the end of this track. Just keep running, that's all.

Ahead, a turn in the track, maybe a place to take shelter. Sean put his head down, kicked the ground hard, felt his shoulder wrenched as Louise's feet left the dirt.

Then the crack of the gun, the pressure in his ears. By instinct rather than thought, he threw himself down, taking Louise with him. Louise cried out, rolling away from him. He looked back, saw Collins at the top of the slope, her pistol pointed skyward, a wisp of smoke taken away by the breeze. Collins lowered the pistol, gripped it with both hands, aimed it at them. She breathed hard, her boots crunching on the ground as she bounded down the slope toward them.

Sean got to his knees, the grit burning the heels of his hands, and turned to see the pistol aimed at his head, only feet away.

"Don't move," Collins said.

He froze, watched as she reached down to grab the back of Louise's T-shirt, haul her upright, put the pistol to her head. Louise stared at him, her eyes and mouth wide. The knees of her jeans torn, the skin grazed and bloody.

"Do you want me to kill her?" Collins said, her eyes glistening with tears and anger. "Is that what you want?"

Sean held his hands up and out, a gesture of surrender. He shook his head.

Collins let go of Louise, pointed her pistol at the ground. Her shoulders rose and fell as she fought for breath. She sniffed and wiped her face with the back of her free hand, leaving smears of dirt on her skin. "All right, then," she said, a quiver in her voice. "Let's go."

Sean helped Louise up, became aware of the sting of his elbows, the tears in his own jeans. Collins pointed back up the slope, and he took his sister's hand, started the climb up toward the van. Collins trudged behind them. On the way, he stooped to pick up Gogo, handed him to Louise. She clutched the pink rabbit to her chest as she sniffed and pouted.

They remained silent as he hoisted Louise up into the van. He followed, careful of splinters from the plywood flooring. Once inside, Sean gathered Louise into his arms. She curled there in his lap and he began to rock her, the way Mom had done for him when he was scared. He turned his head, saw Deputy Collins watching him, saw the fear on her face.

She raised a cell phone, and Sean heard the synthetic whirr and click as she took a photograph.

Then she slammed the doors closed and terrible darkness swallowed them.

CHAPTER 7

AUDRA PACED TO ONE END OF THE CELL, TURNED, PACED TO THE other. Turned again. And again. An hour had passed, maybe more, and her throat burned raw from screaming. She had shouted and yelled until her lungs ached, until her eyes watered.

There were no more tears, but fear and anger still chased through her mind, each threatening to take over, to shred the last of her sanity. It was all she could do to keep them in check, and exhaustion made her want to curl up on one of the bunks and disappear into herself. But somehow she kept upright, kept pacing.

When Whiteside had said those two words, she had stood still and silent for a few moments before asking, "What do you mean?"

Whiteside had said nothing, had simply turned away, back toward the door of the custody suite, through it, and locked it behind him. Her screams had reverberated between the walls until she could scream no more. Now all she had was forward motion, one foot in front of the other. That or go crazy in here. So she kept moving.

The rattle of keys froze her in place, her back to the door. She heard it open, heard the sheriff's heavy footsteps on the concrete, then the door closing again.

"You done hollering?" he asked.

Audra turned, watched him approach the bars. "What did you mean?" she asked, her voice a hoarse croak.

"Mean about what?" he asked, his face blank. Bored, even.

"What you said about my children. Where are they?"

He leaned his forearm against the bars, stared back at her. "You and me are going to have a talk."

She slapped the bars with her palm, hot pain in her bones. "Where are my children?"

"But first, you need to calm down."

"Fuck you. Where are my children?"

"If you calm down, then we can discuss that."

She tried to shout, but her voice cracked. "Where are my children?"

Whiteside pushed himself away from the bars, said, "All right, have it your way. We can talk about it another time."

He turned and headed back to the door.

Audra grabbed the bars and said, "No, please, come back."

He looked over his shoulder. "You ready to be calm?"

"Yes," she said, nodding hard. "I'm calm."

"All right." He took the keys from his belt as he came back to the cell, pointed to the bunk at the far end. "Sit down over there for me."

She hesitated, and he said, "Go on, sit down, or we can talk another time."

Audra went to the bunk and did as she was told. As he slipped the key into the lock, he told her to sit on her hands, and she obeyed. He pulled the sliding door back, stepped inside, and closed it again. He leaned his shoulder against the bars and stowed the keys away.

"You calm?" he asked.

"Yes, sir."

"Okay. Now, I'm going to lay this out for you as best I can, and I want you to stay right there and take it easy. You think you can do that?"

"Yes, sir."

"Good. Now, I'm going to talk with you about your children, and you aren't going to like it. But even so, I want you to keep calm. Will you try real hard to keep calm?"

"Yes, sir," she said, her voice a whisper she could barely hear herself.

Whiteside examined his fingernails for a few moments, a crease in his brow. Then he took a deep breath and looked her in the eye.

"See, as far as can I remember, there were no children in your car."

Audra shook her head. "What are you talking about? Sean and Louise, they were in the car when you pulled me over. The deputy, whatever her name was, she came, she took them away."

"That is not my recollection," Whiteside said. "What I remember is I pulled you over, you were alone. I radioed Deputy Collins to come assist me in searching you, and I asked her to get hold of Emmet to come tow your car. We waited, he came, I brought you here and booked you in. No children."

"Why are you saying this? You know it's not true. They were there. You saw them. You talked to them. For Christ's sake, please, just tell—"

Whiteside pushed away from the bars, put his hands on his hips. "Thing is, what you're saying presents me with a problem."

"Please, just—"

"Quiet, now." He held a hand up. "I'm talking here. You're telling me you had children in that car when you left New York. Now you're here in Silver Water, and no children. Assuming you did set off with those kids, I have to ask you: Where are they?"

"Your deputy, she—"

"Mrs. Kinney, what did you do with your children?"

Audra heard a distant noise like a stampede or a hurricane or a thousand screaming animals. Cold to the very center of her soul, like she'd fallen into an icy lake. She stared back at him, the sound of her own heartbeat building inside her, drowning out everything, even the distant wild clamor.

Whiteside said something. She didn't know what. She couldn't hear him.

Then the distance between them disappeared in a blur and she was on him, her fists smashing into his face, and he was falling, and she was on his chest, her nails scraping at his skin, and then her hands were fists again, and she brought them down and down again as his head turned first one way then the other, her blows glancing off his cheeks.

She didn't know how long she straddled him, striking him again and again, but she didn't stop until she felt his meaty hand at the center of her chest, between her breasts, and she knew she could do this man no harm, not really, he was too strong. Then he pushed, and she flew backward, weightless for a moment before crashing to the floor, jarring her elbows, the back of her head cracking on the concrete.

Through the black dots in her vision, Audra saw Whiteside rise over her, then drop down, his big fists, a telescopic baton in one. She brought her hands and knees up by instinct, and he whipped the baton across her shins. The pain cut through everything, bright and fierce, and she would have screamed if she'd had the voice for it. Then those big hands gripped her shoulders, flipped her over like she was nothing, and he planted his knee in the small of her back.

Audra tried to draw a breath so she could plead, beg for mercy, but she could barely gasp. Whiteside grabbed her left wrist, pulled it back, twisting her shoulder in its socket. He forced the wrist up her back, and she felt certain he would tear her arm clean off, before she felt the metal circle the wrist. Holding her left hand in place, he took her right wrist and did the same, the pain so great her consciousness wavered.

When both wrists were bound, he held them there, and leaned down so she felt his breath against her ear.

"Your children are gone," he whispered. "If you can accept that, you might survive this. If you can't? Well . . ."

And then his weight lifted from her, the cell door opening and closing, the jangle of keys.

Alone on the floor, Audra wept.

CHAPTER 8

D ANNY LEE TOOK THE STAIRS TWO AT A TIME, THREE FLIGHTS up. He paused at the top, let his heartrate settle. Then he walked along the corridor, counting off the doors in the dim light, until he reached 406. The number the boy's parents had given him.

A good boy, Mrs. Woo had said. But he'd changed lately. Stopped talking, become sullen and quiet. His respect for them gone.

Danny knew the story. He'd heard it plenty of times before.

The door rattled along with the bass notes from inside, hip-hop music rumbling within. Must drive the neighbors crazy, he thought. Not that the neighbors would complain.

He made a fist, hammered the door, and waited. No answer. He hammered the door again. Still no answer. Once more with his fist, and a couple of kicks to get the point across.

Now the door opened a few inches, revealing the face of a young man Danny vaguely recognized. One of Harry Chin's boys.

"What the fuck?" the young man said. "You want to lose your hand, just knock one more time, motherf—"

The sole of Danny's shoe hit the door hard, sending the Chin boy staggering back. He barely kept himself from falling, cursing as his hand grabbed at the wall.

Danny stepped inside, surveyed the room. Half a dozen young men, counting the Chin boy, all staring back at him. Five of them sat on a couch and a pair of armchairs surrounding a coffee table laden with loose marijuana and rolled joints, a bag of coke, a few lines on the table's glass top. Another bag of crystal meth, though it didn't appear that any of them had partaken yet.

The Chin boy had the wide-eyed look, the flaring nostrils, and the sheen of sweat on his forehead that said he'd had at least a line or two of coke. But Danny didn't care about him. His only concern was Johnny Woo, the youngest of the boys, who sat in the middle of the couch. A faint wisp of hair on his upper lip, pimples across his nose and forehead. A child, really.

"Johnny, come with me," Danny said.

Johnny said nothing.

Danny heard a snick-click at his left ear. He turned his head, saw the Chin boy and the .38 in his hand, cocked and ready.

"Get the fuck out of here," the Chin boy said, "before I take your head off."

Danny said nothing.

"Yo, man," one of the other young men said. "That's Danny Doe Jai."

The Chin boy turned to his friend. "Danny who?"

A child, Danny reminded himself, nothing more. So easy. He simply reached up and grabbed the boy's wrist, pushed it away, twisted, squeezed. The pistol dropped to the floor, a heavy clunk, and the boy fell to his knees. He squealed, and Danny squeezed harder. Felt bones grind beneath the flesh.

Danny turned to the young man on the couch. "Don't call me that."

The young man dropped his gaze, mumbled, "Sorry, Lee-sook."

The boys all nodded, called him uncle, showed the respect he was due. Danny returned his attention to the Chin boy.

"Any reason why I shouldn't break your goddamn arm?" he asked.

The boy whined. Danny twisted a little more, squeezed a little harder.

"I asked you a question," he said.

The boy opened and closed his mouth, said, "Sorry . . . Lee . . . sook."

Danny let go, and the boy collapsed onto the floor, hugging his wrist to his chest.

Johnny Woo picked at his nails, didn't look up.

"Come on," Danny said. "Your parents are waiting for you."

Johnny lit a joint, took a long hit, and said, "Fuck you."

The other young men winced. One of them nudged Johnny's elbow, said, "Just go, man. Do what Lee-sook says."

"Fuck you, I ain't going nowhere. You nod your head and call him uncle all you want, go ahead and be a pussy. He don't scare me."

"Listen to your friends," Danny said. "Let's go."

Johnny took another hit, exhaled a long plume of smoke, and looked Danny in the eye. "Fuck. You."

Danny reached down, grabbed a leg of the coffee table, threw it aside, scattering green flakes and white powder. It crashed into the wall, shattering the glass. The other boys dived out of the way as Danny stepped forward and slapped the joint from Johnny's mouth. He put a hand at either side of the kid's throat, hoisted him up by his neck. Johnny gave one strangled croak as Danny dragged him across the room, then threw him against the wall. He slapped the boy again, rocking his head on his shoulders, bringing tears to his eyes.

"You a tough guy now?" Danny asked.

Slapped him again, his hand powering through, even as Johnny tried to shield himself.

"You a gangbanger?"

Slap.

"You ready to take me on?"

Slap.

"Go on."

Slap.

"Go on and try, boy, if you're such a big man."

Johnny slid down the wall, his hands over his head. "Stop, stop! I'm sorry! Stop!"

Danny reached down, lifted Johnny up by his collar. "Get the fuck out of here."

As Johnny stumbled out through the door, Danny kicked him once in the ass, almost knocking him off his feet. He gave the other boys one last hard look. None of them returned it, suddenly more interested in their shoes or their fingernails. He followed Johnny out, closed the door behind him. Johnny looked back to him, a child now, seeking instruction.

Danny pointed at the stairs and said, "Go."

The air was damp and cold out on Jackson Street, a breeze blowing straight in off San Francisco Bay. Danny pulled his jacket tight around him. He pushed Johnny between the shoulder blades, told him to keep walking. The boy wore nothing but a short-sleeved 49ers shirt, and Danny could almost see the goosebumps on his skin.

They passed a beauty salon, lit up bright in the darkness, the sound of chattering women from inside. A seafood market, the ripe smell of fish and salt. It was relatively quiet here compared to the hubbub and the glare of Grant Avenue, where the sidewalks were perpetually crammed with Chinatown tourists. Less chance of the boy running and losing himself in the crowds.

Johnny looked back over his shoulder. "Hey, why they call you Danny Doe Jai?"

"Shut up and keep walking," Danny said.

The boy looked back again. "Doe Jai. Knife Boy. You don't get a name like that for nothing."

"Your mom told me you were a smart kid," Danny said. "Prove her right and shut your mouth."

"Come on, man, just tell—"

Danny grabbed Johnny's shoulder, spun him around, threw him against the shutters of a closed-down catering wholesaler. The metal rattled and boomed. Danny grabbed the boy's throat in his right hand, squeezed his windpipe tight.

Two young couples, Chinatown tourists, skipped out of the way, understanding this was none of their business.

Danny brought his nose to the boy's, their eyes two inches apart.

"Ask me again," he said. "Just ask me one more time and I'll show you why they call me Knife Boy."

The boy blinked and Danny eased off the pressure on his throat.

"What?" Danny asked. "You not interested anymore?"

"No, Lee-sook," the boy croaked.

"Good." Danny let him go, gave him another kick in the pants. "Now move your stupid ass."

A thirty-minute walk—Johnny pouting and dragging his heels, Danny nudging his back—took them to the Woo house over in the Richmond. Mrs. Woo answered the door, gasped, then called back into the house for her husband in Cantonese.

"It's Lee-gor! He's brought Johnny home."

Mr. Woo came to the door, nodded respectfully at Danny, gave his son a withering look. The boy said nothing as he slipped past his father into the hall where his mother waited. Mrs. Woo tried to embrace him, but he shrugged her off and disappeared into the house.

"Thank you, Lee-gor," she said, nodding, her eyes wet. "Thank you so much."

She elbowed Mr. Woo's flank, and he took his wallet from his pants. Two hundred-dollar bills. He took Danny's wrist with his left hand, nodded again, pressed the money into the palm with his right. Danny's pride might have told him to hand the two hundred dollars back, but his rational mind remembered the rent was due. He slipped the money into his pocket and gave a nod of thanks.

"Keep an eye on him," he said. "He's probably too embarrassed to go back to that apartment, but you never know. Don't go too hard on him. Don't give him a reason to leave again."

"We won't," Mrs. Woo said. She turned to her husband, gave him a hard stare. "Will we?"

Mr. Woo looked at the ground.

"We don't want trouble," Mr. Woo said. "The Tong, will they . . . ?"

He couldn't finish the sentence. He didn't have to.

"I'll see what I can do," Danny said.

LESS THAN an hour later, he found Pork Belly sitting on a corner stool at the Golden Sun bar, an upstairs drinking hole in a back alley off of Stockton Street. The kind of alley the tourists hurried past, not looking too closely at the men who lingered there.

Pork Belly's stomach sagged between his thighs, his shirt gaping between the buttons, showing the white undershirt beneath. A sheen of perspiration permanently glossed his forehead, and he kept a handkerchief on him at all times, should his brow be in need of mopping. Rumor was that Pork Belly's grandmother, impressed by his appetite and girth, had given him the nickname as a child—Kow Yook, in her tongue—and it had stuck. He nursed a dark rum and sipped at a beer as he watched a college basketball game on the TV over the bar. Danny knew the rum was for show, that Pork Belly would make that glass last all night long, contenting himself with a mild beer buzz.

Used to be different. There was a time Freddie "Pork Belly" Chang would have swallowed a whole bottle of rum and barely felt a thing. Not anymore. Not since three years ago when he had hit a young homeless man with his car, down among the warehouses and waste ground at the tip of Hunter's Point. He had sat in the car for a half hour, the drunk still heavy on him, before he called Danny. And Danny had helped him deal with it, even though it had sickened him to his very core. Because Pork Belly was a brother of the Tong, and you don't say no to a brother.

The only condition Danny had attached to his assistance was that Pork Belly kick the booze. And he had done so, more or less, with Danny's help. Since that time, as far as he knew, Pork Belly had stayed close to sober, so Danny could live with what he'd helped his old friend hide away. And from time to time, he could call on the big man for a favor.

Like now.

"Hey, Danny Doe Jai," Pork Belly said as Danny approached along the nearly empty bar. "What'll you have?"

"Coffee, decaf," Danny said. He hadn't touched alcohol in years either, not even beer, and it was too late in the evening for caffeine. Sleep was difficult enough without it. He took the stool next to Pork Belly's, nodded his thanks to the barman who set a cup in front of him, and poured from a glass pot.

"How you been?" Pork Belly asked.

"Okay. You?"

"Meh." Pork Belly wavered his hand and shrugged. "My knees are no good. They hurt like a motherfucker, sometimes. Goddamn arthritis, the doctor tells me. Says I gotta lose weight, take the pressure off my joints."

"Be good for your heart too," Danny said.

"Listen to him, Doctor Danny."

"Swimming."

Pork Belly turned his head toward him. "What?"

"Swimming's good for arthritis. You get a good workout, but it's easy on your joints."

Pork Belly's gut jiggled. "Get the fuck out of here. Swimming? You see me at the lido in Speedos and one of them little rubber skull-caps?"

"Why not? Get you an inflatable ring, maybe some armbands."

"Yeah, I go in the water, some motherfucker come at me with a goddamn harpoon gun."

Danny smiled around a mouthful of stale coffee, then swallowed. The TV switched to the ten o'clock news, the pomp of music over the titles.

"I guess you know why I'm here," Danny said.

Pork Belly nodded. "Yeah, I got a call. Been expecting you."

"The Woos are good people," Danny said. "Mrs. Woo knew my mother years ago. Johnny, her boy, he's no gangbanger. He's a good kid. Used to be, anyway. He was doing all right at school. He would've graduated next year; he still might, if he can make up his grades. Maybe have a shot at college."

The mirth left Pork Belly's face, the eyes deadened. "You should have come to me first."

"And what would you have done?"

"Maybe nothing," Pork Belly said. "Maybe something. But that was my choice to make. Not yours. You bypass me, you make me look like a bitch in front of all my boys. I ain't called the Dragon Head yet. When I do, he's gonna tell me to smash your kneecaps, maybe take a couple of fingers. What do I say to him?"

As Danny opened his mouth to speak, a movement on the TV screen distracted him. Fuzzy CCTV footage: a jail cell, a cop standing at one side, a woman sitting on a bunk at the other. Then the woman threw herself at the cop, knocked him to the ground, clawing and punching the big man.

"You talk him out of it," Danny said, turning his attention back to Pork Belly. "Tell him Johnny Woo was too soft for the life, he'd have been more trouble than he was worth, that I did you a fav—"

Two words from the television stopped him. Missing children, the newsreader said. He looked back to the screen.

"I'll try," Pork Belly said. "I don't know if he'll accept it, but I'll try, just because I love you like a brother. But you pull that shit again . . ."

The news ticker along the bottom of the screen read: "Woman left New York days ago with her children, but local sheriff found no children in the car when it was stopped for a minor traffic offense."

The same image again: the woman throwing herself at the cop.

Cut to the anchor, a serious expression on her face. "State police and FBI agents are traveling to the small town of Silver Water, Arizona, to question the as-yet-unnamed woman about the whereabouts of her two children. More on this story as it unfolds."

Pork Belly said something, but Danny didn't hear. His gaze remained on the television, even though the anchor had moved on to some other story. A woman traveling alone with her children, then she's picked up by a cop, and the children are gone.

Chills ran across Danny's skin. His heart raced, his lungs working hard.

No, he thought, shaking his head. You've been wrong before. Probably wrong this time too.

Pork Belly's hand gripped his arm. "What's up, man?"

Danny's head snapped around to him, staring, as his mind tumbled.

"Shit, man, you're creeping me out."

Danny climbed down from the stool. "I gotta go. We good?"

Pork Belly shrugged. "Yeah, we good."

"Thank you, dailo," Danny said, putting a hand on Pork Belly's shoulder, squeezing. Then he walked out of the bar, onto the street, without looking back. His phone in his hand before his feet hit the sidewalk, his thumb picking out the search letters, looking for more on this woman in Arizona and her missing children.

As the screen filled with a list of results, he wondered if the woman had a husband. A husband whose world was being blown apart right now, just as Danny's had been five years ago.

CHAPTER 9

EAN SAT ON THE FLOOR, HIS BACK TO THE WALL, KNEES UP TO his chin. A blanket wrapped tight around his shoulders. Louise lay on the mattress in the center of the room, her eyelids rising and falling in a sleepy rhythm, a candy wrapper still in her hand. The deputy had left them a bag of candy bars, a few bags of potato chips, along with a case of water bottles. She said she'd be back later with some sandwiches. Sean didn't think she was coming back at all.

Cold in the basement, the air damp in his lungs. A smell of mold and moss and rotten leaves. Both the floor and the walls were lined with wooden boards, the packed earth visible between the slats. Sean wondered how it didn't all cave in on them, bury him and his sister alive.

The cabin had looked old, from the little he'd seen of it as they approached the clearing. Collins had let him and Louise out of the van on a trail deep in the forest and made them march through the trees. He had been glad of the walk after the time spent in the van, but Louise mewled for the duration of the trek, coughing as she walked. She had wet her pants, and now she complained her jeans were cold and stinging. Sean had barely managed to hold on himself as he sat in the dark.

It had seemed to grow cooler as they drove. Shade had kept the van from becoming an oven while it was parked by that shack, but it had warmed as they traveled, making the air thick and heavy. Sean could feel the rise and fall of the road, more up than down, and after some time he began to feel pressure grow in his ears, like in an airplane. They were going somewhere higher up, maybe into those mountains that had seemed to haunt the horizon as Mom drove across Arizona. He didn't know much geography, but a vague recollection told him Arizona's desert gave way to forests in the north, rising thousands of feet above sea level. That would explain why the temperature had dropped so fast, he and his sister sweating one minute, shivering the next.

Louise had cried hard when she wet herself, desperate, shameful tears, punctuated by the coughs and rattles from her chest, even as Sean said it was all right, he'd never tell anyone. He felt bad now for edging away from the wet spot on the van's plywood flooring when he should have held his sister in his arms. However ashamed Louise might have been for not holding on, he was more so for not comforting her.

He remembered quite distinctly the feeling of the van leaving the road, and the judder and rattle as it crossed rough ground. Not long after, the sound of branches against the outside, scraping and clanging. What kind of trees did they have in Arizona? High ground, cooler weather. Sean guessed pines. He was proven right when the van stopped and Deputy Collins opened the rear doors.

Sean and Louise both shielded their eyes, even though by that time the sun had sunk well below the trees, making the light beneath the canopy a milky blue.

"Out," Collins said.

Sean and Louise stayed where they were.

Collins reached out a hand. "Come on, now. You're going to be all right. There's nothing to be scared of."

Sean wanted to tell her she was a liar, but he kept his mouth shut.

"I had an accident," Louise said. "I'm all wet."

Collins looked confused for a moment, then she nodded in understanding. "It's okay, honey, I've got clean clothes for you. Come on."

Louise crawled to the rear lip of the van, allowed Collins to help her down. The deputy turned back to Sean, keeping hold of Louise's hand.

"Sean, it's okay, really. Everything's going to be all right. You just need to come with me."

Sean weighed his choices and realized he had none. He couldn't stay in the van forever. If he ran, he had no doubt both he and his sister would be shot. So he got to his feet, walked to the back of the van. He ignored Collins' hand, her offer of help, and jumped down. The ground was soft beneath his sneakers, carpeted by years of shed pine needles, skeletal cones here and there. A freshness to the air after the stuffiness of the van.

He turned in a circle as he looked around. A narrow trail in a forest, nothing but trees in every direction and as high up as he could crane his neck to see.

"Where are we?" Louise asked.

Collins opened her mouth to answer, but Sean said, "Somewhere safe?"

The deputy gave him a look, flint in her eyes, her free hand on the grip of her pistol. "That's right," she said. "Somewhere safe. Let's take a walk."

She led Louise by the hand, and Sean had no choice but to follow.

An age later, they arrived at the log cabin, its windows and door boarded up, parts of the roof beginning to sag with neglect. Collins climbed up onto the porch, sidestepping broken boards, and opened the unlocked door. Darkness inside. Louise stopped at the threshold.

"I don't want to go in," she said.

"It's okay, nothing to be scared of." Collins looked back to Sean, that hard look in her eyes again, her hand returning to the butt of her pistol. "Tell her there's nothing to be scared of."

Sean stepped onto the porch, took Louise's other hand in his. "Yeah, there's nothing scary in here. It's just dark. I'll be right behind you."

Collins gave him a nod, then spoke to Louise. "You hear that? Your brother's not scared. Come on."

Weak light crept into the cabin, enough to reveal the old furniture piled up at one side, and the trapdoor in the middle of the floor. About three feet square, with a sliding bolt, a new-looking padlock hooked into it. Collins released Louise's hand, crouched down, and undid the lock. She put her hand to the bolt and looked up at Sean.

"You're going to be a good boy, right? You're going to help me. 'Cause if you don't, if things go bad . . ."

She let the threat hang in the cold air between them.

"Yes, ma'am," Sean said.

"Good," she said, then slid the bolt back, grunted as she hoisted open the trapdoor.

A pair of taut chains prevented the door from swinging back onto the floor, held it upright over the opening. Louise stopped, planted her feet firmly on the wooden boards.

"It's too dark," she said.

Collins pulled her a step closer. "There's a light. I'll switch it on. There's a big battery to run it. You can keep it on all the time, if you want."

"No, I want my mommy." Louise tried to tug her hand away, but Collins held firm.

"Sean, tell her."

He watched Collins' fingers circle the pistol grip, saw the hardness to her features and a panicky fear in her eyes. Like this could all go terribly wrong. Even as bad as things were, even if she didn't want them to, they could get so much worse.

"We'll see Mom soon," Sean said, guiding Louise toward the door. "I promise."

Louise began to cry again, and Sean had to fight back his own tears. Collins took the flashlight from her belt and shone the beam into the trapdoor's mouth, revealing the steep wooden stairs down into the dark. He could feel Louise's tremors through his fingers. He put an arm around her shoulder, and Collins released her other hand, allowing him to help his sister down the steps. One at a time, slow and easy, the deputy's heavier feet a couple of steps behind them.

The basement floor was lined with wood that creaked and flexed under their feet. Collins went to the far wall and an old bookcase that leaned there. On top was an electric lamp wired to a large battery, just as she'd said. She flipped a switch, and pale yellow light washed across the room. Sean saw the items that had been left here—a mattress, a pair of buckets and toilet paper, water, candy bars, some books and comics—and felt a new dread, colder and heavier than before.

This had been planned for. These things had been here for weeks, maybe months, waiting for children like them.

"Eat something," Collins said, tossing a few candy bars from the bag onto the mattress. She took two bottles of water from the case, set them on the floor. "Drink."

She went to another bag, rummaged inside. She removed items of clothing, pants, underwear, checked labels before pushing them back in. Eventually she found a pair of faded jeans and underpants that looked about Louise's size. She beckoned to Louise.

"Let's get those wet things off you."

"No," Louise said. "Mommy said I can't let anyone take my clothes off but her, or my teacher in school."

"Your mommy's right to tell you that, but you see, I'm a police officer, so it's okay. You can't stay in those wet things."

Once again, Collins looked to Sean for help, and he nudged Louise, said, "It's okay. Go on."

Sean watched as Collins undressed his sister, cleaned her with a wet wipe, and put the fresh clothes on. What was he watching for? He wasn't sure. He knew there were some bad adults who wanted to do things to kids, to touch them in bad ways. If he saw anything wrong, any bad touching, what would he do? He had no idea, but he watched anyway until it was done.

Collins stood and said, "Now eat. And drink some water. I'll be back later tonight with some sandwiches."

She said nothing more as she climbed the stairs up to the trapdoor. The door slammed shut, and Sean felt the pressure in his ears, and a coldness like never before. He wanted to cry so badly it caused an ache behind his eyes, but he knew if he did, if he let his terror show, then Louise's fragile mind would crack. So instead they sat beside each other on the mattress and ate candy and potato chips until Louise announced that she was tired. She lay down and Sean pulled a blanket over her, and he tried to remember one of her favorite stories, the one about the mouse and the deep, dark wood, and the monster who turned out to be real after all.

HOURS PASSED. Sean wished he had his watch, so he could tell how many. His father had given him one for his last birthday, said a man should have a good watch, but Sean could never get used to the feel of it on his wrist. The clingy leather, the fiddly clasp, the cold of the metal. Always either too tight or too loose. He stopped wearing it after a few weeks, and Mom hadn't said anything, even though it was an expensive watch. It cost more than the watches most grownup men wear, his father had said, because his father cared about such things.

Sean's right hand went to his left wrist, the memory of the watch still on his skin there. He sometimes dreamed about his father. Angry, frightening dreams from which he awoke breathless and confused. He supposed he should hate Patrick Kinney, though that was a big emotion for a man he'd seen so little of in his life. Breakfast, usually, sometimes dinner, they had shared a table, but there hadn't been much conversation. Now and again his father might ask about his grades, his friends, his teachers. One or two questions met by Sean's stumbling answers, and that was that.

Mostly when he thought of his father he felt a hollow space inside, as if he had never had a father at all. Not in a real way.

Didn't matter now. The watch was in one of the boxes in the back of Mom's car.

Louise moaned and stirred, neither awake nor fully asleep, and hacked out a series of phlegmy coughs. Sean resisted the urge to lie down beside her, close his eyes, and—

What was that? A buzzing noise through the basement walls, getting louder.

Then it stopped somewhere overhead, and Sean heard a metallic clank. He wondered if it was Collins coming back, like she said she would.

Part of him sparked with the hope that she might take them both away from here, take them back to Mom. But the grownup part of Sean's mind—the part that Mom called the Wise Old Man—told him no, they weren't going anywhere. Nowhere good, at any rate.

Footsteps across the floorboards above, and Louise gasped as she bolted upright on the mattress, wild eyes staring as the lock rattled.

"It's okay," Sean said.

He couldn't help but flinch at the bolt sliding open, like a rifle shot above their heads. Then the creak of the trapdoor, and Collins grunting again as she pulled it up and over. She peered inside, and once satisfied, climbed down the stairs, a brown paper bag in her right hand. She no longer wore her uniform. Now she was dressed in jeans and a jacket, and motorcycle boots. Sean understood what the buzzing noise from above had been.

Collins looked at him and pointed to the empty spot on the mattress beside Louise. He got to his feet, kept the blanket around him, crossed the floor, and lowered himself to the mattress beside his sister. He felt heat where their shoulders touched. Collins dropped the paper bag on the floor, knelt down, and opened it. The dark smell of cigarettes tainted her breath. She reached inside the bag and produced two sandwiches.

"Peanut butter and jelly," she said. "Okay?"

Hunger pangs blotted out Sean's caution, and he reached for one, took a bite. His stomach growled as he tasted the sweetness and the salt. He gave a sigh in spite of himself.

After he swallowed, he said, "You look tired. What time is it?"

"I am tired," Collins said, reaching a sandwich out to Louise. "It's a little before midnight, I think."

Louise shook her head. "I don't like the crusts."

Collins pushed the sandwich at her. "Just eat it."

"Mom cuts them off," Louise said.

Collins gave her a hard look, then sighed, spreading the paper bag flat on the floor and putting the sandwich on top of it. She reached into her back pocket and pulled out what looked like a short metal bar. With her free hand, she pulled a vicious-looking blade from the bar, then snapped it into place. Sean had never seen a lock knife before, but he'd heard of them, and he guessed this was one. Collins proceeded to hack at the edges of the sandwich until the crusts were gone. She lifted the bread and held it out to Louise once more.

"Now eat," she said.

Louise took the sandwich and bit into it once, before shoving more and more into her mouth, barely chewing. Collins' expression softened as she put the lock knife away.

"I know you're both scared," she said. "But you don't need to be.

You're going to be fine, and so is your mom. Everything's going to be straightened out, maybe not tomorrow, but the day after, or the day after that at the latest. And here's what'll happen: you're going to go on a trip."

"Like a vacation?" Louise asked.

Collins smiled. "Yes, like a vacation."

"Where to?" Sean asked.

"You're going to stay with a very nice man."

"Our father?"

Collins hesitated, then said, "A nice man."

"Where?" Sean asked again.

"In his house. It's a nice house, a big house."

"Who is he? Where's his house?"

Collins' smile faltered. "He's a nice man, and it's a nice house. He's going to take good care of you." She leaned forward and looked Louise in the eye. "And you know what?"

Louise blinked. "What?"

"Your mom's going to be there too."

"I think that's a lie," Sean said.

Collins turned her gaze on him, and he wanted to back away. "Don't call me a liar, Sean."

Sean looked down at his hands.

"I'll be back in the morning," Collins said, standing. "Both of you get some sleep. And try not to worry."

As she climbed the creaking stairs, Sean took Louise's hand in his. The trapdoor closed, wood on wood, the bolt snapped, the padlock rattled. Sean lay down on the mattress, pulled Louise in close, and wrapped the blanket around them, trying not to wonder about the nice man and his nice house.

CHAPTER 10

Private Forum 447356/34
Admin: RR; Members: DG, AD, FC, MR, JS
Thread Title: This Weekend; Thread Starter: RR

From: RR, Wednesday 8:23 p.m.
Gentlemen, I assume you all got my message. A potential seller has been in touch. The goods are excellent, going by the photograph. Minor damage, but nothing to be concerned about. Initial checks are satisfactory, the seller seems genuine. I will of course carry out further checks, but at the moment, I'm happy.

As the goods are a pair in good condition, I suggest we offer $3M (three million), meaning a $500k contribution from each of us. I will expect to have received your contributions via wire transfer by noon on Friday at the latest, assuming we're all still solvent? Lol. I'll offer a further $250k bonus if the goods receive no further damage, but I'll cover that out of my own pocket.

You'll notice a change in the membership list. After his behavior at our last gathering, CY will not be joining us in future. He has assured me of his discretion, and I have assured him of the consequences if his discretion slips. In more pleasant news, however, allow me to introduce JS, vouched for by DG. I have personally looked into JS's background and have found no cause for concern, so please welcome him to our little group. All being well, you'll have a chance to meet him in person on Saturday evening.

Speaking of which, the next gathering will be at the usual place. My driver will pick you up at the airport; as ever, please don't bring any of your own staff. I know you trust them, but the fewer in the know, the safer for all of us. Please confirm your attendance, and let me know your arrival times, but try to keep it between 4:00 p.m. and 6:00 p.m.

Until then, take care, and do post here if you have any questions.

From: DG, Wednesday 8:36 p.m.
Thanks, RR, I'll definitely be there, and will give you my arrival time ASAP. And please, everyone, welcome JS to our group. He's an old college friend and a good guy.

From: JS, Wednesday 8:41 p.m.
Message deleted by the forum administrator.

From: RR, Wednesday 8:47 p.m.
JS—I appreciate you're new to the group, but please show more tact. Yes, this is a private forum, but discretion is still required. Our gatherings are fun, of course, but this remains a serious business, with serious consequences for all of us should anything go wrong.

From: JS, Wednesday 8:54 p.m.
Gentlemen, my sincerest apologies for getting out of line—not a good introduction to the group! What I meant to say was, simply, thank you all for accepting me as a member, especially to DG, who vouched for me. See you all on Saturday—my flight is already booked, getting in at 4:55 p.m.

From: AD, Wednesday 9:06 p.m.
I'm in. Will come back with arrival time.

From: MR, Wednesday 9:15 p.m.
Me too—and thanks, RR, for offering to cover the bonus. Very generous of you. Wheels down at 5:40 p.m. Saturday. Anyone for a quick nine holes on Sunday morning?

From: FC, Wednesday 9:47 p.m.
Sorry to keep everyone waiting for an answer. I have a prior engagement on Saturday afternoon and I'm trying to see if I can get away in time to

make it there. I hope I can, but I'll let you know one way or the other by tomorrow morning.

From: RR, Wednesday 10:12 p.m.
Thanks for the quick replies, gentlemen. FC, I've had a better look at the photograph now—you really don't want to miss this. Clear your schedule and get here, my friend, you won't regret it. They're beautiful. They really are.

CHAPTER 11

AUDRA DRIFTED IN AND OUT OF SLEEP ON SLOW, SICKLY WAVES. Every time the darkness took her, a jagged dream shook her loose again. Over and over, she jerked awake on the bunk's thin mattress, terrified, disoriented, pain clamoring from her shoulders and wrists. The night dragged its hours out until she lost all sense of their passing. By the time dawn light crept through the skylight outside her cell, the quiet of the place had grown so heavy that she thought she might be crushed by it.

At one point in the darkest hours she had roused from her shallow sleep to see that Whiteside was watching her from just beyond the bars. She had lain there, frozen, afraid to move in case he came at her once more. After a minute or two, keeping his silence, he had turned and left the custody suite.

Whiteside had reminded Audra first of her father, but now he made her think of her husband. She remembered the nights she awoke in their bed to find Patrick sitting at the other side of the room, watching her. Only once did she make the mistake of asking him what he was doing; he had crossed the room in the time it took for her to gasp a breath, grabbed her by the hair, and dragged her from the bed. As she lay on the floor, Patrick leaning over her, he told her it was his apartment, his bedroom, and he didn't have to explain himself to her.

They had met ten years ago. Audra Ronan had been working at the gallery on East 19th Street—it was named Block Beautiful after the cluster of townhouses it nestled between—for six months, using her evenings to paint. She had enjoyed the job, walking each lunchtime to Union Square to eat whatever she'd been able to afford to pack for herself. The pay was terrible, but what she earned on the occasional sales commission gave her enough to get by. Sometimes enough to go to the big Barnes & Noble at the northern end of the square, or south along Broadway to the Strand Book Store, to treat herself to something from the art section. All the while, she cultivated contacts with the agents of the artists whose work passed through. A couple of them had seen her paintings, told her to keep them in mind when she felt she was ready to start selling.

But somehow she never seemed to be ready. Every piece began with hope that this time the vision in her head would make it onto the canvas unspoiled, but it never did. Her friend Mel told her she was too much of a perfectionist, that she was a classic case of the Dunning–Kruger effect: those with the most talent can't recognize it in themselves, and those with the least can't see how little they have. Audra wasted hour upon hour reading articles about the Dunning–Kruger studies, and imposter syndrome, trying to convince herself she could do this. In one piece she found a quote from Shakespeare's *As You Like It*:

*The Foole doth thinke he is wise, but the wise man knowes himselfe
to be a Foole.*

She printed it out in big letters and pinned it to the wall of her little studio apartment.

Audra had tried cocaine because she'd heard it boosted confidence. She'd smoked weed at college, just like everyone else, and she imagined cocaine wouldn't be much different. But she found it made her nauseous, the crackling in her brain too much to bear, so she had stopped using as quickly as she had started. She still smoked the occasional joint, but not often. Sometimes it relaxed her, but other times it made her jittery and nervous.

Instead, she drank.

It had started at college, all those parties, and she always seemed to be the last one standing. She can hold her liquor, they'd say. After college, she dialed it back a little, kept it for weekends. But as time went on, and more failed canvases stacked up in the corner of her studio, she started drinking more. Soon, it was every night.

But she kept it under control. At least, that's what she told herself.

"Just give some of the pieces to an agent," Mel had said over and over, "see what happens. What's the worst that could happen?"

Rejection could happen. The agent could tell Audra her work was good, but not good enough. And she knew, if that occurred, what little confidence she had would be stripped away. So she kept trying for the perfect piece that never came.

Patrick Kinney had come to the opening night of a new exhibition. Audra had been applying a red sticker to a large canvas on which someone had just dropped twenty-five thousand when a smooth voice spoke over her shoulder.

"Excuse me, Miss, is this one sold?"

She turned to the voice and saw a tall and slender man, perhaps ten years her senior, in a suit so well made it seemed almost a part of him. When he smiled at her and said, "Miss?," she realized she had been frozen there, staring, for some time.

"I'm sorry," she said, feeling heat on her neck and cheeks. "Yes, it sold a few minutes ago."

"Pity," he said. "I like it."

Audra cleared her throat and said, "Maybe I can show you something else?"

"Maybe," he said, and she was struck by the way he looked her in the eye, his utter confidence, and whether she realized it at the time or not, she was his from then on. She had to force herself to look away.

"Are you thinking of an investment, or do you just want something for your wall?"

"Both," he said. "I moved into my apartment six months ago and I still don't have a single thing to look at, other than the TV or the window."

He had a place in the East Village full of bare walls, he explained as she walked him around the gallery. Patrick bought two pieces that night, totaling forty-two thousand. He left with a receipt and her telephone number.

She got drunk on their first date. Half a bottle of Sauvignon Blanc before she left her apartment to meet him. For the nerves, she told herself. At some point in the evening, she'd had to excuse herself and go to the restaurant's bathroom to throw up. The next morning she awoke in her own bed with a thunderous hangover and sickly, greasy shame.

That's that, she thought. I blew it. She was surprised, then, that Patrick called in the afternoon and asked when he could see her again.

Four months later, he proposed, and she accepted, knowing even as they embraced that it was madness. She caught the first glimpse of his true nature a week after that when he arranged an introduction to his parents at their Upper West Side apartment.

Patrick came out to her loft in Brooklyn that evening, let himself in with the key she had given him. Audra remained behind the folding screen that separated her bed from the rest of the place, her clothes hung on rails or folded in wire baskets. She had no money for real furniture. Her nerves had jangled all afternoon in anticipation of the dinner. Would his parents approve? After all, they were from old money, while Audra's mother came from the wilds of Pennsylvania, her father from Ohio, neither of them with a college education. Patrick's parents would smell the poor on her and take their son aside, tell him he could do better.

She had chosen her clothes carefully. With three good dresses to her name, four decent pairs of shoes, and only a scattering of costume jewelry, there hadn't been a huge range to choose from, but still, she had given it much consideration.

Audra trembled as she stepped around the screen, doing her best to move with the elegance that she had always felt eluded her.

Patrick stood quite still in the center of the room, staring, his face blank.

When she could stand it no longer, she asked, "Well? Do I pass?"

Another pause, and Patrick said, "No."

Audra felt something crack inside.

"Do you have something else?" he asked, flexing his hands, his face hardening.

"I like this," she said. "I like the color, it's a good fit, and—"

"Audra, you know how important tonight is to me," he said, rubbing his eyes with his fingertips. "Now, what else have you got?"

She was about to argue, but something in his voice warned her against it. "Come and look," she said.

Patrick followed her to the sleeping area on the other side of the screen, and the two dresses still on the rack. She lifted them from the rail, held each in turn against her body.

"I've seen these before," he said. "You wear these all the time."

"I'm sorry," Audra said, "I don't have the money to spend on clothes. I make the best of what I have."

Patrick looked at his watch, a chunky Breitling tonight, and said, "There's no time to buy anything else. Jesus, Audra, you knew how much I wanted to impress them. And I have to take you looking like that."

"I'm sorry," she said, holding back tears. "We can cancel, say I'm sick."

"Don't be stupid," he said, and her teeth clicked together as she closed her mouth. "Come on, we'll be late."

He hailed a cab outside, and they did not speak for the entire journey into Manhattan. She stood on the sidewalk while he paid the driver, facing the end of the block, watching the trees of Central Park sway in the evening breeze. Patrick took her arm, led her to the stone steps of his parents' building.

As they rode the elevator up to the penthouse, he leaned in and whispered, "Don't drink too much. Don't make a fool of me."

In the end, the evening wasn't entirely unpleasant. Patrick turned on his charm in the way that he always did, and his mother gushed over Audra, how pretty she was, and didn't she dress well? And the ring—just beautiful, where's it from? How much did it cost? Oh, and you're Irish too? Where are your people from?

Audra made the one glass of wine last all night, barely wetted her lips with it, while Patrick and his mother emptied two bottles between them.

Patrick's father—Patrick Senior—drank only water, barely spoke through the evening, offering only a few disjointed comments here and there. Instead, his mother, Margaret, steered the conversation between occasional barks at the help. And how Patrick gazed at his mother. For a moment, Audra wished he would stare at her like that, but she found the idea too uncomfortable to let it linger in her mind for long.

Afterward, Patrick brought Audra back to his apartment—he had never spent the night at her place—and led her straight to his bedroom. He took her with such force that she had to bite her knuckle to stifle a cry. When he was done, sweating and breathless, he rolled off and held her hand.

"You did well tonight," he said. "Thank you."

While he slept, Audra decided to call off the engagement. Just walk away. She hated the hard bead of self-doubt that he had found in her and worked so skillfully. A lifetime of that? No thank you.

She spent the next fortnight trying to figure out a way to break it off, to find the right moment, the right place. But Patrick was so charming and kind those two weeks that thoughts of splitting went to the back of her mind. And then she realized her period was late, and there was no further thought given to leaving.

Almost twelve years between there and here, her bed in a Brooklyn studio gone, a bunk in an Arizona cell in its place.

She thought: Did Patrick do this? Could he?

Audra supposed Sheriff Whiteside must have been here all night, keeping an eye on her. The camera up in the corner had remained on her all that time, its little red light staring at her. She had turned away from it, but she felt it burning like a laser between her shoulder blades. Now, as the custody suite's shadows sharpened, she lay on her back, watching it watching her.

Then the light went out.

Audra stayed quite still for a few seconds, waiting for it to come back on again. When it didn't, she sat upright, ignoring the fresh flares of pain as her feet dropped to the floor. An alarm sounded somewhere inside of her, telling her this was wrong, this shouldn't be. The camera should not be switched off. Why would it—?

Before she could finish the question in her mind, the door to the custody suite opened, and Whiteside entered, followed by Collins.

Audra's hands gripped the edge of the bunk as her heart quickened. Whiteside marched to the cell door, unlocked it, slid it aside.

"What?" Audra asked, her voice rising in fear.

Whiteside stood aside to let Collins enter, then followed her inside.

"What do you want?"

Neither of the police officers spoke as they approached the bunk. Audra's hands went up, a reflex, an act of surrender.

"Please, what do—?"

In one motion, Collins took Audra's arm, hoisted her up, and threw her to the cell floor. Audra sprawled there, her palms and elbows stinging. She put her hands over her head, ready for a blow from either of them.

"What do you—?"

Collins grabbed the collar of Audra's T-shirt, pulled her up onto her knees. Audra looked up at Whiteside's blank face, opened her mouth to speak again, to plead, but Collins gripped the back of her neck, forced her head down, so she could only see the sheriff from the waist up.

Enough to see him draw a revolver from behind his back.

"Oh God, no."

He pressed the muzzle against the top of her head.

"Oh, God, please, don't." Audra's bladder ached. "Please don't, please don't, please—"

He cocked the pistol, the metallic sound of it bouncing between the walls and bars. Collins tightened her grip on Audra's neck.

Audra raised her hands as if in prayer. "Oh, Jesus, please, no, please, don't—"

A single hard SNAP! as Whiteside pulled the trigger, the hammer falling on an empty chamber.

Audra cried out, a long guttural wail. Collins released her neck.

Whiteside returned the pistol to his waistband.

Audra collapsed to the floor as they left. She curled in on herself, knees to her chest, hands clasped over her head. In the dim early light, even though she didn't believe, she prayed.

CHAPTER 12

SHERIFF RONALD WHITESIDE FOLLOWED DEPUTY COLLINS OUT through the side door onto the disabled access ramp. The sun hung low in the sky, promising heat to come, glinting off the metalwork of their parked cruisers. Collins took a pack of cigarettes from her shirt pocket, and a lighter. She lit one, took a long drag, tucked the pack away as she exhaled blue smoke that hung still in the air, no breeze to move it along.

"You want me to stick around?" she asked.

"No," he said. "Go and check on the other two. Make sure they're okay. I'll say you're out on patrol."

She took another pull. "That boy might be trouble."

"Not if you handle him right. Give me one of those."

Collins stared at his outstretched hand. "You don't smoke."

"I'm considering starting." He clicked his fingers. "Come on, give me one."

She retrieved the pack from her pocket, handed it and the lighter over. He took one, gripped it between his lips, and flicked the lighter's wheel. The smoke filled his lungs, and he couldn't help but cough it out again. He gave her back the pack as his eyes watered. It had been twenty years since he had last smoked a cigarette, and he savored the nicotine crackle in his brain. Another lungful, and this time he kept it in.

"It's not too late," Collins said.

Whiteside shook his head. "Don't."

"We give her back the kids, make her promise not to say what we did, and we can just forget the whole—"

"Goddamn it, shut up," he said, regretting his anger as he spoke.

"We're in it now, and we're going to see it through. You had your chance to back out yesterday when I radioed. You remember what we agreed."

The call for the tow truck, for Emmet. They'd talked about it for months. If and when he found the right kids in the right situation, he'd radio her to ask for Emmet's tow truck. All she had to do was say Emmet couldn't be raised, if she wanted to back out.

"I know, but . . ."

"But what?"

She shook her head. "I just never thought we'd actually do it. It was one thing talking about it. Even yesterday, when you radioed. It didn't feel like a real thing. But last night, when I went up there to bring them food, I thought, Christ, this is for real. And I don't know if I'm strong enough for it."

"It's done," Whiteside said. "We quit now, we might as well hand ourselves over to the feds."

Collins went quiet, staring up at the hills, flicking ash from her cigarette. It had burned halfway down to the butt before she spoke again.

"You should've killed her," she said.

"*I* should've? Not you?"

"All right, *we* should've killed her. Out there on the road. Buried her someplace and got rid of the car."

"That's not how the buyer wants it done," Whiteside said. "He wants it so the trail ends with the parent. Otherwise there's a hunt out for the bodies. This way, there's someone to blame it on. All we have to do is keep her scared, see if we can force her into a breakdown. Any luck, she'll do the job for us."

"Even so," Collins said, "it'd be simpler if she was dead."

Whiteside took the revolver from his waistband, held it out grip-first to Collins. "All right, then. There's a box of .38 rounds in my desk drawer. You go on and load this up, go back in the cell, and put one in her head. Better yet, go out to the desert and do it."

She glared at him.

He pushed the pistol against her hand. "Go on. Go and do it."

Collins dropped her cigarette to the ground, crushed it with her heel. She gave Whiteside one more hard look before walking down the ramp and over to her car. The engine roared as she sped out of the lot. He returned the pistol to his waistband, tucked it into the small of his back. Another drag on the cigarette, the gritty heat becoming more pleasing with each inhalation.

She was right, of course. The simplest thing would have been to drive the Kinney woman way out into the wilds, put a bullet in her head, and let the crows and the coyotes have her. But that wasn't how the buyer played these things. And there was a detail he hadn't told Collins. He'd heard that the buyer—the Rich Man, some called him—liked to watch things play out on the news. He enjoyed the anguish of others.

Whiteside wondered if there'd been any word.

He finished the cigarette, killed the butt under his boot, and went to the passenger door of his cruiser. Inside, he opened the glove compartment, reached back and up, found the pouch fastened to the underside of the dash. He retrieved the cheap cell phone and switched it on. Once it had powered up, he launched the web browser, opening a private window so that no cookies or history would be recorded. He navigated to a proxy server, then from memory typed out the forum's URL, an obscure string of numbers and letters. The login screen appeared, and he entered his details.

One new direct message. He tapped the link.

From: RedHelper
Subject: Re: Items for sale
Message:

Dear Sir,

Thank you for your offer. We have carried out checks and believe your goods to be genuine and safe. Our offer is three million dollars ($3,000,000). We note that both the items show some minor damage. An additional amount of two hundred and fifty thousand dollars ($250,000) will be paid, provided no further damage occurs. These terms are final and non-negotiable. We trust they are to your satisfaction.

Exchange must take place between 3:00 p.m. and 4:00 p.m. on

Saturday; no other timeframe will be acceptable. Please confirm acceptance of these terms and we will be in touch within twenty-four hours to make arrangements for transfer.

We need not remind you that any attempt to disrupt our operation will be met with swift and harsh retaliation.

Regards,

RedHelper

"Jesus Christ," Whiteside said.

Cold sweat prickled all over his body. Three million. No, three and a quarter million. The forum members had said there would be extra for a pair, but he hadn't anticipated so much.

A year ago, Sheriff Ronald Whiteside had killed a man for fifteen thousand dollars, and it had seemed like a fortune until it all blew away. The same forum had brought him that job. A dark corner of the Internet, in the underbelly, where the perverts, the pedophiles, the snuff-hounds, all the worst filth of humanity met to trade in sordid pleasures. The Dark Web, they called it. A fancy name for a place where, no matter how bad you were, there was always somebody worse.

Within that place, in its own shielded corner, there lay a forum, a message board. A place for cops and military people who could provide certain services. You needed something done that only a connected man could do, you sent word to this forum. Whiteside had been introduced by an old army friend. Weeks of checks, and they let him browse the top layers. Another six months, and he was into the inner core. The place where the real money could be made.

The hit had been a low-level dealer in Phoenix. Whiteside never knew what it was over, probably a bad debt, or maybe the mark was threatening to turn informer. He didn't really care. He simply accepted the job and got on with it. A few days of watching and following, then he blew the mark's head off outside a lowlife Tolleson bar. He sped away on a motorcycle he'd salvaged from a scrapyard, the helmet hiding his face, not that anyone outside that particular bar would ever breathe a word to the cops. The money appeared in his offshore account the next morning.

Simple.

After that, another level of the forum opened up to him, one he hadn't known existed. A core within the core. And there they talked about the big money. Hundreds, not tens of thousands. And there was a thread with a simple request. A buyer for a very specific kind of item, who was willing to pay into seven figures. A sequence of instructions, methods, requirements. And an email address, should anyone be able to fulfill the request.

Now, his hands shaking, Whiteside read the message again. Then he pressed reply.

To: RedHelper
Subject: Re: Items for sale
Message:

Dear RedHelper,
    Thank you for your prompt reply. I confirm that your offer is acceptable and await your instructions.
    Regards,
    AZMan

He pressed send, waited for confirmation that the message had sent.

Done.

He switched the phone off and returned it to its pouch beneath the dash.

CHAPTER 13

AUDRA SAT IN SILENCE. CUFFS AROUND HER WRISTS, JOINED by a chain threaded through a metal loop on the table. The room was painted battleship gray over cinderblock, chipped linoleum on the floor, one small grimy frosted window reinforced with wire mesh. The table's vinyl top flaked in places, showing the particleboard beneath. The whole station was like that, verging on ruin, as if the people here had simply given up.

It occurred to Audra that one good yank would probably pull the loop out of the tabletop. And what then? The state patrolman by the door would have her facedown on the floor within seconds, that's what.

The patrolman stared straight ahead, hadn't moved a muscle in the hour she'd been in the interview room, not even to clear his throat. She had tried talking to him, asking about her children, asking for a lawyer. Nothing. He was a big man, all biceps and belly, with meaty fists. His uniform was an almost identical beige to the sheriff's; Audra wouldn't have known he was a state cop had she not been told.

A knock on the door, and Audra's gaze jerked toward it. The patrolman turned and opened it a few inches. A string of whispers, then the patrolman stepped aside to allow a young well-dressed man to enter. A conservative suit, a plain tie. The patrolman had said the FBI were coming, and this young man had to be one of them.

He carried a tripod, its legs bunched together, a small camera mounted on top. A minute of fussing and adjusting and he had it set up in the corner, the lens aimed at Audra. He pressed a button, then another, rotated a display so he could see it. Once satisfied, he nodded, and went to leave.

"Excuse me," Audra said.

The FBI man ignored her, grabbed the door handle.

"Sir, please."

He stopped, turned back to her.

"Please, sir, tell me what's happening."

He allowed her a pained smile. "We'll be with you presently, ma'am."

As he opened the door and stepped through, Audra called after him, "Have you found my children? Are you looking for them?"

The door closed. Audra dipped her head, brought her hands to her mouth, whispered into the cup of her palm, "Goddamn you."

The patrolman looked at her now. "Excuse me?"

Audra held his gaze. "Are they looking for my children?"

"I wouldn't know anything about that, ma'am." He returned his attention to the far wall.

"When can I get a lawyer?" she asked.

The patrolman remained silent.

Audra exhaled, spread her hands on the table, willed her mind to level out, to be calm. She found a crack in the vinyl that looked like a black lightning bolt. She stared at it, followed its arcs and branches, focused in on the details, felt order restored within.

Another knock on the door, harder this time, and the trooper had to sidestep it as it swung open. A woman and a man entered, both suited, her attire crisper than his. She was tall, long-limbed, dark-skinned, her Afro hair cut tight to her scalp, bright eyes that suggested a deep intelligence. The man shambled behind her, a nest of gray-blond hair on his head, the lined face of a smoker. He gave a phlegmy cough and drew out a seat and dropped into it. The woman remained standing, an iPad tucked beneath her arm, along with a notepad and pen.

"Mrs. Kinney, I'm Special Agent Jennifer Mitchell from the Child Abduction Response Deployment team, Federal Bureau of Investigation, based out of Los Angeles. May I sit down?"

Audra nodded.

Mitchell smiled, said thank you, and took her seat. The man bristled and coughed again. Audra caught the stale cigarette smell drifting across the table.

"This gentleman is Detective Lyle Showalter from the Arizona Department of Public Safety, Criminal Investigations Division, based out of Phoenix. Detective Showalter is here strictly to observe. Let me be clear, I am in charge of the investigation into your children's whereabouts."

As Showalter rolled his eyes and shared a smirk with the patrolman, Audra opened her mouth to speak. Mitchell silenced her with a raised hand.

"Before we begin," she said, "there are a few things you should be aware of. Firstly, although you are under arrest for possession of marijuana, this interview does not concern that. Further, you are not under arrest in connection with the disappearance of your children, and you have no entitlement to the presence of a lawyer during this interview. You are therefore free to terminate the interview anytime. I should warn you, however, that failure to cooperate in this matter will not help you. Finally, you see that camera?"

Audra nodded.

"That camera is recording this interview, and I will share footage of this interview with as many other investigators or agencies as I deem necessary to the advancement of this investigation. Mrs. Kinney, do you understand everything I've just told you?"

"Yes, ma'am," Audra said, her voice small and whispery in her throat.

Mitchell pointed at the shackles on Audra's wrists. "Officer, I don't think those are necessary, do you?"

The patrolman looked to Showalter, who nodded. He left his position at the door, taking a key from his pocket as he approached the table, unlocked the bracelets, let them clatter on the tabletop.

"Are those the clothes you were wearing when you were arrested yesterday?" Mitchell asked, pointing with her pen.

"Yes," Audra said.

Mitchell closed her eyes and sighed. She opened them again and said, "They should have been removed as evidence. Once we're done here, we'll get you something else to wear. Now, shall we start?"

"Okay," Audra said.

Mitchell smiled. "Comfortable? Would you like some water?"

Audra shook her head.

"Mrs. Kinney . . . Audra . . . may I call you Audra?"

Audra nodded.

Mitchell took a breath, smiled, and asked, "Audra, what did you do with your children?"

Audra's head went light and full of sparks. She gripped the edge of the table to steady herself. Her mouth opened and closed, no words to fall from it.

"Audra, where are they?"

Stay calm, she thought. Reason with her. Explain.

Still gripping the table, Audra took a long deep breath, filled her lungs. "They took them."

"Who took them?"

"The sheriff," Audra said, her voice rising. She waved her hand at the wall as if Whiteside was on the other side, ear pressed to the cinderblock. "And the deputy, the woman, I don't remember her name."

"Do you mean Sheriff Whiteside and Deputy Collins?"

"Yes, Collins, that's her." Audra became aware of the brittle edge to her voice, breathed again, tried to smooth it. "Deputy Collins took Sean and Louise away while I was in the sheriff's car waiting for the tow truck."

"Is that right?"

"Yes, that's right. They took them."

"I see." Mitchell gave her a small, kind smile. "Thing is, Audra, Sheriff Whiteside doesn't remember it like that. He told me this morning that there were no children in the car when he pulled you over."

"He's lying," Audra said, her nails digging into her palm.

"And Deputy Collins says she was nowhere near the County Road when you were stopped. She drove over there to assist Sheriff Whiteside in searching you."

"She's lying too. Don't you see that?"

"I also spoke very briefly with a Mr. Emmet Calhoun just about thirty minutes ago, and he tells me there were no children around when he towed the car. He thought it odd at the time, because of the booster seat and various bits and pieces he saw in there. He said it was just you in the back of Sheriff Whiteside's cruiser."

"But he came after," Audra said, loud enough to make Showalter wince. "Of course he didn't see them, he didn't get there till after my children had been taken."

Mitchell laid her hands flat on the table, spread her fingers, like smoothing a sheet. "Audra, I need you to calm down. I need you to try to do that for me, okay? I can't help you unless you're calm."

"I'm calm," Audra said, lowering her voice. "I'm calm. But I want my children back. They took them. Why aren't you out looking for them?"

Showalter spoke for the first time. "We've had a helicopter up in the air since first light, searching from here down to Scottsdale. My colleagues are liaising with police and sheriff's departments in neighboring counties, getting search parties together. Don't worry, Mrs. Kinney, whatever you did with those kids, we're going to find them."

Audra slapped the table with her palm. "I didn't do anything with them. Whiteside and Collins have them, for Christ's sake, why won't you listen?"

Mitchell held her gaze for a moment, before turning it to the iPad that lay on the table in front of her. She entered a passcode, illuminating the screen.

"Audra, I need to show you something."

Audra sat back in the chair, fear tightening her chest.

Mitchell said, "Agents from the Phoenix field office have given your car a preliminary search before it goes to the CID pound for a more detailed analysis. They took a few pictures. Do you recognize this?"

She pulled up an image, turned the iPad so Audra could see it. A striped T-shirt. Sean's. A reddish-brown stain on the front.

"Wait, no—"

Mitchell swiped a finger across the screen, replacing that image with another. "And this?"

The interior of Audra's car, the rear footwells, the back of the passenger seat, the passenger-side rear door. With the tip of her pen, Mitchell indicated several points across the image.

"I'd say those look like bloodstains. What do you think?"

Audra shook her head. "No, it's Sean, he gets nosebleeds. He had one day before yesterday. I had to pull over and get him cleaned up. I wiped around the car, but I couldn't do it properly, there was no time, it was getting dark."

Mitchell swiped again. Another image.

Audra said, "Oh God."

"Audra, tell me what you see in this picture."

"Louise's jeans," Audra said. Fresh tears came as she began to quiver. "Oh God. And her underpants."

"Lying in the rear passenger-side footwell," Mitchell said. "They were tucked underneath the passenger seat."

"How . . . how . . . ?"

"Audra, can you make this out?" Mitchell put the tip of her pen to the image. "The jeans appear to be ripped, with blood on them. You can't tell from the image, but they're also damp with what seems to be urine. Is there anything you want to say about that?"

Audra studied the photograph, the jeans, the stitched tulips for pockets.

"She was wearing them," she said.

"Your daughter was wearing these jeans," Mitchell echoed. "When was she wearing them?"

"When she took her."

"When who took her?"

"Deputy Collins. When she took my children away, Louise was wearing those. But they weren't torn. There was no blood on them."

"Then how did these jeans wind up back in your car? After it was towed away, how did they get there?"

Audra shook her head, tears free-flowing down her cheeks, dropping fat and heavy on the table. "I don't know, but the sheriff and the deputy, they took my children, they know where they are. Please make them tell you."

An idea sparked in her mind so bright and clear that she gasped. She put a hand to her mouth.

Mitchell leaned back. "What?"

"The cameras," Audra said, feeling a giddy fizz behind her eyes. "The police cars, they all have cameras, right? Like you see on TV, when they do a traffic stop, they record it all, don't they? Don't they?"

Mitchell gave her a sad smile. "No, Audra, not in Elder County. Deputy Collins' cruiser is almost fifteen years old, it's never had a dashcam fitted, and the one in Sheriff Whiteside's car stopped working three years ago. There's never been spare change in the budget to fix it."

"What about GPS, anything like that?"

"Nothing like that."

The weight of it settled on Audra's shoulders again—the fear, the anger, the impotence. She covered her eyes with her hands as Mitchell spoke.

"Now, I've listened to what you've told me about Sheriff Whiteside and Deputy Collins, and believe me, I will speak with them about that. But right now, even if I discount the things we found in your car, it's your word against theirs. And I've talked to some people today. Including at the diner you ate in early yesterday morning. The manager confirmed Sean and Louise were with you then. As far as I know, she's the last person to have seen you and your kids together. She said you looked nervous."

"Of course I was nervous," Audra said through her hands. "I was trying to get away from my husband."

"I spoke with him too."

Audra's hands dropped away from her face. "No. Not him. Don't listen to him. He's a liar."

"You don't know what he told me yet."

"He's a goddamn liar." Audra's voice rose again. "I don't care what he said. He did this. He paid Whiteside and Collins to take my children from me."

Mitchell sat quiet for a moment, let the silence dampen Audra's anger.

"I spoke with Patrick Kinney early this morning while I was waiting to board the flight from LAX to Phoenix. He told me about the problems you've had in the past. The alcohol. The cocaine."

"The cocaine was a long time ago, before the children, before Patrick even."

"Maybe so, but not the alcohol. Or the prescription meds. He told me you had three different doctors handing out uppers and downers like they were candy. He told me there was a time you barely knew your own children."

Audra closed her eyes and whispered, "Goddamn him. He did this. I know he did."

"Mr. Kinney told me since you left and took the kids, he's been trying to get them back."

"There, see?" Audra said, ignoring Mitchell's irked expression. "He's been trying to take them from me. He paid the sheriff—"

"Let me finish, Audra. You've had New York Children's Services circling, threatening to take the children back to their father. That's why you upped and ran four days ago. Isn't that right?"

"I wasn't going to let him take my—"

"What happened, Audra?" Mitchell leaned forward, her forearms on the table, her voice smooth and soft and low. "I have three kids myself, and an ex-husband. I'm lucky my mom's around to help, but even so, they're a handful. Raising children is hard. *So* hard. It's stressful, you know? Even with all the love I have inside me, when they push hard, I can only bend so far. Every mother should get a medal, I think, just for getting through a day with children."

She leaned closer still, her voice dropping in pitch, honey-sweet, her brown eyes fixed on Audra's.

"So tell me what happened. You've been driving for four days straight, you're tired, you're scared, the heat is getting to you. Maybe Sean and Louise are bickering in the backseat, you know the way children do. Maybe they keep asking for things they can't have, even though you told them no a hundred times already. Maybe they're shouting and screaming, over and over and over, louder and louder, and they just won't stop. Did you do something, Audra? Did you pull over someplace out in the desert and go back there to them? Maybe you only meant to chew them out. Maybe a little smack on the leg or the arm. Maybe a shake, that's all. I know that's all you meant to do, I've wanted to do it to my own kids plenty of times, but you just lost control for a moment. Just for a split second, that's all, and you did something. Is that what happened, Audra? I know it's eating you. All you have to do is tell me, and we can go get them and this will all be over. Just tell me, Audra, what did you do?"

Audra stared at Mitchell, something burning inside her chest.

"You think I hurt my children?"

Mitchell blinked and said, "I don't know. Did you?"

"My son, my daughter, they're both out there somewhere, and you're not looking for them because you think I hurt them."

The same soft smile, the same honey voice. "Did you?"

With no conscious thought, Audra's right hand lashed out, across the table, her palm striking Mitchell's cheek hard and clean. Mitchell recoiled, anger in her eyes, the sting blooming on Audra's hand.

Audra got to her feet and said, "Goddamn you, find my children."

She didn't see the patrolman come at her, only felt his bulk slam into her body, the floor racing up at her. Her chest hit the linoleum, crushing all the air from her lungs, the patrolman's knee on her back, big hands seizing her wrists, forcing them up behind her shoulders.

Audra kept her gaze on Mitchell, who stood at the far wall, breathing hard.

"Find my children," Audra said.

CHAPTER 14

"JESUS," WHITESIDE SAID, TURNING HIS ATTENTION AWAY FROM the video feed on the laptop's display to the young fed who'd set it up. He gave the kid the full force of his sneer. "That went well."

The fed—Special Agent Abrahms, if Whiteside recalled correctly—did not reply. Instead, he tapped a few keys, making windows appear and disappear on the screen.

The laptop had been placed on the rearmost desk in the open office, a handful of state cops looking on, a couple more talking on the phones, taking calls, organizing a search operation. Already a map of Elder and the surrounding counties had been stuck up on a wall, a red pin marking the spot where he had picked up Audra Kinney, more pins marking her last known locations, a string from one to the next giving an approximation of her route over the last few days. More feds and state cops were due to arrive in the county between tonight and the morning, the motel over in Gutteridge about ready to burst. Talk was they'd move the operation over to the town hall soon.

Collins haunted the spaces between the station's desks, pacing the room, sometimes meeting Whiteside's eyes, sometimes not. A couple of the state cops tried flirting with her and got shot down pretty hard.

The door to the interview room opened and the patrolman emerged, one big hand on Audra Kinney's arm, her other held by the detective. Whiteside stood and went to the far wall, leaned his back against it. Collins came to his side.

Audra saw them both and bared her teeth. As the two cops led her back to the custody suite, she craned her neck so she could keep them in sight.

"Where are my children? What did you do with them? What did my husband pay you? You bastards, you tell the truth. Tell them where my children are. You hear me? You tell them. I swear, I'll . . ."

Her voice faded to a muted cry as the door closed behind her.

"Hold your nerve," Whiteside said, low enough so only Collins would hear.

"I'm trying," she said, her voice wavering.

"Trying won't do it. You keep it together or we're dead."

"You think I don't know that?"

"Keep your mind on what comes after," he said, "what that money's going to do for you."

"Won't do me any good if—"

"Shut up."

Mitchell approached, her iPad in one hand, her notebook and pen in the other. Her gaze traveled from Collins to Whiteside and back again, her face unreadable. Then she smiled and said, "Sheriff Whiteside, can you spare me a minute?"

"Sure I can," he said.

He left Collins where she stood and went to the station's side door, Mitchell following. Heat blasted in as he pushed the bar to open the door. He held it wide for Mitchell to step through, closed it behind them both. A sliver of shade on this side of the building shielded them from the worst of the sun, but still the air bore down on Whiteside, the glare on the fleet of state police cars and black federal SUVs making him squint.

"What's that over there?" Mitchell asked, pointing. "Those orange streaks on the hills. Like steps."

"Copper mine," Whiteside said. "Used to be, anyway. Open pit, all the work on the surface. The red is the clay they laid on top of the earth they exposed; they did it when the mine closed. Supposed to stop rainwater leaching acid and stuff into the environment. Not that it rains enough to wet much more than a tissue around here. They call it 'rehabilitation.' Isn't that just great? They rehabilitated the mine like it was some dealer just got out of the penitentiary."

Mitchell shielded her eyes from the glare as she studied the hillside. "What happened to it? Why did they close?"

"Stopped being profitable," he said. "They weren't getting enough out for the work they put in, so, pfft! Gone. This town used to make its living from that mine. Whole damn county, in fact. This used to be a wealthy place, believe it or not. Sort of place a young man could raise a family and know he could provide for them. There's still copper up there, but the suits figured out it was cheaper just to leave it in the ground, and that was all she wrote. The world still needs copper, needs it more than ever to make all our laptops and cell phones and whatnot, but the world wants it cheap. Just you wait, sooner or later, the bean counters are going to figure out it's more cost-effective to get all our copper from China, same as they did with steel, and then the whole country's screwed. It starts in places like this, but it doesn't end here. Towns living or dying by whatever some Ivy League college boy works out on his calculator or his spreadsheet. They closed that mine, it was a death sentence for us. Anyone fit to work got out long ago. What's left is living from one Social Security check to the next, just waiting to die, along with Silver Water."

"I suppose that's why you haven't got the money to fix your dashcam," Mitchell said.

Whiteside let the air out of his lungs in a long exhalation before turning to look at her.

"Special Agent Mitchell, what is your salary like?"

She shook her head. "I'm not going to answer that."

"Well, I've had to take a pay cut for five years straight. Either that or lose my job, that's how the mayor put it to me. I'd wager you pay more in taxes than I take home in a year. You know, I voluntarily gave up my salary for three months last year, just so there was money to pay Deputy Collins. And as shitty as my pay is, hers is worse, and she needs it more. Right now, you might be standing on the poorest patch of ground in the United States, and I've got a budget of about two quarters, a nickel, and a stick of gum to keep it safe."

Mitchell stared at the distant mountains for a time, her lips sealed tight, before she said, "You know I'm going to have to ask the question."

Whiteside nodded. "Yeah, I figured that. Go on, then."

"Is there any truth to what she said? Did you or Deputy Collins play any part in the disappearance of Audra Kinney's children?"

She turned her eyes to him and he held her stare, hard as it was.

"You know we didn't," he said. "It's a fantasy. Maybe she believes it. Maybe it's easier for her to dream up a story than it is to face the truth."

"Maybe," Mitchell said. "But I have to investigate all possibilities. Whether you like it or not."

"I got nothing to hide," Whiteside said.

"I'm sure. I'll have Special Agent Abrahms send that video to the behavioral analyst at the Phoenix field office. We'll know soon whether or not she's lying. And I'll have my team search the back of Collins' cruiser. If there's no truth to Audra Kinney's allegations— well then, you have nothing to worry about. Do you?"

"No," Whiteside said. "I don't."

Mitchell smiled, nodded, and opened the door. She stepped into the station, let the door swing closed.

Whiteside put a hand against the wall to stop himself from falling.

CHAPTER 15

AUDRA WOULD HAVE SCREAMED IF SHE'D HAD THE VOICE FOR it. Every time she tried to shout, it turned into a squeak and whisper in her throat. She paced the cell, willing herself not to bang her head on the bars. A coiled spring strained at the middle of her chest. Panic lurked at the edge of everything, threatening to swoop in and take her control away. So she focused on the anger. Anger was more use to her now than fear.

No one would listen. No one. As though what she said meant nothing to them. She had felt certain when Mitchell walked into the interview room that this woman would at least consider there might be truth in her words. But no, Mitchell was just another cop in a suit, unable or unwilling to look past what Whiteside had put in front of them.

By the clock on the wall, forty-five minutes passed before Mitchell entered carrying a Styrofoam container in one hand, a plastic bag in the other, and a large paper sack tucked under her arm. Audra kept pacing as Mitchell approached the cell.

"Have you eaten since yesterday?" Mitchell asked.

As if woken by the words, Audra's stomach let out a long, deep growl. She stopped walking, wrapped her arms around her belly.

"I guess not," Mitchell said. "I got this from the diner down the street. It smells pretty good."

She placed the container on the desk by the door, a napkin and a plastic fork beside it, along with the paper sack.

"First, though, I want those clothes. I went over to the Goodwill store and got some things. I had to guess your size, but they should do for now. They didn't have any underwear, so I put in some things of mine."

Mitchell unlocked the cell door, slid it aside, and tossed the bag of clothes across the floor to land at Audra's feet. Audra stayed put, didn't reach for it.

"I need your clothes," Mitchell said. "I don't want to have to get some of those state cops in here to strip you by force. The camera's off, and I'll turn my back."

She turned away and Audra opened the bag, pulled out a shirt, a pair of jeans. She found a sports bra that looked like it would fit well enough, two pairs of panties, and a single pair of socks. As quickly as she could, she stripped and dressed again.

She brought her clothes to Mitchell, who bundled them into the clear bag and left them on the desk. Mitchell lifted the polystyrene container, the fork, and the napkin, and brought them back to the cell. Audra kept her hands by her sides.

"Come on," Mitchell said. "You need to eat."

Audra stepped closer and took the box from Mitchell's hand. She opened it and the aroma of beef and tomato and rice swamped her senses. Her stomach growled again, and her mouth filled with saliva.

"Chili," Mitchell said. "Strange, isn't it? The hotter the place, the hotter the food. You'd think people would want to cool down."

Audra retreated to the bunk, sat down, dug in with the plastic fork. She couldn't help but give a moan of pleasure as she chewed.

"I got you this too," Mitchell said, taking a plastic bottle of Coke from her jacket pocket. "Can I come in?"

Audra nodded as she swallowed, as if she had any control over who came and went from between these bars. Mitchell indicated the camera in the corner.

"We're not being watched," she said. "But I know you won't try anything stupid."

"They turned it off last night," Audra said.

Mitchell crossed the cell, placed the bottle of Coke on the bunk, sat down beside Audra.

"Turned it off?"

"Whiteside and Collins," Audra said. "They came in here during the night and put a gun to my head. Whiteside pulled the trigger. I thought I was going to die."

"That's a serious accusation," Mitchell said.

"A serious accusation," Audra echoed. "More serious than taking my children, or less?"

Mitchell leaned in. "Audra, you have to realize the position you're in. Sheriff Whiteside and Deputy Collins have years of public service between them, unquestionable records. Sheriff Whiteside is a war hero, for God's sake. He served in the first Gulf War, got medals and everything. You're a former addict running from Children's Services. How much do you think your word means against theirs?"

The meat and rice in Audra's mouth lost their flavor, turned to ash on her tongue. She dropped the fork into the box, wiped her mouth with the napkin.

"Here," she said, pushing the food back at Mitchell.

The agent took them. "Audra, I want to help you. Don't pull away from me."

"Can I make a phone call?"

"Whatever you've seen on TV, you don't have an automatic right to—"

"Can I make a phone call?"

Mitchell closed her eyes, opened them again, and stood up. "All right."

She reached into her jacket pocket and retrieved a smartphone, entered a code to unlock it.

"You're aware there's about a dozen cops on the other side of that door who want to tear you to pieces, right?"

"Yes," Audra said.

"Well, then," Mitchell said. "Act accordingly."

Audra stood, walked to the far side of the cell, and tapped out the only number she could think of. A few moments of silence, then the purr of the tone, before a woman's voice answered.

"Hello?"

Audra opened her mouth, found it empty. She listened to the hiss and whine of the signal traveling all the way from California. I should be there now, she thought. Me and Sean and Louise, out there by the sea. Not trapped here, not like this.

"Hello? Who's calling, please? If this is a reporter, I don't want to—"

"Mel?"

Silence for a moment, then, "Audra? Is that you?"

"Yeah, it's me. It's good to hear your voice."

"Audra, what's happening?"

"I need help."

"Do the police know you're calling me? Are you calling from jail?"

"Yeah." She forced a smile into her voice. "I know, it's crazy, isn't it? Me in jail. Mel, can you help me?"

"Jesus, the press have been calling me nonstop since this morning, asking about you. I only picked up the phone because I was expecting Suzie's school to call. What do you want?"

"I want help. Mel, I'm in trouble. Whatever you saw on the TV, I didn't do it. The sheriff, he's trying to set me up. Him and his deputy, they have my children. I think if I could get someone, like a private investigator, he could do something. If I had the money to pay him, I could hire one. But I don't have any. I've got nobody else to turn to. Mel, can you help me?"

Audra listened to her friend breathe, in and out, in and out. Mitchell watched, her face blank.

"You want money," Mel said.

"Yes," Audra said. "Can you help me?"

"I'm sorry I ever met you," Mel said. "Don't call me again."

A click, then a series of beeps.

Audra stared at the phone. She wanted to smash it against the wall. She wanted to beat herself around the face with it. Instead she swallowed her anger, did not allow its destructive energy out into the world. She had done that too many times before and it never solved anything. She gripped the phone tightly between her hands and forced herself to think.

Who else?

Audra's parents were long gone. Her one brother was eking out a living as a musician somewhere in Seattle. Even if they'd had any kind of relationship, he'd never kept a dollar in his pocket longer than it took to walk to the nearest bar.

Who, then?

"You done?" Mitchell asked.

"Wait," Audra said.

She screwed her eyes shut, tried to think of someone. Anyone. Only one name came to her mind, and she would not dial that number. Not if her life depended on it.

"You don't want to call your husband?" Mitchell asked, as if reading her mind.

"What good would that do?"

"He's the father of your children."

"That's right," Audra said. "He's my husband. And he's the father of my children. And he's the kind of man who'd pay someone to take my children, just to try and break me. He's been trying for a year and a half to grind me down. I won't let him get me now."

Defeated, she went back to the bunk and returned the phone to Mitchell.

"You have some thinking to do," the agent said, standing.

Audra didn't answer. She sat on the bunk, buried her head in her hands as Mitchell exited the cell and locked the door behind her.

Memory bore down on her like a river on rock, wearing her away.

The first months of her marriage to Patrick had been good. They got married at City Hall, only a handful of people present. Patrick's mother was initially displeased, even used the term "shotgun wedding," but the idea of a grandchild won her over. And when Margaret was happy, Patrick was happy. Or as close as he ever came to it. Audra had grown used to his constant criticism by then, in the way one gets used to a toothache or an arthritic joint. But now his carping had become a nagging concern for the growing life inside her belly. Suddenly his two-bed-two-bath apartment in the Village was no good anymore. Patrick's mother insisted that they move closer to his parents' place on the Upper West Side.

But we can't afford it, Audra had protested.

Maybe not, Margaret had said, but I can.

It was then Audra learned that Patrick's lifestyle was provided for less by his job on Wall Street than by his mother's indulgence. It wasn't that he lacked money; he was, by any measure, a wealthy man. But not Upper West Side wealthy. So, when Audra was five months pregnant, they moved to a three-bed-two-bath in the West Eighties. Unlike her mother-in-law's place, the apartment afforded no view of the park from its window, but it was still greater luxury than Audra had ever hoped to live in.

Even with all that space, there still wasn't a room for her to paint in. While Patrick's mother picked out wall coverings and carpets, and hired the very best contractors to carry out the work, Audra moved her easel from corner to corner, ever cautious of spilling a yellow ocher or a burnt sienna, of letting a brush too near a drape, of knocking over a canning jar full of turpentine or linseed oil.

Some days she didn't paint at all. The smell made her nauseous, and the baby made it uncomfortable for her to sit in a working position. Some days became most days, and by the time Sean was born, she hadn't touched a brush in weeks.

Looking back, Audra could remember that first week with her new baby with utter clarity. She had wanted to breast-feed, even though Patrick's mother said nonsense, a bottle had been good enough for her son, and it would certainly be good enough for her grandson. But Audra had insisted, not that it was any of that old bat's business anyway. She had spent days and weeks reading up on the topic, watching videos on a new website called YouTube, rapt by the simple beauty of the act. It might be difficult at first, all the books and websites said, but don't worry, baby will soon get the hang of it.

But Sean would not latch. And when he did, it hurt so bad it brought Audra to tears. And how he cried, his hunger driving him to sound like a revving chainsaw. No bottle, everyone said. Even if Audra expressed her milk, a bottle would ruin the chances of successful breast-feeding. So she had held Sean upright on her knee, tipping milk from a tiny cup into his tiny mouth. She sniffed back tears as most of the food that she had endured terrible pain to provide for him ran down his chin and his chest. And still he cried as Patrick and Margaret watched, their faces hard and unpitying.

It lasted almost a week. The doctor weighed Sean, said he wasn't too concerned about the lack of weight gain, that they'd figure out the feeding soon enough. But Patrick's mother wouldn't hear any of that.

"You're starving my grandson," Margaret said on the sixth night as Audra took a cup of expressed milk from the fridge.

"No, I'm not," Audra said.

Tiredness made her mind a swamp, thick and heavy in her skull. She still burned and itched between her legs, even though the tearing hadn't been too bad, and the bleeding had lessened over the last twenty-four hours. Her abdomen felt as though it had been used as a punching bag, like she'd been turned inside out, her breasts hard and aching, her nipples stinging. Every single minuscule action seemed like a grinding effort, but still she pushed on.

"Listen to him, for God's sake." Margaret pointed to the door, Sean screeching on the other side. "Just give him a bottle and be done with it."

"No," Audra said. "I want to keep trying. The doctor said he's—"

"I don't care what the doctor said. I know what a suffering child sounds like."

Audra slammed the fridge door shut. "You think I don't hear him?" She tried to keep her voice down, but couldn't. "You think I don't have that noise drilling into my head night and day?"

Margaret glared at her for long seconds before she said, "Please don't raise your voice to me."

"Then don't tell me how to feed my baby," Audra said.

Margaret's eyes widened. She marched out of the kitchen, the door swinging closed behind her. Audra cursed and poured a little of the milk into the small cup she used for feeding. A few seconds in the microwave, and she brought it out to the living room where Patrick waited, his hands in his pockets, Sean still squealing in the bassinet.

"I thought you'd have lifted him," she said. "He needs comforting."

"What did you say to my mother?" Patrick asked.

"I told her to butt out. Not in so many words, but that was the gist of it."

Audra set the warmed cup of milk on the coffee table and took a muslin cloth from the folded stack. She shook it loose, draped it over her arm.

"She's very upset," Patrick said.

"I don't give a—"

The back of Patrick's hand rocked Audra's head on her shoulders, left a hot ball of pain to swell inside her cheek. She staggered two steps to her left, her vision wavering, put her fingertips to the arm of the couch to keep herself upright.

Patrick stood still, blinking, his mouth tight and small.

"I'm sorry," he said, his lips barely moving. "I didn't want to do that. I mean, I didn't mean to. Please don't be angry."

Audra waited for the dizzy waves to abate, then she said, "I need to feed the baby."

"Sure," Patrick said. He shuffled his feet, put his hands back in his pockets. His eyes on the carpet, he left the room.

Audra sniffed hard, wiped her eyes with the heel of her hand. Then she went to the bassinet, lifted Sean out. So small, so delicate, like a rose whose petals would fall if you breathed on it too hard. His cries softened as he nuzzled the skin of her throat.

Try again, she thought.

She brought him to the couch and lay down on her side, opened her dressing gown, and guided his mouth to her breast. He squirmed there, his tiny feet kicking at her belly. She placed her nipple at his upper lip, and on cue, his mouth opened.

Please God, she thought. This time, please.

His mouth closed around her, drew her in.

"Oh God," she said. "Please."

No pain. Pressure, yes, but not the stinging pain she'd felt before. She watched as Sean's jaw worked, up and down, his cheek filling out. Then a pause. Then a swallow.

"Yes," Audra whispered. "That's it, little man. That's how you do it."

Tears rolled across her cheek into her hair.

"Good boy," she said.

Over the next hour, Sean drank his fill. Even when Audra turned to her other side, moved him to the other breast, he latched on again, kept suckling, and she giggled with joy, the heat from her husband's hand forgotten.

When Sean was done, almost passed out from gorging, Audra poured the cup of expressed milk down the kitchen sink and brought her son to the bedroom. She swaddled him in a clean muslin cloth, and he barely stirred as she lowered him into the crib by her bed. The bedclothes swallowed her up, the pillow drawing her head down into its cool embrace. She closed her eyes and knew nothing until sunlight through the bedroom window touched her face.

Audra dragged herself upright, untangled her limbs from the sheets. She checked the clock by the bed: just past six in the morning. How long had she been asleep? Seven hours at least. She reached for the crib, looked inside, found it empty.

"Sean?"

She had felt fear before in her life. Those times she hid from her father, hearing his heavy footsteps on the stairs as he came looking for her, his belt in his hand. Or the time she had gotten stuck on a climbing frame, couldn't find a way down, and no one was around to help her. But this—this was different. This was a cold dagger in her chest, twisting at her core.

Audra threw the sheets off and ran for the door, her bare feet slapping on the varnished floorboards. She pulled the bedroom door open, out into the hall, calling her son's name.

Margaret and Patrick looked up at her as she burst into the living room. Smiling. Why were they smiling?

Then she saw Sean in Margaret's arms. The teat of a bottle in his mouth. His cheeks bulging as he sucked, exhaling from his nose after every swallow.

"What is that?" Audra asked, pointing.

"It's formula," Margaret said, her smile widening. "Look at him go. Such a hungry boy."

"Mom brought it over during the night," Patrick said as if it was a tremendous kindness. "It's his second feed. He's been belting it down."

"I couldn't bear to hear him cry like that," Margaret said. "Not when there's a Duane Reade right around the corner. Did you know you can get it ready-made now? In a carton? Just like orange juice."

Audra's hand went to her breast. She still felt her son there, the warmth of him.

"Why did you do that?" she asked.

"It was no trouble," Margaret said. "Like I said, the drugstore's right there, it's so easy to make up. You just put it in the microwave and—"

"Why did you do that?"

Sean flinched at the sound of her scream. The smiles left Patrick's and Margaret's faces. They stared up at her.

"I want to feed him," Audra said.

"If it means that much to you," Margaret said, taking the bottle from Sean's mouth, holding it out to her. "Here, go ahead."

"No!" Audra clutched at her breasts. "*I* want to feed him. *Me*."

Margaret turned the corners of her lips down in distaste. "Really, I don't see what's wrong with—"

"Give him to me," Audra said as she crossed the room, her hands outstretched.

Margaret stood and said, "All right. But remember, your baby's health is more important than your pride."

Audra took Sean from her, gathered him in close as he snuffled and mewled.

"I'd like you to leave now," she said.

Patrick shot up from the couch, his mouth open, but Margaret waved at him to be quiet. "It's all right, dear, she's bound to be emotional. The first weeks are always the hardest."

As she walked to the door to the hall, Audra said, "I think you should know something."

Margaret stopped, turned to her with a raised eyebrow.

"Last night, your son hit me."

Margaret looked to Patrick, who looked at his feet. "It's hard on the father too, but he shouldn't have done that. Though I imagine you deserved it."

She left the room, silence in her wake until Patrick spoke, his voice quivery and wet.

"Don't ever do anything like that again," he said.

"Or what?"

"What happens between us stays between us," he said.

"I'm going to put Sean down for a sleep," Audra said. "I'm going to take a shower, then I'm going to pack."

"You have nowhere to go," Patrick said.

"I have friends."

"What friends?" Patrick asked. "When was the last time you saw any of those artsy shitbags?"

"Don't talk about them like that."

Sean stirred in her arms, agitated by her rising anger.

"Whatever, when was the last time you saw one of them?"

When Audra couldn't think of the answer to his question, she turned and left the room, went to their bedroom, and closed the door. She swaddled Sean once more and went to the en suite bathroom. With the door open, she showered, her tears melding with the hot water, flushed away into the drain. A cold feeling in her gut as she accepted that Patrick was right: she had nowhere to go. He had never wanted to be around her friends when they were dating, and she had drifted away from them, quietly pulled from their orbits and into his.

Once she'd dried off, she wrapped her dressing gown around her and lay on the bed, watching Sean through the bars of his crib. Listened to his breathing, allowed herself to be carried away by it.

Hours later, he woke, hungry again. Audra lifted him from the crib, brought him back to the bed, where she offered him her breast once more.

He refused it, and she wept bitter tears of defeat.

Even so, she tried again through the day. And still he squirmed and fussed, his lips slipping away from her. The screeching returned, that drill bit boring into her head. The small cups of expressed milk did not satisfy him, most of it spilled and wasted. She caught glimpses of Patrick watching her from doorways, saying nothing, and she knew what he was waiting for.

At ten o'clock that night, twenty-four hours after the first and last time that Sean would ever drink from her breast, Audra went to the cupboard by the fridge and took down one of the small cartons of formula. As easy as Margaret had said. Just put it in the bottle, heat it in the microwave. Simple as that.

She sat on the couch, Sean gulping at formula, nothing but a dry hollowness inside her. Patrick came to her then, sat down beside her. He put an arm around her shoulders, kissed her hair.

"It's for the best," he said. "For you and for him."

Audra had no strength left to argue.

CHAPTER 16

D ANNY LEE WATCHED THE ROLLING NEWS AS HE WORKED OUT IN his living room. He raised the pair of twenty-pound dumbbells from his thighs to his shoulders and back again, keeping his breath steady, not rushing the lift or the drop, letting his biceps do the work. Ten reps in a set, thirty seconds between sets.

That image of the woman launching herself at the sheriff, over and over. Nothing new had emerged through the afternoon into the evening, yet he kept watching.

He moved on to lateral lifts, swapping to twelve-pound weights. Sweat-drenched hair fell into his eyes, and he shook it away. On the television, a detective from the Arizona Department of Public Safety, Criminal Investigations Division, talked about search parties and aerial scans. The picture changed to a police helicopter circling over a desert road, then teams of uniformed men picking through the scrub and the rocks and the cacti, two highway patrolmen hunched over a map that was spread across a cruiser's hood.

Then a photograph of the woman, a mug shot, her face reading fear and bewilderment. The woman had a history, the anchor explained, of addiction. Booze and prescription drugs, an overdose two years ago. Destroyed her marriage. And Children's Services had been on her back recently, trying to get the children signed over to the husband. So she had put the kids in the car and taken off. Four days later, she'd made it as far as Arizona.

But no children.

Now a photo of the kids, at least a couple of years younger than they were today. Both of them beaming amid piles of torn wrapping paper and Christmas toys. Next, the anchor addressing the camera, saying the search was on to find Sean and Louise Kinney before it was too late. But he couldn't hide that tone in his voice, the one that said it was already too late, these children were gone as gone could be.

Danny lowered the weights to the floor, rolled his shoulders, worked the muscles with his knuckles. He closed his eyes for a moment, savored the weary tingle through his upper arms and back, the rush of oxygen as he breathed in through his nose, out through his mouth.

Mya's face shimmered in his mind.

Five years she'd been gone. Sara six weeks before that. Mya just couldn't take it. Danny had tried to be strong for her. He couldn't have done any more. By the end, Mya asked him again and again if he believed her.

Did he believe those policemen took Sara away?

Of course he did. Of course.

But she must have seen something in his eyes, some vein of doubt. And hadn't he asked himself that question some nights? What if the police were right? What if Mya was lying? What if she really did do that awful thing the police and the feds had suggested?

When Mya took her own life, the cops stopped looking for Sara. But Danny didn't. Even though his rational mind told him she was almost certainly dead, he had to keep searching until the trail went cold. As senseless as it was, there remained a flicker in him even now, like a candle that won't be blown out. Maybe Sara was still out there somewhere.

Almost certainly not. But maybe.

And now this woman all the way out in Arizona. She looked like Mya, a little. Both of them white, of course, but it was more than that. The cheekbones were alike. The good strong jawline, the curve of the lips.

"Did they take your children from you?" Danny asked his empty living room.

He scolded himself for talking to thin air like a crazy man, drained the bottle of water on the side table, and switched off the TV set. Ten minutes later, he was climbing into his cold and empty bed.

Mya had never slept in this one—he had replaced their bed after she died, unable to face lying in it without her—but still he missed her shape, curled beneath the sheets, her cheek resting on her palm, the faint purr of her breathing.

Mya had saved him. There was no question. Were it not for her, he would have wound up locked away, maybe a big man inside, but inside all the same. She knew they called him Danny Doe Jai, Knife Boy, but she never asked why. And he never told her.

He'd been drawn into the Tong at fifteen. Pork Belly had vouched for him, taken him under his wing. By sixteen, he was living in an apartment off Stockton Street with five other young men with more anger than brains. Collected a few debts here, sold a few wraps there. When he was nineteen he was working the door at a brothel above a restaurant, making sure the drunks stayed out, that the johns had the cash to pay for their pleasure. Making sure the girls didn't get slapped around by anyone other than the men who owned them.

It was there that he came to the Dragon Head's attention. A drunk sailor in his Navy duds had come in when Danny was on a piss break, and whoever was keeping an eye on the door hadn't had the nerve to send him away. The sailor had broken a girl's nose and was refusing to leave. Danny came out of the restroom, got hold of the sailor, and threw him down the stairs. At the bottom, Danny drew his knife and cut him so bad that Pork Belly had to come pick the sailor up and dump him out on one of the piers. Danny never found out if he lived or died. Wouldn't be the last man he killed, anyway.

Danny never moved up much. He was too useful on the streets, even as smart as he was. Too good with a blade. He hurt a lot of people.

Until he met Mya.

She'd been at the next table when Danny was eating and drinking with Pork Belly and his friends in the restaurant below the brothel. The boys had all sniggered as she stood from her table and crossed to theirs.

In the most musical Cantonese he'd ever heard, this white girl said, "You boys ought to watch your language in public. What would your mothers say?"

The boys had roared with laughter, and Mya had returned to her friend, seemingly defeated. She took the other young woman by the arm and led her to the counter, where she talked to the cashier before leaving.

When the check came for Danny's table, Pork Belly held it at arm's length.

"This isn't right," he said. "Who had this?"

They passed the check around the table and no one had the answer.

But Danny knew. By the time Pork Belly had called the waiter back over, Danny was already laughing fit to burst.

"The young lady," the waiter said. "She said you'd offered to pay for their dinner."

Pork Belly had sat quiet and still for a few moments, his eyes burning. Then he threw his head back and his gut wobbled with a peal of laughter.

It took a week to find her. Another week to convince her that she should allow Danny to take her out sometime. Two more weeks to fall so in love that he knew he would never again take a breath without her approval.

She was teaching part-time at USF's Asian Studies Department while working on her doctorate. Her father had been a banker based in Hong Kong through much of her childhood, only returning to the States when he was diagnosed with the cancer that took his money and his life. She was fluent in Cantonese, had a workable grasp of Mandarin, and smatterings of Korean and Japanese. Danny's friends had at first warned him that she was a tourist, attracted to his exoticism, a rough-boy trophy to parade in front of the other white folks.

But they were wrong. Danny knew it beyond all certainty. On the day they married, Mya became the first person to call him by his Chinese name since his mother on her deathbed: Lee Kai Lum.

It was Mya who put him straight. Mya who encouraged him to use his contacts to help keep kids out of the gangs. To work with the police and the community. Make his neighborhood a better place, not worse.

Danny proposed the night Mya told him she was pregnant. She had come close to a termination, she said, agonizing over the choice, before she accepted that she could be a mother. He swore he would never abandon her, that the life inside her, even if it was only a cluster of cells, was a part of him. And therefore he was a part of Mya. They were tied together forever, like it or not, so why not make it real?

When those cops stopped Mya on a lonely road and took Sara from her, they might as well have put a gun to her head. They killed her then, even if she seemed to go on living for the six weeks it took for her to give up. And still her death, and Sara's, did not sever the tie between them. Slowly, steadily, Mya had been dragging him after her into the grave.

But he still had business to settle.

Every breath he took now felt like a debt to her, as if the five years between here and there were simply borrowed. God, he missed her and his daughter like they were bones ripped from his body. Especially nights like this, when all he had were the ghosts in his head.

Somehow, somewhere in the next hour, sleep took him, swallowed him whole. Bloody dreams stalked him; they always did. But now there were new faces among the old: two children and their mother. All the things he could not change, could not reach, and here they were, and maybe if he stretched far enough, bled enough, maybe he could reach them.

Danny jerked awake in the darkness, his heart thundering, lungs heaving, nerves carrying a jangling charge like bell wire. He checked his clock: not long past midnight.

When his heart had calmed, and he had his breathing under control, he pulled aside the sheets and got out of bed. Wearing only his underwear, he left the bedroom and walked down the stairs. Only when he reached the bottom did he wonder why he had come down at all.

"Thirsty," he said aloud.

He wiped the back of his hand across his mouth and thought, yeah, thirsty. He remembered the almost full carton of orange juice in the fridge and padded through the living room out into the kitchen.

Fetched a glass from the cupboard and poured himself a generous serving. One swallow half emptied the glass, and he turned away from the fridge.

His laptop sat closed on the table.

Without thinking, he sat down, set the glass beside it, and opened the computer. The screen flickered on and he entered his password. The web browser opened on the Google home page.

He typed: *Fly SFO > PHX*

"Huh," he said as a list of travel sites and ticket prices filled the screen. "So that's what I'm doing."

CHAPTER 17

THE NIGHT HAD DRAGGED ON LONG AND SLOW FOR SEAN. AT least, he thought it was night. The temperature had gone from cool to cooler, the quiet entering a deeper silence. Louise had slept on and off for much of the day and night, and her forehead had become hot to the touch, even though she shivered and complained of being cold.

Sean knew his sister was becoming sick, but he didn't know what to do about it. He supposed he would ask Deputy Collins for some medicine when she came back.

If she came back.

She hadn't been by since the morning, when she left some more sandwiches, potato chips, and fruit. Sean had devoured two bananas and a fistful of chips. Louise had taken a bite from an apple and had eaten nothing since.

"When can we go?" Sean had asked.

"Maybe tomorrow," Collins had said. "Day after at the latest."

"The police will be out looking for us," Sean said. "There'll be search parties. You won't move us until it's safe. Until you won't get caught."

Collins smiled. "You're a smart kid. You know, I have a boy maybe a year younger than you."

"What's his name?"

Collins hesitated, then said, "Michael. Mikey."

"What's he like?"

Her eyes went distant. "Smart, like I said. And funny."

"Does he have a dad?"

She shook her head. "He's not around anymore. Truth be told, he was a bit of an asshole."

"Mine's not around, either," Sean said. "I guess he's an asshole too."

"You shouldn't say words like that."

Sean ignored her admonishment. "What does Mikey like to do? Does he play sports?"

"No," Collins said. "Mikey gets sick a lot. He has a problem with his heart. Means he can't do stuff like that. He has to stay in bed a lot of the time and take medicine. So he reads mostly. Comic books and stuff."

"Me too," Sean said. "Not the staying in bed part, I mean the comic books. I like comic books. Maybe I could meet Mikey sometime. Maybe we could be friends."

Suddenly Collins came back to herself, her eyes hardening, her lips thinning. She reached down and grabbed Sean's shirt in her fist, pulled him close, so he could feel her breath on his skin.

"I know what you're doing, you little shit. You're smart, but you're not that smart. Now keep out of my head."

Sean watched her eyes while she spoke and saw no anger there. Collins couldn't hold his gaze, looked away as her cheeks grew red. She turned and climbed the steps, let the trapdoor drop closed behind her, bolted it, locked it. Sean heard the buzz of the motorcycle, its engine note rising in pitch as she sped away across the forest.

How long had passed since then? Could it be twenty-four hours yet? Sean simply didn't know.

He reached across the mattress and placed his palm on Louise's forehead. Still hot, still damp with sweat. Louise moaned and swatted his hand away.

"Don't worry," he said. "I'm going to get us out of here. We'll find Mom and we'll go to California, to San Diego, and we can go to the beach. Just like she promised. You hear me?"

Louise blinked and said, "I hear you."

"Good," he said. "Now let's get some sleep."

He watched her close her eyes, then he closed his own, his arm around his sister, her warm body pressed against his. Sleep came like a shadow, slipped over him, and he knew nothing more until the trapdoor opening overhead pulled him awake.

Sean blinked up at the rectangle of light and the silhouette of Collins descending the steps, a bag of food in one hand.

"I think Louise is sick," he said.

Collins set the bag on the floor and came to the side of the mattress. She hunkered down and reached across to feel Louise's forehead, then down inside her top. Louise barely stirred at her touch.

"Goddamn it," Collins said.

Sean sat up on the mattress. "You need to get medicine for her," he said.

"I don't know if I can get any."

"What if she gets worse?"

"All right," Collins said, standing up. "Make sure she takes plenty of water. Take the blanket off her, maybe take her top off, try to cool her down. I'll be back later."

She turned and walked back toward the steps. Sean called after her.

"Deputy Collins?"

She stopped, looked back over her shoulder.

"Thank you," Sean said.

Her eyelids flickered. She turned and climbed the steps, locked the trapdoor without replying.

CHAPTER 18

AUDRA'S MIND ACHED. THE WORLD HAD STRETCHED SO THIN she imagined she could tear a hole in it with a fingertip. Everything moved in jerks, either too slow or too fast, and everyone spoke in jumbles of sound. Part of her knew it was exhaustion, but the other part felt she moved through a dream, that none of this was real. That it was happening to some other woman in some other town, as she watched it all play out like a strange television show.

She had lain awake through the night watching the red light on the camera, waiting for it to blink out, fearing that when it did, they would come again, put a gun to her head. At moments she wondered if that had really happened at all. Had she simply dreamed it, one of those nightmares that follows you into waking? But she did fall asleep at some point, only to wake again, like dragging herself up through tar, her heart hammering, lungs unable to grab the air they needed.

When she opened her eyes, Whiteside stood over her.

He hunkered down next to the bunk.

"You've got to let them go," he said. "They're gone, and that's all there is to it."

Paralyzed, she couldn't raise a fist to strike him.

Part of her mind asked, am I dreaming? Is he really there?

His hand came into her view, the fingers open as if reaching for a glass of water. They slipped around her throat. Pressure. Just a little. Enough to hurt.

"Don't think I won't," he said. "If I have to."

Then he let go and stood upright, turned, left the cell.

Alone again, she gasped, her heart suddenly beating hard and fast. Chest rising and falling, grabbing at air.

She couldn't tell how long it took for the waves of fear to ebb away, only that the sun had risen over the world outside, coloring everything around her in deep blues and grays.

After a while, Audra became less certain that Whiteside had been there at all. He might have been a phantom of her sleep-deprived brain. Another piece of her sanity breaking and falling away.

Perhaps that was the point. To get inside her head, break her from within. Make her crazy, keep her scared. Because scared is easy to control. Just as Patrick had done all the years they were together.

Her husband had made her doubt every single facet of her being, kept her constantly off balance until she barely knew up from down. Every morning, he'd berate her for her hangover. Every evening he'd come home with another bottle. One day telling her how pathetic she was for needing the pills, the next day getting another prescription filled for her.

It had started the evening after her defeat, when she gave Sean a bottle of formula for the first time. Patrick had come home from work with a bottle of white wine. He held it out to her as she fed their son.

"What's that for?" Audra asked.

"If you're not breast-feeding," Patrick said, "there's no reason why you can't have a drink."

"I don't want it," she said.

She hadn't touched alcohol since she'd discovered she was pregnant, had sworn she wouldn't touch it again after the baby was born. Too many nights had been lost to the blur. She wasn't going to get pulled into that mire again.

Patrick shrugged and nodded. "Okay. It'll be in the fridge if you change your mind."

If she had possessed the clarity of mind to ask why he'd brought home the bottle of wine, why he wanted her to be drunk again after all these months of sobriety, things might have been different. But she didn't ask. She was too broken for rational thought.

The night feeds came and went, Audra's mind dimming with each one, sleep seeming like a strange and vague notion, not something she could actually indulge in. In the morning, Margaret appeared, volunteered to take over and let Audra rest. Audra tried to resist, but Margaret's insistence and Patrick's hard stare won out. She handed Sean over to his grandmother and went to the bedroom, where she dreamed her milk had poisoned him, made him sick, and she woke with an aching sorrow that did not leave her as the day dragged on.

Audra saw the bottle of wine there in the fridge that evening, but she ignored it, even though she was very, very thirsty.

Another night of fragmented sleep and toxic dreams, and even as she held Sean close, listening to him gulp down formula, she felt something had broken between them. She had let him down, and she had lost something she could never get back, no matter how hard she wished for it.

In the morning, Margaret came again. And, again, Audra handed her baby over. Once more, she went to bed. Now the mattress and the sheets felt like quicksand, and she wanted to be swallowed up, to stay in the dark forever.

That night, she poured herself a glass of wine. But just the one.

The night after, she had another glass. And a second.

A day later, another bottle of wine appeared in the fridge. Audra finished the first, and opened the next. She didn't stop until she had passed out drunk on the couch. Patrick woke her in the morning, told her she should be ashamed of herself.

That night, he brought home a bottle of vodka.

Again, looking back, she should have asked why. But the lure of the haze was too strong to resist, when all she wanted was to blot everything out.

Weeks passed like that, nights and days blurring into drunken hazes and oily hangovers. The nanny had been in the apartment almost forty-eight hours before Audra noticed her. Jacinta was her name, a pretty young woman from Venezuela who looked at Audra with an expression of pity when they met in the hallway.

"You're not fit to care for Sean," Patrick explained, "so I hired someone who is."

Audra went to bed for four days, only emerging for another bottle of whatever Patrick had left in the fridge or cupboards for her. On the fifth day, a doctor came to the apartment. One Audra didn't recognize. He smelled bad, sweat and mildew, masked with aftershave. He asked her a few questions, scribbled on a pad, and gave the paper to Patrick. Her husband came back after an hour with a bottle of pills and a glass of water. She refused the water, downed two pills with a mouthful of neat vodka, and went to sleep.

Looking back, it seemed to Audra that she had been sucked down by a sinkhole, unable to climb out again. Every time she resolved to go without a drink or a pill, Patrick would appear with a full glass, or another rattling bottle.

Sometimes she wondered about her child. She was surprised one day to pass through the living room on her way to the kitchen and see Sean walking across the room into Jacinta's arms, a tottering gait, his hands up and flapping, giggling as he went.

"When did he start that?" Audra asked, suddenly aware that months must have passed without her noticing.

"A week ago," Jacinta said. "You saw him do it yesterday. You asked me the same thing."

Audra blinked. "Did I?"

"Do you want to hold him?"

Audra didn't answer. She went to the kitchen and fetched another bottle of wine.

She remembered Sean's third birthday. They had a small gathering at Patrick's parents' apartment. Patrick had hidden the booze and the pills, told her he wanted her sober.

"Don't show me up," he'd said. "Don't embarrass me."

The fog had drifted from her mind that morning, and she studied herself in the mirror after she showered. The darkness around her eyes, the blotches on her cheeks. The skin too loose on her bones. But she did her best with the makeup and the new clothes Patrick had bought. She presented herself to him before they left to walk the few blocks south.

"You'll do," he said, a weary exhalation.

She walked next to Patrick along Central Park West, Jacinta

holding Sean's hand as he tottered ahead. The buzz of the traffic fizzed in her brain, the cool air on her skin making her tingle, aware of the sensation of her clothing against her body, the weight of her feet on the ground. In spite of the rumbling ache behind her eyes, she felt something she hadn't experienced for so long: she felt alive.

"Patrick," she said.

"Mm?" He kept his gaze ahead, didn't turn to look at her.

"Maybe I should get some help."

He didn't answer, stopped walking. Audra stopped too, both of them standing like islands, the flow of people like water around them.

"Maybe I should talk to somebody," she said. "About the drinking. And the pills. Try to change."

Patrick remained quiet, but his jaw worked as he ground his teeth.

"I didn't know it was my son's birthday until you told me."

Tears came, hot on her cheeks.

Patrick took her hand, squeezed it hard, squeezed until it hurt. "We'll talk about it when we get home," he said. "Pull yourself together. Don't embarrass me in front of my mother's friends."

"Why do you keep me like this?" she asked. "Why keep me around at all? I'm not a wife to you. I'm not a mother to my son. Why don't you just let me go?"

He squeezed her hand again, harder, and she had to bite her lip to keep from crying out.

"Do you want to humiliate me?" he asked, leaning in close. "Is that what you want? So help me, I will beat you senseless right here on the street. Is that what you want me to do?"

Audra shook her head.

"Then shut your fucking mouth and start walking," he said.

Audra wiped at her cheeks, sniffed, got herself under control, and walked with her hand in his, the bones aching.

At his parents' apartment, people milled between the tables laden with finger food and glasses of sparkling wine. Audra watched the bubbles, imagined the feel of them on her tongue, the sweetness of the swallow. She and Patrick sat at a table in the center of the room, Sean in a highchair, Jacinta feeding him a piece of cake.

Patrick Senior sat quiet in a corner, his hands quivering in his lap, the dementia by now evident for all to see. The guests ignored him, as did his son and wife. From the other side of the room, his distant eyes met Audra's, focused, only for a moment, but long enough for her to wonder if the old man saw her. Did he recognize her, the way she recognized him, each lost and alone in a room full of people?

Margaret came to sit with Audra and Patrick Junior. Father Malloy—the priest who had christened their son—followed behind, smiling. Margaret took Patrick's hand in hers.

"Now, you two," she said, "isn't it time you gave me another grandchild? We can't have Sean growing up an only child, like Patrick."

Patrick blushed and smiled as Margaret squeezed his knee. And Audra caught a glimpse of her function in the marriage, then. She shivered and counted the minutes until she could go home and retreat to the haze.

CHAPTER 19

D ANNY STEERED THE RENTAL CAR OUT OF THE LOT AT PHOENIX Sky Harbor, followed the GPS directions for the Ak-Chin Pavilion to the west of the city. A Mexican eatery near there, with a bar, popular with the locals, he'd been told.

This goddamn heat. Christ, he was used to the cool of San Francisco, never too hot, never too cold. Not like this. The goddamn air cooked the inside of his throat. He'd made the mistake of putting his hand on the hood of the Chevrolet when he collected the car, and it recoiled as if he'd stuck it on an electric burner.

The journey took twenty minutes along the highway, then only a handful of turns until the sprawling grounds of the amphitheater came into view. He headed west for two blocks and found the restaurant. A hand-painted sign over the door, big red letters, green cacti wearing sombreros. Plenty of space at the curb this time of day, he pulled in.

Danny put his fingers to the door handle and braced himself. The car's AC had barely begun to cool it down, and sweat pooled in the small of his back, in the crack of his ass. He opened the door, and the heat roared at him.

A few paces took him to the restaurant door. Inside, ice-cold air gushed down from an AC unit over the threshold. He stayed there for a moment, savored the feel of it on his body. A young Hispanic woman approached, took a menu from the table by the sign that said PLEASE WAIT TO BE SEATED.

"For one?" she asked, a broad smile on her face.

Danny returned the smile. "Hey, how are you? I'm here to see George. I think he's expecting me."

Her smile disappeared. "Wait right here," she said and dashed over to the bar to speak with a large man. His black hair was greased back, his arms sleeved with tattoos. He glanced over at Danny as the girl spoke. He lifted a telephone receiver, spoke a few words, listened, then hung up before saying something to the girl.

She came back to Danny, nervous now, and said, "This way, please."

He followed her to the restaurant's dim interior, weaving through the tables and the scattering of afternoon diners. A doorway veiled by stringed beads, the sign above reading PRIVATE DINING. The girl slipped a hand between the beads, pulled them back to allow Danny to step through. On the other side, the beads rattled and whispered across his back as she let them go.

The room held one large circular table. Big enough to seat a dozen comfortably, more if patrons were willing to touch elbows. It had been set for a gathering, a clean white cloth, sparkling cutlery and glasses. At one of the chairs, George Lin.

"Long time, Danny Doe Jai," George said.

"Ten years," Danny said.

"I was sorry to hear about your wife and your little girl. No man should have to deal with that shit. Come, sit down."

Danny walked around the table, took a chair two away from George's. A little more than arm's length. He wasn't afraid of George Lin, but that didn't mean he trusted him.

Danny cast his eyes around the room. "Mexican?"

"When in Arizona," George said.

"How can you stand this heat?"

"What, you don't like it? It's always wet and cold in San Fran. Here, it's summer all year long. Why do you think I moved out here? I got a pool in my yard and everything."

Danny shook his head. "I don't think I could take it. Drive me crazy after a while."

George smiled. "Man, just chill out and eat some ice cream, drink some water, you'll be fine. Anyway, you ain't here to talk about the weather."

He reached under the tablecloth for something on the seat to the far side of him. A large padded envelope, creased and torn. He set it on the table, a weighty clunk from within.

"Here you go," George said as he sat back, one hand waving at the envelope. "Check it out, see if it fits."

Danny pulled the envelope toward himself, parted the opening with his fingers, peered inside. He tipped it up and a Smith & Wesson Model 60 tumbled out, followed by three boxes of ammunition and a speedloader.

George tapped each box in turn. "Hollow point .357, FMJ .357, and FMJ .38 Special. Unless you're thinking of starting a war out here, I figure that should cover you."

Danny lifted the pistol, kept the short muzzle aimed at the wall, and opened the cylinder to check that the five charge chambers were empty. He gave it a spin, closed it, then cocked and dry-fired three times.

"That'll do," he said. He packed the pistol and the ammo back into the envelope.

George extended his open hand. Danny fished a roll of bills out of his pocket, counted out hundreds into George's palm.

When he was satisfied, George asked, "So, you just doing some target practice while you're here?"

"Something like that," Danny said as he grabbed the envelope and stood to leave. "Good to see you again, George."

As he walked to the beaded doorway, George called after him.

"Whatever you got going on, Danny Doe Jai, just be careful, all right?"

Danny glanced back over his shoulder and said, "I'll try."

He slipped through the hanging beads, back out through the restaurant, the package under his arm. The young lady who'd greeted him gave him a nervous smile as he passed on his way to the door. As he reached the cool draft of the AC unit, a thought occurred to him. He turned back to the girl.

"Hey," he said. "Is there a hardware store near here?"

CHAPTER 20

THE SUITED MAN EXTENDED HIS HAND ACROSS THE TABLE AND said, "My name is Todd Hendry, I'm a public defender."

The chain rattled as Audra lifted her hand to shake his. "You're what?"

"I'm your attorney," he said.

The interview room's fluorescent light reflected off his freckled scalp. He placed a thin file, a notepad, and a pen on the table as he sat down.

"Why are you here?" Audra asked.

"You can't go to an arraignment without representation," he said. "Well, you can, but I wouldn't advise it."

"Arraignment?"

"The possession with intent charge," Hendry said. "The hearing's in an hour. Didn't they tell you?"

"No," she said. "All they've done is question me about my children."

Another session with Mitchell last night, one first thing this morning. The same questions over and over, the same answers. No matter how often she told the FBI agent that Whiteside and Collins had taken Sean and Louise, that her husband had to be behind it, Mitchell kept turning it around, pointing the question back at her. And always that kindness in her eyes and in her voice.

At one point this morning, during a brief break in the questioning, when she was alone with the patrolman in this room, an idea crept into Audra's addled head: What if she really had hurt her children? What if they were right? Maybe her mind couldn't cope with the truth, so she had created another reality? None of this felt quite real, did it?

That had been the closest she'd come to breaking. She had felt herself crumble, like a wall with no foundation.

Hendry opened the file, what looked like some sort of police report, clicked his pen, and placed the tip close to the pad. "So, tell me exactly what happened on the morning of the fifth."

She told him. The general store by the roadside, Whiteside's car parked out front, driving away, the flashing lights in her mirror, the stop, the search.

"Wait a moment," Hendry said. "Before Sheriff Whiteside opened the trunk of your car, did he seek your consent to search it?"

"No," Audra said.

"Was the bag of marijuana visible from outside the vehicle?"

"It was never in my car in the first place. He planted it there to—"

Hendry raised a hand. "Listen, let's not say anything about planting things in your car. Assuming—just assuming—the marijuana was in fact in your car, where he found it, would it have been visible from outside the vehicle?"

"No," Audra said. "He reached under some blankets to get it, but it wasn't—"

"That's all I need to know," Hendry said, smiling.

JUDGE MILLER peered over the top of her glasses, her gaze somewhere over Audra's shoulder.

"Sheriff Whiteside, is this true?" she asked, the lines of her face deepening, puckering around her mouth. "Didn't you seek consent to search the vehicle?"

Audra turned her head, saw Whiteside stand up from his chair among the crowd of onlookers, his hat gripped in his hands, and clear his throat.

"No, Your Honor," he said, "it's not true. I had consent to search."

"The defendant says different," the judge said. "I need better than your word, Sheriff."

Whiteside met her stare, straightened his back, raised his head. "My word is all I have, and if that's not good enough for—"

"No, it is not good enough for me, Sheriff. Let's try applying some logic to this, shall we?"

Whiteside seemed to lose an inch in height. A twitch below his left eye.

A hush fell over the press people who occupied the rear part of the town hall's meeting room. Tables had been arranged in an approximation of a court layout, one each for the defense and the prosecution, both facing another, where Judge Miller now sat, a weary expression on her face. She removed her spectacles and placed them on the notepad in front of her.

As soon as they'd arrived, Hendry had gone to the middle-aged man at the other table, the one whose suit was too tight and too old, and they had huddled together, whispering into each other's ears. The state prosecutor, Audra had guessed. Hendry had explained that Joel Redmond would have shown up expecting a simple plea to a minor offense. He certainly didn't look prepared for what Hendry told him. The prosecutor had sat back in his chair, shaking his head, then stood and walked to where the judge sat. Judge Miller had shook her head in much the same manner as Redmond, as he went back to the table to pack up his things.

Now Judge Miller spoke again.

"So, you spot this car that you deem to be overloaded. You pull it over, find a lone woman inside."

Audra went to speak, but Hendry took hold of her wrist, silenced her.

"What was it about this scenario that gave you probable cause to search the vehicle?" She raised a hand before Whiteside could reply. "Let me answer that for you: Nothing. You had no good reason to search the vehicle, so you had no good reason to seek consent. Therefore I'm inclined to believe the defendant's version of events."

Whiteside shuffled his feet, fingered the brim of his hat.

"Well, Your Honor, I was already in the trunk, with the idea of moving some of the boxes over to my car, thus alleviating the load on the defendant's rear axle. Since I was already there, I felt permission to search was implicit."

"Sheriff Whiteside, did you just become a law-enforcement officer in the last five minutes?"

"No, Your Honor."

"The last five days? Five weeks? Five months?"

Whiteside sighed. "No, Your Honor. I joined this sheriff's department when I left the military in 1993."

"So you've been an officer of the law for almost a quarter of a century," she said, a hint of a smile on her small mouth.

"Yes, Your Honor."

Her face hardened, her eyes fixing Whiteside like green lasers. "Then you know damn well that trunk was private property, and you had no business opening it and rooting around, and nothing you found there is admissible as evidence before any court, even one as half-assed as this."

"Your Honor."

Whiteside's eyes met Audra's. Another twitch.

Judge Miller returned the spectacles to her nose, scribbled something on the pad. "Mr. Redmond tells me he's going to save wasting any more of our time and drop this stupid case like a hot potato. Sheriff Whiteside, I do not appreciate being asked to drag my ass all the way to Elder County, only to find I'd have been better off staying home. Is my displeasure clear to you, Sheriff?"

"Yes, Your Honor," he said.

Judge Miller turned her attention to Audra.

"Mrs. Kinney, as I understand it, you have not been arrested in relation to the whereabouts of your children, nor have you been charged with any other offense. As such, you are free to go."

Audra fought the urge to cry. The reporters hummed and rattled like an engine come to life. The prosecutor closed his briefcase, stood, and headed for the exit.

"However," Judge Miller said. She slapped the table with a bony palm. "Goddamn it, shut the hell up back there. Go on outside if you need to yammer at each other, goddamn pack of vultures." She waited a moment for the hush to return. "However, I believe Detective Showalter has something for me."

"Yes, Your Honor," Showalter said, getting to his feet. "May I approach?"

"You may."

Showalter stepped past the desk where Audra sat next to the lawyer. He did not look around at Audra, walked straight to the judge, and handed over a manila envelope.

"Your Honor," he said, "as you know, Audra Kinney is at the center of an ongoing investigation into the disappearance of her children. I traveled back to Phoenix this morning and applied to the Family Court for a special order against Mrs. Kinney, barring her from leaving the town boundary of Silver Water until our investigation is concluded."

Judge Miller pulled a letter and a form from the envelope, gave them a cursory glance.

"Does Mrs. Kinney have accommodation?"

"Your Honor, I spoke to Mrs. Anne Gerber, proprietor of River View guesthouse. She hasn't let a room in some time, but she has agreed to rent a room to Mrs. Kinney for the next few nights."

"Very well," Judge Miller said. "Mrs. Kinney, do you understand? You are free to leave this court, but you are not free to leave this town. If you put one foot beyond the town boundary, you'll be put straight back in a cell. Is that clear?"

Audra had stopped listening.

Out.

She gripped the table as a dizzy wave washed through her.

I can get out of the cell.

No matter that she couldn't leave the town, she didn't want to. But now she could try to find her children. She had no idea how, but at least she'd have space to think.

"Yes, Your Honor," she said.

Judge Miller went to gather up her things. "This court is dismissed," she said. "Good day, everyone."

Audra stood. "Ma'am, may I speak with you, please?"

Judge Miller removed her glasses once more, sighed, then beckoned with one long finger.

Audra approached, unsure if her legs could support her for the few steps that would take her to the judge's table. But she reached it, and once there, she lowered herself so that their eyes were on a level.

"Ma'am, I—"

"Please, address me as Your Honor."

"Your Honor, I need help."

"Sweetheart, that ain't news to anyone."

Audra pointed back over her shoulder at Sheriff Whiteside. "That man, him and the deputy, they took my children. Sean and Louise. I think my husband paid them to do it. I need to get my kids back. They're all I have in the world. I'll die without them. Please help me. Please do something."

Judge Miller gave her a kind smile. She reached across the table and took Audra's hand in hers.

"Honey, the only help I can give you is advice. Just tell the truth. Whatever happens, whatever they say to you, just tell the truth. It's the only thing that ever helps anyone. You hear me?"

Her fingers tightened on Audra's wrist.

"Just tell them what you did with your children," she said. "Just tell them where the bodies are and it'll all be over. I promise."

CHAPTER 21

THE WALK FROM THE TOWN HALL TO THE GUESTHOUSE TOOK less than five minutes, but for Audra it lasted a lifetime. Hendry had refused to escort her, saying as he walked away that he'd discharged his responsibilities. As they huddled around the table in the makeshift courtroom, Sheriff Whiteside offered to do it, but Audra said no, she'd rather brave the journalists on her own.

"Shit," Special Agent Mitchell said. "I'll do it. Detective Showalter, Special Agent Abrahms, you're coming too. Let's go."

Showalter stood back from the table, said, "Nuh-uh, not me. No thank you."

"I wasn't asking, Detective," Mitchell said. "Abrahms, take off your jacket."

Audra resisted for a moment as Mitchell's strong fingers gripped her upper arm and hoisted her up out of the seat, but then she allowed herself to be guided toward the door. The press had mostly left the meeting room, and Audra could hear them buzzing outside the town hall's main entrance, waiting to get a shot of her, maybe throw questions at her. They had all been crammed into the makeshift courtroom when she arrived, a constrained murmur running through them as she entered, wrists cuffed, a state patrolman at each arm. Now they were out in the wild and sounded ready to bite.

Mitchell spoke to Whiteside. "Is there another way out?"

"Fire exit out to the side," he said, jerking a thumb in that direction. "Through the main hall there, over to the right. Probably alarmed, but—"

Mitchell didn't wait to hear the rest. She dragged Audra toward the large doors to the hall, then through, letting them swing closed. One caught Showalter on the knee and he cursed.

A dozen or more police officers turned to look. The hall had been turned into some kind of operations center, a large map of Arizona mounted on an easel, red pins tracing a line across the state. The cops watched as Mitchell guided Audra through them toward the pair of doors to the right-hand side. A green sign above the push bar declared it an emergency exit. Mitchell didn't break stride until they reached it. She paused there, nodded to her colleague.

Abrahms draped his jacket over Audra's head and shoulders, leaving her a narrow opening to see through. She heard rather than saw Mitchell hit the push bar, then the blare of the alarm, felt the heat of the afternoon sun as she was guided out. Not far away, reporters shouted, "There, down there, there she is."

"Move," Mitchell said.

Abrahms holding one arm, Mitchell the other, Audra's feet skipped over the ground in the alleyway, out through a parking lot, then turning onto a sidewalk. Behind, the sound of running feet. And the voices, calling her name.

"Audra, where are your children?"

"Audra, did you hurt them?"

"Audra, what did you do with Sean and Louise?"

Mitchell's hand tightened on her upper arm. "Just keep your head down, keep moving."

All Audra could see were her own feet skimming the cracked sidewalk. The footsteps coming from behind, running, passing her.

"All right, get back, out of the way." Showalter's voice, hard and angry.

"Audra, where are the bodies of your children?"

Had it not been for Abrahms and Mitchell holding her upright, she would have fallen then. The realization hit her: They think I killed my children. Of course the authorities believed it, but now she knew that the world believed it too. The thought horrified her.

Mitchell said, "This way," and pulled Audra along another alleyway, back to the main street. Still the footsteps all around, the questions, the shouts, the accusations. Audra focused on keeping her feet moving, not stumbling. All she could think of was getting off the street, out of the way of the reporters.

The dogs, the dogs, they're chasing me.

A flash of a memory, a little girl near her grandfather's yard, a neighbor's terriers scrabbling after her, barking, teeth bared.

Help, they're chasing me.

She wanted to run, adrenaline hitting her hard along with the fear.

"Almost there," Mitchell said. "Almost there."

They reached a short flight of wooden steps, and now Audra did stumble, her fall caught by her escorts, but not before the edge of a step caught her shin and knee. The voices all around, the questions, reached a crescendo, and she heard the same words over and over, hurt, bodies, harm, children. And their names. They kept shouting her children's names and she wanted to scream at them to shut up, to leave her alone, to never utter another word about Sean and Louise.

As Abrahms and Mitchell hauled her upright once more, a door opened, and Audra was swallowed by the building's cool interior. She heard the door slam shut behind her, Showalter's voice on the other side telling the reporters to back off, now, that's enough, just back off.

Her arms free, Audra pulled the jacket from over her head, threw it down on the floor. Her heart thundered so hard she felt it in her head, in her neck. The adrenaline had turned to a queasy rattle around her body as she tried to breathe. She leaned against a wall, her forehead against her forearm.

"You're all right," Mitchell said, breathless herself. "Just take it easy."

"What was that?" Audra asked between gulps of air.

"You're big news," Mitchell said. She bent down, picked up Abrahms' jacket, and handed it back to him. "Didn't you know that?"

Audra looked to the door, through the glass, and saw the wall of men and women. The microphones and cameras. Showalter with his hands up and out, trying to placate them.

"Jesus," Audra said.

"Worry about them later," Mitchell said. "Let's get you some-where to sleep."

Audra looked around, found herself in the hallway of what was once a grand old house, with its wide staircase and high ceilings. A small reception desk at the foot of the stairs, a dozen empty hooks that once held keys on a board behind. A musty scent about the place, the smell of disuse, abandonment, of doors kept closed.

An elderly lady stood by the desk, her gray-eyed gaze hard on Audra.

Mitchell placed her palm at the small of Audra's back, guided her deeper into the hallway, closer to the desk.

"Audra, this is Mrs. Gerber. She has very kindly agreed to let you a room for a few nights."

Audra was about to thank her, but Mrs. Gerber spoke first.

"As a mother, I'd like to kick you out on the street," she said. "But as a Christian, I won't turn you away. Now, it's almost a year since I let a room, so don't expect much. I've aired it best I can, changed the sheets and whatnot. There'll be no meals prepared, I'm not willing to share a table with you, so you'll have to figure something out for yourself."

Mrs. Gerber reached into the pocket of her cardigan and pro-duced a long brass key with a leather fob attached, the number three barely legible. Audra reached out her still-shaking hand, but Mrs. Gerber ignored her, instead placed it in Mitchell's palm.

"Thank you, ma'am," Mitchell said. "We can find it."

She told Abrahms to wait there, then guided Audra to the stairs, up to the second floor. Audra waited while Mitchell unlocked the door, opened it, stepped aside to let her in. The room was modest, a queen-sized bed, a bathroom. The sole window overlooked a garden and the rear of another property, an alley in between.

Mitchell placed the key on a dresser. "Lock the door behind me when I leave. I'll come back this evening, bring you something to eat, some more clothes, some wash things. All right?"

"Thank you," Audra said. "For everything."

Mitchell's expression hardened, as if Audra's gratitude offended her. She came a step closer. "While I'm gone, I want you to think very hard about what you're going to tell me. Your children have been missing for at least forty-eight hours now. I hope they're alive, but everything in my experience tells me they're not. And everything in my experience tells me you know where they are. When I come back, I want you to tell me. I'm running out of patience with you, Audra. There's only one way to fix things now. You know what to do."

The agent walked back to the corner, where an old cathode-ray television sat on top of a dresser. Mitchell pressed a button and its screen flickered into life, the image distorted and jittery. She scrolled through the channels until she found a news station.

Audra saw her own face and felt a cold dread.

"You better watch this," Mitchell said, tossing the remote control onto the bed on her way to the door. "Maybe help you think."

CHAPTER 22

"UP NEXT," THE FEMALE ANCHOR SAID, "DISTURBING NEW DE-
tails emerge in the case of missing children, Sean and Louise
Kinney, in Silver Water, Arizona."

The male anchor turned to the camera. "And, believe me, you
don't want to miss this latest turn in a story that has already gripped
the nation."

"Oh God," Audra said, putting her hands on either side of the
screen as if the images would burst it at its seams.

A fanfare, the station's logo spinning through space, then an ad
break. A pharmaceutical commercial for a prescription antidepres-
sant. A grayed-out woman turning to beaming color as she said how
glad she was she talked to her doctor about it. Then a man's voice
with a long list of possible side effects, including suicidal thoughts.
Audra might have laughed if she wasn't holding her breath, waiting
for the next news segment.

Another fanfare, another spinning logo, and the hosts reappeared.

"Welcome back," the woman said. "As we said before the break,
disturbing new details have emerged in the case of the missing Kinney children, ten-year-old Sean and six-year-old Louise. The children's mother was arrested on Wednesday evening just outside the
small Arizona town of Silver Water, for possession of an illegal drug.
The thirty-five-year-old woman left Brooklyn, New York, four days
prior to that, with her children in the backseat. When the Elder
County sheriff stopped her car for a minor traffic offense, the children were nowhere to be seen. In a surprise twist today, the possession case was thrown out of court, Judge Henrietta Miller ruling the

search of the car to have been illegal. Our reporter in Silver Water, Rhonda Carlisle, has more."

Cut to an attractive young African-American woman on the town's main street, other press people milling around in the background.

"Yes, Susan, dramatic scenes here in Silver Water today, as Judge Miller found that Sheriff Ronald Whiteside had not sought proper consent to search the station wagon Audra Kinney was driving, thus rendering the physical evidence inadmissible. She had no choice but to throw the case out, leaving Mrs. Kinney free to go. But not quite."

Cut to Audra hunkered down before the judge, the judge holding her hand. Then Audra being rushed along the street, the jacket over her head, flanked by Mitchell and Showalter. The reporter spoke over the footage.

"A detective from the Arizona Department of Public Safety, Criminal Investigations Division, had obtained an order from the Family Court in Phoenix, forcing Audra Kinney to stay within the town boundary of Silver Water while the investigation into her children's disappearance is ongoing."

Audra stumbling on the steps of the guesthouse, Mitchell helping her up.

"Kinney is being accommodated at a local guesthouse, effectively under house arrest. FBI and state police are concentrating their search for the missing children along the route Kinney took from east to west across Arizona, using her cell phone's GPS data. They know she crossed into the state from northern New Mexico around twenty-four hours before she was stopped by the Elder County sheriff, and witnesses at a roadside diner said they saw the children the following morning, so the authorities know that whatever happened to Sean and Louise, it happened in Arizona."

Cut back to the studio, and now the male anchor spoke to a picture-in-picture image of the reporter.

"Rhonda, we understand that some disturbing new details have emerged about Audra Kinney, the mother of the missing children."

Back to Silver Water.

"That's right, Derek. As has already been reported elsewhere,

Audra Kinney separated from her wealthy husband eighteen months ago, taking her two children from their Upper West Side home to a one-bedroom apartment in Brooklyn. The children's grandmother spoke to reporters outside her home close to Central Park earlier today. She painted a worrying picture of Audra Kinney, a woman with a history of problems with mental health and addiction."

Rhonda Carlisle looked off camera, a serious and concerned expression on her face.

"Oh no," Audra said.

There on the screen, Margaret Kinney, her dyed red hair, her pale stony face. She stood on the sidewalk outside her building, a doorman waiting to let her in. Father Malloy by her side, his expression one of warm sympathy.

"I curse the day my son met that woman," Margaret said. "She's given my son hell over these last few years. With the alcohol and the prescription drugs. Wine and vodka, mostly, and whatever antidepressants or sedatives she could talk a doctor into prescribing for her. She barely knew those children, I did most of the raising of them myself, along with their nanny."

"You liar," Audra said. "You goddamn liar."

"Before she and my son split, things had gotten worse and worse, she could barely get out of bed. Then she overdosed and wound up in the hospital. My son, out of love, did his best to get her back on her feet, but then she moved out with the children. He's been trying for eighteen months to get them back, because they're just not safe with her. Children's Services agreed, they were about to get an order to force her to hand them over to their father, then she took off. And now this. Excuse me?"

A knot on her brow as she tilted her head, listening.

"Yes," she said. "Yes, I am very worried."

Her eyes brimmed. Father Malloy put his hand on her shoulder.

"We're trying to stay positive, I've been praying around the clock, but I do fear the worst for those babies."

She tilted her head again, wiping a tear away.

"What would I say to her? Just tell us what you did with them."

Margaret looked into the camera, her resolve disappearing, Father Malloy seeming to keep her upright in her distress.

"Audra, whatever you did with my grandchildren, wherever they are, please just tell us. Don't torture us like this. I can't stand it. Patrick is in pieces. We're all barely hanging on. Just do the one decent thing you can do now. Tell the truth."

She disappeared, Rhonda Carlisle and Silver Water's main street taking her place.

"Powerful words there from Margaret Kinney, the grandmother of the missing children. Back to the studio."

The anchors reappeared, thanked the reporter.

"What about Whiteside?" Audra said to the television. "What about Collins?"

She slapped the screen with her palm, made the image roll away, then come back.

The female anchor's expression darkened. "Of course we'll keep you up to date as this case unfolds, but it's now coming up on forty-eight hours since the children disappeared." She turned to her colleague. "Derek, surely the authorities must be fearing the worst by this stage."

Derek nodded gravely. "I think all of us are."

Audra slapped the screen once more. "They're alive, you son of a bitch."

Derek turned to the camera again. "Join us in the next hour as we ask: Who is Audra Kinney? From the attractive young woman who married into one of New York's elite families, to the allegedly drug-addicted mother suspected of committing the worst crime imaginable, find out more, after the break."

Audra hit the off button with her fist, skinning her knuckles.

"Goddamn them," she said.

Anger flared in her, hot and bright. They'd all but said she'd killed her children and dumped them in the desert somewhere. No mention of what she'd told Mitchell. No one questioned Whiteside's story. The anger turned to cold fear as she realized what the whole country must be thinking. That she was a monster. She had never bothered much with social media, Facebook, Twitter, all of that, but she could only imagine what they'd be saying there. They'd be ripping her to pieces.

Audra went to the corner of the room, pressed herself into it, her head in her hands. She wrapped her fingers around her skull, trying to contain it all. The crushing weight of it on her shoulders, snaking around her chest.

"Keep it together," she told herself. "They want you to break."

From here, she could see the yard below the window, the weathered fence beyond that. And on the other side, standing on something to get a better vantage point, a young man with a video camera looking right back at her.

"Jesus," Audra said. She crossed to the window, pulled down the blind.

She flopped onto the bed, pulled her knees up to her chest, folded her arms around them.

Lying in the semidarkness, she remembered a hospital room far from here. A room where she had woken with a grinding behind her eyes. Confusion and fear. A doctor had explained to her that she'd taken an overdose. The nanny had found her on her bedroom floor, he said, half naked, barely conscious. Audra would probably have died otherwise. The paramedics had pumped her stomach and shot her full of Adrenalin.

Patrick had visited her later that night, stayed for only a few minutes. "How could you be so stupid?" he asked.

Another visitor came by the following day. She wore a plain gray dress with a crucifix around her neck. Her name was Sister Hannah Cicero, and she asked why Audra had taken so many pills, why she had taken them with neat vodka. Audra told her she couldn't remember.

"Did you overdose on purpose?" Sister Hannah asked. "Did you try to kill yourself?"

"I don't remember," Audra said.

And she wondered: Had she? Had she finally reached the point where dying seemed a better choice than living? She knew that the last months had been dark, that she felt certain the world would be no poorer without her.

"Would you like to pray?" the nun asked.

"I'm not religious," Audra said.

"That's okay," Sister Hannah said. "I'm a qualified counselor as well as a nun. The first part and the second part don't always overlap."

"A counselor," Audra echoed as she remembered the conversation she'd had with Patrick on Sean's second birthday.

Sean was eight and a half now, Louise not quite four. At Patrick's insistence, Audra quit drinking as soon as the pregnancy test showed positive and they knew she had another baby inside her. She was allowed to keep taking the drugs, but at a reduced dosage. When Louise was born, Margaret swooped in once more and took over. Audra didn't even get to try breast-feeding this time. In fact, she couldn't quite remember feeding Louise at all. Three days after the baby was born, Patrick gave Audra a bottle of wine, and so she descended into the pit once more.

"Do you feel like talking?" Sister Hannah asked.

Audra said nothing. She rolled onto her side, faced the other way.

"Would you rather I left?"

Audra opened her mouth to say yes, but the word did not come out. A silence hung in the room, and it terrified her so much that she had to say something.

"I don't know my children."

"Do you know their names?"

"Sean and Louise."

"Well, that's something. How old are they?"

"Eight and three. Well, maybe closer to four. I'm not sure."

"And that's something else. Try for a third thing."

Audra thought for a moment. "Louise has a pink bunny. She calls it Gogo."

"What do you feel in your heart when you think of your children?"

Audra closed her eyes, concentrated on the ache in her breast. "That I miss them. That I let them down. That I don't deserve them."

"No one deserves children," Sister Hannah said. "They're not a prize you get for being a good girl. I understand the children's nanny found you unconscious. Who hired her?"

"My husband," Audra replied. "He said I wasn't fit to care for my son. She's been in our home ever since. I see my children at the dinner table, and they kiss me goodnight. I see them at breakfast, and they kiss me good morning. They call me Mother. They call Patrick Father. Not Mommy or Daddy. That's not right, is it? I should be their mommy."

"You should. Then I guess the question is, why aren't you?"

"Like I told you, I don't deserve them."

"Bullshit," Sister Hannah said. "You tell me that again, I'm going to kick your ass. Does Patrick drink?"

"No," Audra said. "Not like I do."

"What about the drugs, the antidepressants, all that? Does he take them too?"

"No. Never."

"What does he say about your drinking?"

Audra's mouth dried. She imagined the cold sweetness of wine on her tongue. The feel of it in her throat.

"He stays out of my way when I'm drunk," she said. "He tells me I'm shit when I'm hungover in the morning. Then when he comes home from work, he brings me more. Wine, usually, sometimes vodka."

Sister Hannah was quiet for a moment, then she asked, "Does he get you the pills too?"

"Yes," Audra said. "What I don't understand is: Why? Why does he keep me around? What good am I to him? If I'm not a mother or a wife, what am I for?"

Another silence. Audra could feel Sister Hannah's gaze on her back.

"Tell me, do you have any friends?"

"No," Audra said. "Not anymore."

"But you used to."

"Before we were married. But Patrick didn't like them."

"So you and your friends drifted apart," Sister Hannah said.

"Yeah."

"Do you ever go out without Patrick? To the store, for a walk, anywhere?"

"No," Audra said.

"Has he ever hit you?"

Audra felt herself shrink down into the pillow, withering under the sheets. "Sometimes. Not often."

She felt Sister Hannah's hand on her shoulder. "Audra, listen to me very carefully. You are not the first woman to go through this. God knows, you won't be the last. I've seen all kinds of abuse. Believe me, beatings aren't the only kind. Your husband is an enabler. He's keeping you drunk and drugged, so you'll be quiet and easier to manage. He doesn't love you, but for whatever reason, he can't let you leave. You have to understand, he's holding you prisoner. The alcohol and the medication are what keep you tied down."

"What can I do?" Audra asked. "How do I get out?"

"Leave. Just go. When you're discharged from this hospital, don't go home. I can get you a place in a refuge where you'll be safe. Patrick won't be able to touch you there."

"But my children . . ."

"You can't help them until you help yourself. You need to get well, then you can worry about them."

"I want to sleep now," Audra said, and she burrowed down into the bed. She was gone before the nun left the room.

CHAPTER 23

DANNY TOOK A BITE OF THE CLUB SANDWICH. WASN'T BAD. Pretty good bacon, turkey wasn't too dry. He'd slipped the sliced tomatoes out from between the toasted bread and left them on the plate. Danny didn't like tomatoes.

The waitress stopped at his booth by the window to freshen his coffee. Tasted pretty good too. But the service was slow. He guessed this place hadn't seen so much business in years.

"Thank you," he said. He dabbed at his mouth with a napkin. "Say, what's going on around here?"

The waitress—her nametag said SHELLEY—laughed, then the smile dropped from her face. "You don't know?"

Danny looked back out to the street, at the reporters wandering around like zombies looking for a scent of flesh. "Know what?"

"Sorry, I just assumed . . ." She waved a hand in front of his face. "I mean, you're not from around here, so I assumed you were a reporter. Like them."

Danny smiled and said, "No, I'm just passing through. Lady in a store out the road said you had good coffee. She was right. So what's happening here?"

"Oh my God," Shelley said, sliding into the seat opposite him, coffee pot in hand. "It's terrible. I've never seen anything like it in my life. I mean, this little town, what's left of it, biggest news is if someone farts in public."

Danny snorted.

Shelley lowered her voice, hooked a thumb toward the counter. "Couple of days ago, Sheriff Whiteside pulls this woman over."

Danny glanced across the room, saw the sheriff. A big man, wide at the shoulders and waist. Sat on that stool like it was a throne, and he the king of the land.

"He found drugs in the car," Shelley continued in a loud whisper. "News said it was pot, enough for a dealer, but I heard there was more. Like cocaine and crystal meth, and whatnot. So he takes her in. Turns out she left New York three or four days before with her two children, but they weren't in the car when Ronnie, the sheriff, he pulled her over. She has a history, mental problems and like that, and they reckon she did something to the kids, maybe out in the desert somewhere."

"Jesus," Danny said. "What do they think happened?"

"Lord knows," Shelley said, shaking her head. "But they got the state police and the FBI here investigating. I hate to think what she did to those poor children. I pray they're alive somewhere, but I don't believe it in my heart. Not really."

"You think she hurt them?"

"Oh, she killed them," Shelley said. "Sure as you and me are sitting here, she took the lives of those little ones. If only she'd tell what she did with the bodies, then we'd all know. How's that sandwich?"

"Good," Danny said.

"You're lucky you got anything. Harvey, my boss, he had to drive all the way to Phoenix last night to pick up supplies. We ain't seen this kind of business since before the copper mine closed. Got to the point last night that I couldn't even pour a cup of coffee."

She reached over and patted Danny's hand.

"Well, you enjoy your meal. Nice talking with you."

"You too, Shelley," he said, giving her his brightest smile.

She returned it, with interest, and slipped out of the booth.

Before Danny could chew another mouthful of sandwich, a shadow fell over the table. He looked up. Sheriff Whiteside looked down.

"How you doing today?" Whiteside asked.

"Pretty good," Danny said. "You?"

"Oh, fair, all things considered. I couldn't help overhearing your talk with Shelley, there."

"She's a nice lady," Danny said.

"She is, and she's been rushed off her feet since yesterday. You be sure and leave a decent tip, won't you?"

"I will," Danny said.

"Anyway, like I was saying, I couldn't help but overhear your conversation. So you're not with these press folks, then?"

"No, sir," Danny said.

"See, now, that strikes me as strange."

"Really?"

"Really," Whiteside said. "Mind if I sit down?"

Danny indicated the seat opposite and said, "Please."

Whiteside slid in next to him, his shoulder against Danny's. "Like I said, it strikes me as strange. I mean, you don't mind my saying, you clearly aren't from around here."

Danny kept his voice low and even. "Why would you think that?"

"Well, I'll come right out and say it, because I don't hold with this political correctness nonsense. See, Silver Water is about as lily-white as a town can be. Since the mine closed, there's not even a single Hispanic within the town boundary. There's a couple of Mormon families, but that's about as diverse as it gets around here."

"I see," Danny said.

"Do you? Do you see what I'm getting at? So, if you're not with the press, what are you doing here?"

"Just passing through," Danny said. "I heard the coffee was good."

"Yeah, the coffee's good, but that doesn't really address my concerns. See, Silver Water is kind of an isolated little town. We're not really on the way to anywhere. Unless you got business here, people don't tend to pass through. Especially not a gentleman like yourself."

Danny smiled. "Like myself?"

"You know what I mean."

"No, I don't."

Whiteside scratched his chin. "Asian-American. Is that the preferred nomenclature these days?"

"Chinese is fine," Danny said.

"Chinese, Japanese, Korean, Outer Mongolian, I don't much give a shit." Whiteside leaned in close. "My point is, you just happen to be passing through a town that no one ever passes through, and you're doing it today of all days, with all this going on. You gonna tell me that's a coincidence?"

Danny held Whiteside's gaze. "I don't know what else to call it."

"Okay, so it's a coincidence. That's fine. But if you stick around here much longer than it takes to finish that sandwich, then I'll be less inclined to see it that way. Do we understand each other?"

"I'm not sure," Danny said. "Let me get it straight. You're telling me that when I've eaten my sandwich and drunk my coffee, I have to leave town. Because I don't look like I belong around here. Is that right?"

Whiteside nodded. "That's about the size of it."

"Because I'm not white."

Whiteside didn't reply, his gaze sharpening.

"First of all," Danny said, "you don't have it within your power to order me to leave town. Second, I think some of these press people would find it interesting that you told me to leave because of the color of my skin."

Whiteside stared, his face cut from stone. Then he spoke.

"Well, I've said my piece," he said, sliding to the end of the booth. "I don't expect to see you around after you're done. Let's just leave it at that."

The sheriff stood, lifted his hat from the table. Danny spoke as he stepped away.

"I know what you did," he said.

Whiteside stopped and turned. "What was that?"

"You heard me."

Whiteside wrapped his thick fingers around Danny's arm. "I think you and me ought to go outside and talk a little more."

Danny smiled at him. "No, I think I'll stay right here and finish my lunch."

"Don't try me, boy." Whiteside leaned down, lowered his voice. "You push me, I will push back, you better believe it. Now come with me."

"Look around," Danny said. "This place is full of reporters. How many cameras do you count? And out on the street. What do you think you can do, in front of all these people? Now get your fucking hand off me."

Whiteside's jaw muscles bunched. He tightened his grip on Danny's arm, then let go.

"I'll be watching you," he said. He straightened, put on his hat, and spoke loud enough for the entire restaurant to hear. "Enjoy the rest of your meal, now. And like I said, make sure you leave a decent tip. Poor Shelley's been run off her feet."

Shelley beamed a smile at him from behind the counter, and the sheriff touched his finger to the brim of his hat, before walking to the door. He kept his gaze locked on Danny as he passed the window, heading toward the station.

Danny took his time finishing the sandwich, enjoying every bite. He watched the guesthouse across the street as he ate, wondering about Audra Kinney, what she was doing in there. Going out of her mind, he guessed. He wondered if she'd eaten.

He pushed his plate away, drained the cup of coffee. Right on cue, Shelley appeared at his side once more.

"You want a look at the dessert menu?" she asked.

"No thanks," he said, reaching for his wallet. "I'll settle up."

"Sure thing," she said, turning to go. "I'll get your check."

"Wait," Danny said. "You do takeout?"

CHAPTER 24

AUDRA FIRST GOT TO KNOW HER CHILDREN IN THE WEEKS AFTER she left the hospital. She slept a lot those first few days at home, hours of black punctuated by screaming nightmares. By the third day she had lost count of how many times she had woken gasping for breath, bed sheets knotted around her. She ate hardly anything. On the fourth morning, while Sean was at school and Louise was having a nap, Jacinta knocked on the bedroom door.

"Come in," Audra said, blinking sleep from her eyes.

Jacinta entered carrying a tray laden with buttered toast, a candy bar, an apple, and two large mugs full of coffee. Without speaking, she set the tray down on the bed beside Audra. She lifted one mug and put it in Audra's hand, lifted the other, and sat in the chair under the window.

"How do you feel?" she asked.

"Like I've got the worst hangover in the history of hangovers," Audra said, laying her palm on her forehead.

"I heard you screaming," Jacinta said. "Mr. Kinney wouldn't let me come into you. But I snuck in when he went to work."

"You did? I don't remember."

"I've seen it before." Jacinta looked down at her coffee. "My father was an alcoholic. He had it worse than you when he tried to quit. Hallucinations. He said the devil came to him. Chickens were running around the floor, and the devil grabbed them and snapped their necks. If bad dreams is all you have, then it's not so bad. It's been a week since the overdose. You should be over the worst of it now."

"At the hospital, they said you found me. You saved my life."

Jacinta shrugged. "I just called for the ambulance."

"Even so, thank you."

"You should eat something."

Audra shook her head. "I'm not hungry."

"You should eat anyway. You'll feel better. Even just the candy bar."

Audra reached for it, a Milky Way, and peeled back the wrapping. Chocolate and caramel mixed on her tongue, and dear Lord, it was good. The rest of the bar was gone in less than a minute.

Jacinta smiled and said, "Told you."

Audra took a sip of the coffee, rich and warm, felt it in her throat and stomach, heating her from the inside. Jacinta indicated the bottle of pills on the nightstand, half empty.

"Are you taking those again?" she asked.

"My husband got them for me," Audra said, avoiding the question.

"I don't think you should." Jacinta dropped her gaze. "If you don't mind me saying."

An empty wine bottle stood next to the pills and a glass with a mouthful left at the bottom. Jacinta looked from one to the other, her expression clouded.

"What?" Audra asked.

"There was a phone call yesterday," Jacinta said. "You were asleep. Mr. Kinney was at work. It was a lady from the hospital."

"Sister Hannah," Audra said.

"That's right."

"What did she say?"

"She asked how you were doing. If you were taking any pills. Drinking anything."

"And what did you tell her?"

"I said I wouldn't know anything about that."

"I haven't," Audra said.

"Haven't what?"

"I haven't taken any pills. I haven't been drinking."

Jacinta pointed to the items on the nightstand. "But . . ."

"Down the toilet," Audra said. "Don't tell Mr. Kinney."

Jacinta smiled and said, "I won't. And I'm glad. He shouldn't give you those things."

"He's an enabler," Audra said. "An abuser. He uses them to control me. But not anymore."

"Can I tell you something?" Jacinta said.

Audra nodded. Her stomach growled, and she took a slice of toast from the tray, savored the salted butter on her tongue.

"I don't like Mr. Kinney. I would have left this job a long time ago, except that I love your children. I really do. With you the way you were, and Mr. Kinney never being around, I couldn't go. They'd have no one if I left."

Audra swallowed the toast. "Thank you. I'm not going to be like that anymore."

"Good," Jacinta said. Her face brightened. "Louise is going to wake up from her nap soon. Do you want to go get her with me?"

"I'd like that," Audra said.

"In fact, I've got to collect Sean from school in about thirty minutes. Usually I'd take Louise with me, but maybe she could stay here with you?"

"Okay," Audra said.

So Audra sat on the living-room floor, wearing her dressing gown, playing with a little girl she barely knew. Louise had protested a little when it was Audra who lifted her from bed instead of Jacinta, but she soon came around. Now she lifted toys from a large basket in the corner, one at a time, and brought them to her mother, told her their names. Showed her how to play with them.

Gogo was her favorite, mostly intact then, still with both his eyes.

Louise was sitting in Audra's lap, a storybook open in front of them, when the living-room door opened forty-five minutes later. Sean stood in the doorway, schoolbag in his hand, staring at her, his eyes cold and wary.

"Hey," Audra said.

Jacinta nudged his shoulder. "Go say hello to your mother."

Sean entered the room, put his bag on the floor next to the toy basket. He pulled his coat off, dropped it beside the bag.

"Sean," Jacinta said from the doorway. "We don't leave our things on the floor. Do we?"

"No," Sean said.

"Okay. Just this once, bring them to me and I'll put them away properly."

Sean gathered the bag and coat and took them to her. Jacinta closed the door, leaving him staring at the wood floor. A few moments passed before he turned to stare at Audra once more.

"Good day at school?" Audra asked.

Sean shrugged and kept staring.

"You want to come sit next to me and hear a story?"

"Those are baby stories," he said.

"What kind of stories do you like?"

"Comic books," he said. "Superheroes."

"You want to show me some?"

Sean went to the sideboard, opened a door, and pulled out a plastic box. From that he took out a half dozen comic books and spread them out on the floor. "X-Men," he said, pointing. "That's Wolverine, and that's Professor X. And these two are *Star Wars*, they do comic books as well as movies. And this one, this one's my favorite."

"Spider-Man," Audra said.

"You know about him?"

"Sure I do. I used to read those comic books when I was a little girl. I stole them off my brother. He got mad when he couldn't find them, but he never knew they were under my bed."

Sean smiled, and they stayed there on the living-room floor for three hours. Then Jacinta came back and said Patrick would be home soon. Audra kissed her children and went back to bed.

Things went on that way for six months. Patrick brought bottle after bottle of alcohol, bottle after bottle of pills, and every day Audra would flush them away. Before dinner, she would rinse her mouth with vodka or wine, just enough to get the smell on her. Every evening the cook served them dinner, and they ate in silence. Somehow Sean sensed it would be best not to mention their play sessions to his father, and it simply never came up with Louise.

Until one night in September.

That night, Louise—now four and a half—asked, "Can we have ice cream?"

Patrick didn't look up from whatever article he was reading on his phone, his shirtsleeves rolled up, his tie loosened. "No," he said. "No ice cream on weeknights. You can have some fruit."

Louise looked to the other end of the table. "Mommy, can we have ice cream?"

Audra went to answer too quickly, her tongue too sharp. She corrected herself, blinked, let her eyelids droop. "Ask your father," she said.

Too late. Patrick had noticed. He didn't take his eyes off her as he said to Louise, "You don't need to ask your mother. You already asked me, and I said no."

Audra reached for the glass of wine on the table, brought it to her mouth, let it clink on her teeth, before taking a small mouthful. She put it down too hard, let it slop over the rim.

"Listen to your father," she said, softening the sibilants.

"Are you all right, dear?" Patrick asked.

"Never better," Audra said, forcing a sneer into her words. "I'm going to bed."

She stood and left the table without looking back. In bed, the sheets pulled up to her chin, she listened to the voices of her children as Jacinta helped them brush their teeth, read them their stories. All quiet for a time, and Audra might have slept, she couldn't be sure, but the next thing she was aware of was Patrick standing by the nightstand. She could feel him staring at her back.

Audra listened as he lifted the bottle, the remains of the vodka sloshing in it. Then the bottle of antidepressants, a rattle as he examined it and its contents. And then quiet as he stood there, watching. Audra kept her breathing steady and deep, waiting for him to go.

Eventually he said, "I know you're awake."

Audra remained still, breathing in and out, in and out.

"Just think of the things I could do to you," he said, a terrible calm to his voice. "I could open that window and throw you out.

You think anyone wouldn't believe it was suicide? Or you could open the safe in the closet, find the pistol there, blow your brains out. Or maybe run a bath and open your wrists."

He leaned on the bed, his weight rolling Audra over to look straight up at him, no pretending now.

"My point is," he said, "you're an addict, an alcoholic, a pill-popper. Everyone knows. Who's going to believe you didn't kill yourself? Now, tomorrow, I'm going to ask Dr. Steinberger for a new prescription for you. After that, I'm going to stop by the liquor store. Then we're going to get things back to normal around here."

Patrick stood and left the room.

The next morning, after he'd left for work, Audra asked Jacinta to change Sean out of his school clothes while she made a phone call. Sister Hannah answered, gave Audra the address of a shelter in Queens, said they'd be expecting her and the kids.

Jacinta helped them down the stairs with everything they could carry. She embraced the children on the sidewalk, tears in her eyes. As a cab driver loaded their bags into the trunk, Audra took Jacinta in her arms.

"Be careful," Audra said. "He'll be angry."

"I know," Jacinta said. "I will."

Sean and Louise waved at her from the cab's rear window. Louise cried, knowing she'd never see Jacinta again. She clung tight to Gogo, and Audra wiped the tears from her cheeks. As the three of them huddled together in the back of the cab, she felt a joyful terror at what lay ahead.

Eighteen months ago, two years since she'd quit the booze and the pills. Audra swore that she would never be separated from her children again. No matter that Patrick had come after her with everything he had, his mother goading him along. Audra would cling to them until she could cling no more.

And yet they had been taken from her anyway.

AUDRA TOOK a long shower; the guesthouse water was hot and plentiful. She turned the temperature up as high as she could stand it and scrubbed her body pink. The grime seemed embedded in every crease and hollow, and even after thirty minutes there was no clearing it.

But her mind cleared. Fatigued though it was, Audra began to reassemble the previous forty-eight hours into some sort of order. For a few moments she questioned herself again. What if they were right? What if she had done something terrible and couldn't admit it to herself? And then she remembered Sean's face as he told Sheriff Whiteside not to hurt her. Sean, her little man, standing up for her. She almost smiled at the thought, before she remembered Louise's terrified sobs from the back of her car.

The time since then had compressed so that two days seemed like two hours. But her children had been out there, somewhere, all the while. Terrified, wondering why she hadn't come and gotten them yet.

No, Audra knew Special Agent Mitchell was wrong. She had not harmed her children. And Mitchell was wrong about something else: Sean and Louise were alive. Audra felt it in her bones. Not some mother's intuition nonsense; all logic pointed that way. Whiteside and Collins wouldn't have taken her children just to kill them. There was something in it for them; the children were worth something. And they were only worth something if they were alive.

Who would pay someone to take her children? Only one answer made any kind of sense. She imagined her husband handing over a wad of his mother's money, slipping an envelope into Whiteside's hand.

A terrifying idea, but it meant Sean and Louise were alive. If her children were alive, then she could get them back. It was simply a question of how.

Audra shut the water off, stepped out of the shower, pulled a towel from the rack. A few minutes later her body was dry, her hair damp. She pulled on the clothes, the same shabby jeans and top she'd been given the day before. They still smelled of her sweat, but at least her body was clean.

She sat down on the bed, next to the nightstand and the old telephone on it. I must do something, she thought. Anything. The smallest thing would be better than sitting here knowing her children were out in the desert somewhere.

A knock on the door startled her. Audra got to her feet, crossed the room, put the chain lock in place. She unlocked the door and opened it a crack, no more than two inches. The landlady, Mrs. Gerber, waited there, her face flushed.

"There's a man here insists on talking to you," she said, breathless. "I told him no, but he wouldn't accept it. Says he needs to talk to you right away. He damn near kicked his way—"

"A man?" Audra said. "What's his name?"

"Wouldn't say. I told him, tell me who you are and what you want, but he just pushed right past me. I've a good mind to call one of those police officers over here to put him out."

"What does he look like?"

Mrs. Gerber seemed to gather herself as she thought. Eventually she shrugged and said, "Like he doesn't belong around here. He's waiting down in the dining room."

Audra closed her door and followed the landlady down the stairs to the entrance hall.

"I don't like this," Mrs. Gerber said over her shoulder. "Strange men showing up and pushing their way in. I don't need the trouble at my age. He's in there."

Audra followed the direction of Mrs. Gerber's finger to a set of double doors across from the foot of the stairs. One of them stood open, but she could see no one inside. She approached the door, wondering if she should knock. A stupid idea, she pushed the door open and stepped inside.

He stood up from the bare table, his face barely visible in the dimness of the room. But she knew him well enough.

"Hello, Audra," Patrick Kinney said.

CHAPTER 25

AUDRA WANTED TO TURN AROUND, SLAM THE DOOR BEHIND her, and run. But she could not. Instead she asked, "What do you want?"

Patrick remained seated, his jacket slung over the back of the chair. One hand on the table, a bulky watch on his wrist. Rolex, Tag Heuer, something expensive and ugly.

"I want to talk," he said, a tremor in his voice. "Sit down."

She should have said that she didn't want to talk with him, but a possibility floated in her mind. So she went to the table, keeping two chairs between her and her husband, and sat down.

It was a large room, a bay window at one end, a net curtain shielding the interior from view. Large framed photographs lined the walls, sepia-toned Arizona landmarks and famous residents. A wedding photograph stood on the mantelpiece of the grand fireplace, a young Mrs. Gerber arm-in-arm with her new husband. She looked happy. Audra supposed she must have been happy with Patrick once, though she could not remember such a thing.

"What do you want to talk about?" she asked.

"What do you think?"

"Do you want to help me? Or do you want to hurt me?"

He bristled, his handsome face darkening. "I want my children back."

"So do I," she said.

His eyelids twitched. A tell. Anger rising in him.

Caution, she thought. Beware.

"You're the only one who knows where they are," Patrick said. "I want you to tell me."

"Don't," she said.

"Don't what?"

"Don't lie to me. Don't pretend. We both know the truth."

He watched her for a moment, then said, "What are you talking about?"

"You want me to say it out loud?"

He lifted his hand from the table, made a fist beneath his lips, his college fraternity ring glinting. "Yes, I do," he said.

Audra fixed her eyes on his, faced his anger.

"You're behind this," she said. "You paid Whiteside and Collins to take our children."

Patrick tightened his fist, shook his head. "Who?"

"Stop," Audra said. "I give up. I don't know how you pulled it off, but you did. You've won. Just tell me what you want, and you can have it. So long as I know Sean and Louise are safe."

Patrick rubbed his temples with his fingertips. He leaned forward, put his elbows on his knees, breathed in hard.

"You're insane," he said.

Her voice shook as it rose. "For God's sake, just tell me what you want."

He slapped the table hard. "I want you to tell me where my children are."

"Stop it, Patrick, you know where—"

"I don't," he said, hitting the table once more. "You've lost your goddamn mind. Haven't you seen the news?"

"Only a little. They only just let me—"

"They want your blood," he said. "All the networks, all the rolling news channels. Every single one, they have your face all over the screen, asking what you did with our kids. They know what you did before, the drink, the drugs, the craziness. How you ran from Children's Services. They have it on constant rotation. That you're a danger to yourself and to our children. There's not a single soul in this country who doesn't believe you're a monster. That you hurt Sean and Louise. They're calling me every minute of the day wanting a statement. They're calling my mother, for Christ's sake. What do you think this is doing to her?"

Audra let out a dry and brittle laugh. "Well, shit, I wouldn't want to upset Margaret."

Patrick sprang to his feet, his fists ready, took one step toward her. He caught himself, stopped, loosened his hands as he shook his head.

"I just want my little boy and girl," he said. "Please tell me where they are."

In the midst of all this, wherever their children had been taken, he remained concerned only for himself and his mother. He didn't even have the sense to hide it, Audra thought, to pretend he really cared for them.

But if he really were hiding Sean and Louise, he would pretend to care. He was smart and manipulative enough to disguise his true desires.

Audra remained seated as the realization hit her: He didn't know where Sean and Louise were. He didn't know, because he didn't do it. She felt the room chill, as the one hope she'd clung to since all this began crumbled away.

"Oh God," she said, her hand going to her mouth. "If you don't have them . . ."

He stood over her, flexing his fingers. "I'm going to ask you one more time."

"If you don't have them, then who does?" Audra placed a palm on each side of her head, began to rock back and forward. "Oh no, no, no."

"You have to stop this," Patrick said. "You're the only one who can bring this to an end. Tell me where they are."

An idea flickered in her mind, the same one she'd had when she spoke with Mel.

"A private detective," she said.

"What?"

"There've got to be some in Phoenix who could do it. Use your money. Pay someone to investigate Whiteside and Collins, find out what they're after. You can do that."

She looked up at him, her hands clasped in front of her.

He shook his head. "You crazy bitch."

Patrick took his jacket from the back of the chair and walked to the door.

"You won't do it?" Audra asked.

He reached for the handle. "Crazy bitch."

"Patrick," she said.

He stopped and turned, and she saw how old he'd become, how deep the lines of his face, how jagged.

Audra wiped a tear from her cheek and said, "You know, it took me far too long to figure you out. What you wanted with me."

"Now's not the time," he said.

"Seems as good a time as any," Audra said. "You remember I asked you? That one day I sobered up for Sean's birthday. I asked you why you kept me around, drunk and drugged. You had our son. You could've just kicked me out. But you didn't, and I had to almost die before I realized."

He put his fists in his pockets, stared past her. "Realized what?"

"You never wanted a marriage," she said. "You never wanted a family. You just wanted the appearance of it. To look normal. To make your mother happy. Once I gave her grandchildren, I was no more use to you. So you kept me doped up and out of the way. In the end, I was just excess baggage. And that left me with another question. See, I don't remember taking that overdose. Yes, I hardly knew where I was most of the time, but I don't remember making that decision. Did you make it for me, Patrick?"

Now he looked at her, hate in his eyes. "What do you mean?"

"Did you try to kill me?"

"Don't," Patrick said.

"Don't what?" Audra said as she got to her feet, her voice rising with her. "Don't talk back? Don't make you angry?"

Patrick took another step forward, threw his jacket on the floor, put his weight on both feet. "This is not the time for your fucking games, Audra. You're going to tell me where my children are, right now, or . . ."

"Or what?" Now she took a step closer to him. "You're going to slap me around? Give me bruises where they don't show? Make me—"

The thick fingers of his right hand snapped onto her throat, squeezed hard, and he pushed her toward the wall, her feet skimming the carpet. Framed pictures rattled as the back of her head struck the plasterwork. She put her right hand flat on his chest. Let her fingers crawl up as his grip tightened, feeling for the place above his shirt collar. Pressure in her ears, behind her eyes.

He raised his left fist, let her see his hard knuckles. "You tell me where they are, or so help me God, I will—"

Audra's fingers aligned, the tips forming a solid edge, and stabbed at the tender hollow between the top of his sternum and the bottom of his Adam's apple. She followed forward from her shoulder, kept the pressure on his throat even as he pulled away. Before he backed beyond her reach, she curled those same fingers in, leaving the knuckles facing out. She punched once and hard at the same spot.

Patrick's eyes bulged as his hands went to his throat. He staggered back toward the table, his weight carrying him until his thighs met the wooden edge. Then he turned, sprawling over the tabletop, one hand keeping him upright, the other clawing at his throat.

"Breathe," Audra said, moving away from the wall.

Patrick stared at her as he gasped.

"Just breathe," she said, miming with her hands, circular movements like she was coaching a singer. "Big breaths, slow and easy. I learned that in self-defense class. Never had to use it before, but it's good to know it works."

Patrick lowered himself back into the chair he'd jumped from less than a minute before, his rage washed away. Now he looked like his true self: a weak and pathetic man in thrall to his mother.

"Listen to me," Audra said. "Listen good. You don't get to touch me anymore. Not ever. You don't own me, or my children. We are not your possessions. You never really loved our children, but I do. Now, I'm going to find Sean and Louise. You can either help me or get out of my way. Which is it?"

He coughed, spat on the carpet. "You're insane."

"Thought so," she said. "Get out, and don't come back."

He glared up at her. "You think I'm just going to back off?"

Audra pointed at the door. "Go. Now."

Patrick got to his feet, coughed, and spat again. He lifted his jacket from the carpet and walked to the door. Without turning to look at her, he said, "You'll suffer for this."

"I know," Audra said.

CHAPTER 26

PATRICK LEFT THE ROOM, AND A MOMENT LATER AUDRA HEARD the front door open and close, then a swell of voices as the reporters swarmed him. She looked toward the window that faced out onto the street. Through the net curtain she saw them, like crows on carrion. They hushed as Patrick said something, microphones and recorders under his nose. Then a roar as he finished, pushing his way through them.

Monsters, all of them. Ghouls seeking flesh to sell. Yet it was she who was painted as a beast. The killer of her own children.

Audra watched as Patrick fought his way to a car double-parked across the road, the reporters hounding him all the way. He blasted the horn to make them move, then a squeal of tires as he took off, the reporters dancing out of his path.

They drifted, their focus lost, huddled into smaller groups. Women fixed their makeup. Men fixed their hair. Cameramen and sound engineers fussed. Some moved to the diner across the way.

"I'm a monster?" Audra asked the empty room.

"Are you?"

Audra spun around and saw Mrs. Gerber in a doorway at the back of the room, one she hadn't realized was there. She could see over the landlady's shoulder that it led to the kitchen.

"No, I'm not," Audra said.

Mrs. Gerber looked at the carpet, a frown on her lips. "Did that man spit on my floor?"

"Yes," Audra said. "Did you hear that?"

"Yeah," Mrs. Gerber said. She tapped the circular window with her fingertip. "Saw it too."

"I'm sorry," Audra said, turning to leave.

"Sorry? Don't be an ass. Too many women apologize for the behavior of men."

Audra didn't know how to respond. She went to the doorway leading to the hall.

"My husband used to beat me too," Mrs. Gerber said. "Funny thing. Everyone thought he was the nicest man. I'd go out to the store and someone would say, oh, I saw your Jimmy yesterday, isn't he just a sweetheart? But they didn't know. Even when I wore sleeves too long for the weather, no one thought to ask why. They just thought he was the bee's knees."

"I'm sorry to hear that," Audra said.

"Stop apologizing, for goodness' sake. People say the same about Ronnie Whiteside. He's a good man, a war hero, all that. But I know what kind of man he is. I've seen it for myself."

"Tell me," Audra said.

Mrs. Gerber exhaled, her small shoulders sagging inside her cardigan. "One night, not long after they closed the mine, I was upstairs looking out onto the street. Used to be a bar across the way, McGleenan's, not much of a place. I watched Lewis Bodie stagger out of there, hardly fit to put one foot in front of another. Bodie got a payout from the mine for losing his job, same as a lot of the men around here, but he drank his up faster than most. He staggered right out of the bar and into Sheriff Whiteside. They talked a bit, and I could see Bodie getting agitated, and I remember thinking, just shut your mouth and go home, or you'll wind up in a cell. Next thing I know, Sheriff Whiteside just belted him across the jaw. Bodie went down like a bag of sand, and I thought, well, he maybe had it coming. But it didn't stop there."

Mrs. Gerber's gaze went to the window, out onto the street.

"Ronnie Whiteside laid into Lewis Bodie like he was ready to kill him. He beat him and beat him, and I could hear it, the sound of his fists and his boots, and Bodie crying and begging. And even when he went quiet, Sheriff Whiteside kept going. When he finally stopped, he just stood there awhile, breathing hard. Then he bent down, took Bodie's wallet, and helped himself to whatever money he found there. And I remember thinking if it was anyone else doing the beating, I'd call the sheriff. So who do I call?

"Then next morning I look out the window again, and there's an ambulance from Gutteridge General outside the sheriff's station. It turns out Lewis Bodie died in his cell overnight. And I never breathed a word of it to anybody. So now I hear you say Whiteside has your children. Him I could believe it of, but Mary Collins? Her with a sick child and all?"

"That's right," Audra said.

"Everyone around here thinks Ronnie Whiteside is a good man. Same as they thought my husband was a good man. But I know different. Just tell me something."

"What?"

Mrs. Gerber stared at her from one doorway to the other, her eyes hard and sharp like blades. Audra realized that each of them stood on a threshold, and she supposed that should mean something. But she couldn't think what.

"Did you hurt your babies?"

"No, ma'am," Audra said, holding her gaze.

Mrs. Gerber nodded. "Well, then. You go up to your room and try to get a little sleep. I'll bring you up some coffee later on, maybe some cake."

"Thank you," Audra said. "I'd like that."

Mrs. Gerber nodded once more and disappeared back into the kitchen. Audra went to the hall and climbed the two flights of stairs. As she approached her room, she noticed the door was open an inch or two. She remembered she hadn't locked it, but she was certain she had at least closed it behind her. But it was an old house, the kind where floorboards creaked, windows rattled, and doors sometimes didn't latch properly.

Audra entered the room, put her shoulder to the door to close it. She slid the chain lock into place, then went to the bed. Tiredness weighed heavy behind her eyes as she sat on the edge of the mattress and kicked off her shoes.

Only when she lifted her head did she see the man in the corner, the brown paper bag in his hand.

CHAPTER 27

THE MICROPHONES SWARMED AROUND PATRICK KINNEY'S handsome face.

"Five hundred thousand dollars," he said, "for the return of my children. I realize at this stage the chances of finding them alive are slim. Even so, the reward stands. Whether to hold them or to bury them, I want my children back."

"Shit," Mitchell said, closing the laptop on which the news clip played.

"Yep," Showalter said, his elbow on the desk, his chin in his hand. "We did not need that."

Whiteside had stood behind them both to watch. "Doesn't make any difference, does it?"

Mitchell turned in her chair, looked at him like he was an idiot. "It won't help us find them, no, but it does mean the phone lines will be tied up with bullshit leads from idiots with dollar signs for eyes."

"Then you best call down to Phoenix," Whiteside said, "get your field office to send up some more stuffed suits."

Showalter smirked.

Mitchell got to her feet. "Thank you for the suggestion. If you'll excuse me, I've got two lost children to find."

"Oh, come on," Whiteside said. "You know those kids are dead. When are you going to get out of the way and let Showalter and the state cops arrest that woman? She killed her kids, you know she did, she killed them and she dumped them out in the desert."

"No, Sheriff Whiteside," Mitchell said. "I do not know that. And neither do you. We won't know anything for sure until Sean and Louise are found. I'll be over in the town hall, if you need me."

She exited by the side door, let it swing closed behind her.

Whiteside looked down at Showalter. "You know what that woman needs?"

Showalter grinned. "Yeah, I do."

They both guffawed.

Across the room, standing in the corner with his arms folded, Special Agent Abrahms cleared his throat.

"Quiet, Junior, the men are talking." Whiteside lifted the laptop from the desk, held it out. "Here, we're done with your computer."

Abrahms approached, extended his hand, reached for the laptop. Whiteside jerked it away.

"Cut it out," Abrahms said. "Just give it to me."

Whiteside handed it over. "Don't cry, kid."

Showalter snorted.

Abrahms took a step closer. "You're a real asshole, you know that?"

"Better men than you have called me a lot worse," Whiteside said, his voice lowered. "Anytime you want to have a serious conversation about it, just say the word. I'll take you out back, show you just how big an asshole I really am."

"Go fuck yourself," Abrahms said, walking away. He sat down at the desk he'd commandeered when he first arrived, opened the laptop, started typing something.

Whiteside patted Showalter on the shoulder and lifted his hat from the desk. "Keep an eye on the kid. Make sure he doesn't hurt himself with that thing."

He exited through the side door, to the sound of Showalter's chuckling. The sun hit him hard, and he plucked the shades from where they hung from his collar. He walked around the building, out onto the street. A few of the press people approached, questions in their eyes, readying microphones and recorders.

"I got nothing for you," he said, waving them away.

The diner had quieted down when he entered, but it still had more customers than he'd seen there in years. Reporters, for the most part. He ignored them and went to the end of the counter. Shelley came straight over.

"Coffee to go, sweetheart," he said.

"Another one?" Shelley asked. "How many's that today? Sure you don't want a decaf?"

"No, regular's good."

She returned a minute later with a large paper cup with a plastic lid. He dropped a few bills on the counter, plucked a napkin from the dispenser, and wrapped it around the cup to save his fingers from the heat.

"Hey, Shelley, you got a second?"

The waitress had been on her way to the register, but she turned back to him. "Sure," she said.

Whiteside beckoned her in close, lowered his voice. "You remember the gentleman you were speaking with earlier? Over by the window."

She wiggled her fingers at her face. "Oh, you mean the . . ."

"Yeah, the Asian gentleman."

"Sure, I remember. He was a nice man. What about him?"

"What did you two talk about?"

"About this." She waved her hands at the world around her. "Everything going on. He hadn't seen anything on the news, so I told him all about it."

"Did he ask about anyone in particular? Like the Kinney woman? Or me?"

Shelley shook her head. "No, not that I recall. He just seemed interested in the whole affair. Well, I mean, who wouldn't be?"

"No one, I guess. Did you happen to see which way he headed when he left?"

"No, sorry, we were jammed here earlier. I was too busy taking orders to watch him. He got another sandwich to go and left me a nice tip. That was the last I saw of him."

Whiteside leaned closer. "He ordered another sandwich?"

"Yeah," Shelley said. "To go. Must have been hungry."

"Must have been."

"You don't think he's mixed up in all this, do you?"

"No, nothing like that. I was just curious about him, that's all."

He dropped another two bills on the counter. "Don't let Harvey work you too hard now."

Whiteside carried his coffee out onto the sidewalk, slipped his shades back on, put his hat on his head. He looked up and down the street, knowing he wouldn't see the man. A sandwich to go, he thought. Maybe he had been hungry, like Shelley said, but Whiteside had a different idea entirely. He looked across to the guesthouse, wondered if Audra Kinney was eating that sandwich right now.

It wasn't really the color of the man's skin that bothered him, though he was an unusual sight around here. Rather, it was the kind of man he was. Whiteside had met enough over the years. Gets to be you know one on sight. A man is either wired to kill or he's not. Most aren't. But this one had the look about him, the eyes that see farther than they should, the hollowness you see in them, if you look too close.

Whiteside had seen that same hollowness in the mirror. The thought chilled him.

Anyway, why would a man like that show up today, of all days? Could have been a coincidence, but Whiteside believed in coincidences about as much as he believed in Santa Claus. This man was a threat, Whiteside was certain of it. And, right this minute, he believed the man was in the guesthouse, giving Audra Kinney food. All he could do was watch and wait.

Whiteside sat down on one of the benches outside the diner, took a sip of hot coffee. From here, he could see the front of the guesthouse, and a few yards of alley that cut to the north of it.

He hadn't even finished his coffee when everything went to shit.

CHAPTER 28

AFTER HIS RUN-IN WITH WHITESIDE IN THE DINER, DANNY HAD gone for a walk. Along Main Street first of all, from one end to the other. So many places closed up, stores long gone. Guns and sporting goods, pet supplies, a bar, ladies' fashion, home furnishings, a men's store specializing in Western clothing, a pair of boots with spurs painted on its sign along with a Stetson hat. All of them falling into decay, their windows whited out or boarded up.

The few locals on the street had given him second looks. They'd have given him more, if they hadn't assumed he'd blown in with the press. He had nodded and smiled, given polite greetings. Some were returned, some were not.

At the end of the street he came to the bridge that he'd driven across an hour or two ago. He walked along the narrow sidewalk to its center and looked over the railing. The river below had withered to a sluggish red stream at the middle of a wide basin, cracked reddish-brown earth all around. Dying, like the town itself.

Danny made his way back to the town side. A row of houses, mostly empty, faced out onto what would once have been a lovely view of the river. An alleyway cut behind them, bordering their rear yards, and branched back toward the rear of the boarded-up stores that lined Main Street. From this end he could see all the way down, right to the wall that enclosed the sheriff's station parking lot. Halfway along, hot air rippled from the vents at the back of the diner. A dozen properties between here and there, most of them unoccupied. Any one of them suitable for entering tonight, for a place to sleep. He'd try the furniture store first; they might have something left in storage that would be comfortable to lie on. In through a rear window or door, maybe a skylight. Danny was skilled at these things.

He retraced his steps out onto Main Street, looked up and down to see if anyone had noted his coming and going. Then he jogged across to the other side of the street, found the alleyway that mirrored the one he'd just emerged from. This time the alley was truncated by the southern wall of the town hall, its grounds fenced off. He counted in his head. The guesthouse should be eight buildings down. He started walking.

The pine fence stood out from the others; it was the only one that had been freshened with wood stain anytime in the last few years. A row of garbage cans stood alongside a gate. He stepped back and looked up. The house looked tired, but better than its neighbors. All the windows intact, everything still nailed together.

One more look in all directions, then Danny tried the gate. A hole just big enough to slip his hand through and feel the padlock on the other side. No matter. He went to one of the garbage cans, noticed dusty boot prints on its lid. Someone had used it to stand on, maybe get a better view of the house. Danny did the same, then hauled himself up and over. He landed silent as a cat on the other side. A good-sized yard, but parched dry. What was once a lawn had been baked solid. A vegetable patch on one side still held a few living things, but mostly too shriveled to feed anyone.

Danny stood still and listened for a moment, his ears alert for cries of alarm at his intrusion. No one had spotted him. He crossed the yard and climbed the few steps onto the back porch, with its wicker chairs and swing seat. A closed screen in front of an open door. He placed his body between the door and the window, edged closer to the glass, peered inside.

A small television set played the local news, the screen showing images of this very street. He couldn't quite make out the newscaster's breathless voiceover. At the table, an elderly woman chopping up tomatoes.

Shit, Danny thought.

He was about to turn and go back the way he'd come, when the woman's head jerked up. Danny froze, and so did she. Then he heard the jangle of a bell from somewhere inside the house, and the woman rose from the table and exited the kitchen.

Danny took the emery board from his pocket and slipped it between the screen door and its frame, flipped the latch, and entered the kitchen. A ceiling fan moved warm air around the room, a steady hum above his head. He closed the screen again and crept to the open door leading to the hall. Voices out there, resonating beneath the high ceiling. Danny eased through the door, ducked into the space beneath the stairs, as far into the shadow as he could squeeze himself.

Listening, he heard a man's voice, hard and insistent, the old woman's protesting. Then the man being taken to a room, before the old woman climbed the stairs above his head. Danny waited in the dark, hearing another conversation upstairs, followed by two sets of footsteps descending.

He pressed himself into the shadows beneath the stairs as the old woman passed on her way back to the kitchen. A few more seconds as he listened again, voices in the room along the hall. Then Danny slipped out of the alcove and moved to the foot of the stairs. He climbed the two flights to the landing above, checked each of the doors.

All but number three were locked. He went inside and waited.

More than twenty minutes passed before he heard Audra approach her room.

CHAPTER 29

AUDRA SHOT TO HER FEET.

"Who are you? What are you doing here?"

The man put his hands up, the brown paper bag still held in his left. "I'm sorry for sneaking in like this, it was the only way I could—"

She pointed at the door as she backed into the far corner. "Get out!"

"Ma'am . . . Audra . . . please just let me talk to you."

"Get out," she said, still pointing. "Get out of here."

"Please just listen."

"Get out!" Audra ran through her few remaining possessions in her mind, wondering which might serve as a weapon.

"My name is Danny Lee," he said.

"I don't care what your name is, just get out."

"What you're going through now," he said, "I went through the same thing five years ago."

Anger outran Audra's fear. "You don't know shit about what I'm going through."

He took a step forward and she grabbed the empty vase from the windowsill.

"Just listen," he said, his hands up, his head down. "I think I know what they're doing with your children. It might not be too late for them. Maybe I can help you get them back."

She moved the vase from hand to hand. "You're full of shit."

"Will you at least hear me out?"

Audra pointed to his hand. "What's in the bag?"

"It's for you," he said. "A sandwich from the diner. Are you hungry?"

Without thinking, Audra's free hand went to her stomach.

"Take it," he said, and tossed it onto the bed.

Audra left the corner, dropped the vase on the blankets, and lifted the bag. She opened the top and the smell of bacon and warm bread billowed out. Her stomach growled.

"It's good," the man said. "I had one earlier. Eat."

Audra knew she shouldn't. He could have put anything in it. But the smell. And she was so hungry. She reached inside the bag, pulled out half a sandwich, took a bite.

"Why don't you sit down," he said. "Give me five minutes to explain."

She perched on the edge of the bed, chewed, swallowed. "You've got till the end of this sandwich," she said. "Now talk."

CHAPTER 30

D ANNY AND MYA HAD FOUGHT BEFORE SHE LEFT. SARA HAD asked, what's wrong? Danny had stroked her hair and said, nothing, honey. But Sara was smart, and she knew. She saw the tears as she looked at her mother's reflection in the rearview mirror.

Neither of them had called it a separation. Simply a couple of days away, Mya driving the few hours north to her parents' place between Redding and Palo Cedro. She would be back after the weekend, she'd said, and neither of them had believed it.

Two hours into the drive, she had pulled off the interstate to find somewhere to eat. Outside the small town of Hamilton, she was stopped by a police officer named Sergeant Harley Granger for a minor traffic offense. Something so trivial Danny couldn't even remember what it was. According to the officer, Mya was agitated and uncooperative, so he radioed for another car to come and assist. Two of Hamilton Police Department's six-strong fleet of cruisers at the scene. According to Granger and the other cop, Lloyd, Mya had no child in the car with her. She had a booster seat and a bag of clothes, but no sign of Sara.

By the time Danny got to the station in Hamilton, Mya was in a state of near-hysteria.

"They took her," she said, over and over. "They took her."

The FBI arrived the next morning. They questioned Mya for three straight days. On the fourth day, Mya tried to hang herself in her cell. After that, they let her go, and she and Danny drove back to San Francisco. The story made the regional news, and Mya's photograph became a fixture on the evening bulletins. People they knew, old friends, stared at them in the street. The story held the press's interest for about a week before the reporters moved on. But Danny's and Mya's friends did not. They kept staring, kept refusing the couple's phone calls. All the while Danny and Mya voluntarily attended interviews at the FBI field office, while Hamilton PD compiled evidence.

What Danny didn't know was that on that last morning the Hamilton Chief of Police called to tell Mya to surrender to them within twenty-four hours, for arrest in connection with the murder of her daughter. If she failed to do so, a warrant would be issued, and SFPD would execute it.

Danny had embraced her before he left for that evening's Youth Outreach meeting, placed a kiss on her cheek. If he had known the finality of it, he would have held her longer, kissed her harder.

Five years ago, almost to the day. Danny arrived home from the meeting, feeling weary and worn. He called Mya's name as he entered their darkened house, the silence telling him something was wrong. No sign of her in any of the downstairs rooms. As he climbed the stairs, he saw the closed bathroom, and the buckle of one his belts trapped between the top of the door and the frame.

He had to shoulder the door open, and he heard the buckle spring free, and a sickening weight hit the floor on the other side. An age passed as he stood there, knowing what he would find when he finally gathered the courage to look. But he did look, eventually, and he pulled the belt from Mya's neck and sat cradling her for an hour, howling and blinded by tears, before he thought to call an ambulance.

Two months after Mya's suicide, Danny drove back to Hamilton. Through his contacts in the SFPD, he had learned that Sergeant Granger had taken a leave of absence due to the stress of dealing with the case. He had gone to Mexico to recover. No one knew when he would return.

But Lloyd was still around, drinking in the town's one small bar every night. Lately he'd been generous with his tips, bought lots of drinks for his friends. He'd even bought a new car. Nothing too fancy, an Infiniti, but upmarket enough to be noticed by those he drank with.

Lloyd was also known to be an idiot.

Danny waited and watched outside the bar. Lloyd lived only a twenty-minute walk away and would usually leave his new Infiniti parked on the street outside, to return for it in the morning. He was pissing in an alleyway when Danny snatched him.

An hour later, Lloyd was tied up, suspended by his wrists from a roof beam in an abandoned storage shed Danny had found a week before. No one for miles around to hear him scream. Danny took his time with the knife. Lloyd didn't know much, only what Granger had told him. When Lloyd told Danny they'd received less money than they wanted because the little girl was mixed-race, Danny lost the sliver of control he had, and Lloyd died too quickly for his satisfaction. No matter, he would make up for it with Granger, and find out how to get to the buyer.

When he found the buyer, he would keep him alive just long enough to find out what they'd done with Sara. Whether they'd let her live or not. His higher mind knew the answer to that question, but he would ask it anyway. He would ask it hard.

Danny had a flight booked for Cabo San Lucas two days later, but when he arrived in Mexico and asked around, he discovered Granger had been stabbed to death in a bar fight a week earlier. On a beach, sand burning hot on the soles of his feet, Danny mourned for his wife and daughter, knowing he might never find the men who had destroyed his life.

HE DIDN'T TELL Audra about the hours spent with Lloyd, showing the cop pieces of himself before tossing them on the fire. But he told her about Granger. By that time she had grown calm, the food gone. She remained on the bed while he sat on the thinly upholstered chair.

"There's a group of men," Danny said, "very wealthy men. They'll pay a large sum of money for the right child. Seven figures, I heard. There's a ringleader. He holds parties at a mansion somewhere on the West Coast. Him and his friends, they have these children procured and . . ."

Audra looked away. Danny cleared his throat.

"Well, I guess you know," he continued. "They could get traf-ficked children easy, refugees, whatever, but they want American kids. White, if they can get them. There's a specific method, a way of working. They use the Dark Web, it's like the underside of the In-ternet, where criminals and perverts hang out. There's a close circle of dirty cops from around the country who talk to each other there. I've tried to find a way in for years now, but I can't. I was told they discuss ways of making money. Odd jobs for the Mob, evidence tam-pering, sometimes even contract killings. And these wealthy men have a request out for kids. If one of these cops comes across a vul-nerable parent traveling with children, preferably alone, they find an excuse to arrest them, separate them from the kids, then say the kids were never in the car. If they do it right, if they find the right target, suspicion falls on the parent. They can pull it off maybe once a year, twice at most."

"Why don't they kill the parent?" Audra asked. "Why didn't Whiteside just kill me? That'd be simpler, wouldn't it?"

Danny shook his head. "Simpler for the cops, maybe, but not for the men paying the money. See, my theory is if they just snatch the kids and kill the parent, then the authorities know there's a mur-derer out there and they go looking. If the parent's alive, and the suspicion's on them, then the authorities waste days and weeks chas-ing their tails. You look at all those cases where a kid goes missing, there's a big search, and they find a body. How many times does it turn out it was the father, the stepfather, the uncle, the cousin? Naturally the authorities look to the last family member to have seen the child. And if it's a parent who does what my wife did . . ."

Audra finished the thought. "Then the case dies with them."

"Exactly."

She sat still and quiet, her gaze on the floor.

"Do you think I'm crazy?" Danny asked. "Some nut job who just showed up here to mess with you?"

She did not look up. "I don't know what you are. My right mind says to kick you out of here, but . . ."

"But what?"

"But at this moment I don't have anyone else on my side."

Danny leaned forward in the chair. "Let's get one thing straight. I'm on my side. Not yours. If I help you, it's because it helps me get to the men who took my daughter. And, if she's alive somewhere, maybe even find her. I'm not your Good Samaritan."

"Then let me get another thing straight," Audra said. "I'm only hearing you out because I've got no other choice."

"Fair enough," he said. "But here's one more question: Why should I trust you? What if they're right about you?"

"You wouldn't be here if you thought that."

"So neither one of us has reason to trust the other. But here we are."

Audra exhaled and said, "Here we are. If you're right, do you think they'll have handed Sean and Louise over yet? Or are they still holding them somewhere?"

"Hard to know," Danny said. "My guess is they'll want to move them soon, if they haven't done it yet. Either way, there isn't much time."

Now she looked at him, hard. "How do I get them back?"

Danny realized then that this woman was not like Mya. She possessed a strength that Mya had not. Whatever she had survived in her past had put steel in her.

"There's only one way," he said. "We use the cops. You said it was the sheriff who arrested you, and the deputy took your children."

"That's right," Audra said. "Her name's Collins."

"All right, we go through her. We take her, put a gun to her head, and give her a simple choice: she tells us where the kids are or she dies."

Audra got to her feet, started to pace the room, shaking her head. "No. No, I can't do that. I'm not that kind of person."

"Maybe not," Danny said. "But I am."

She stopped mid-stride, looked down at him. "Have you killed someone before?"

He didn't answer the question. "We need to take the deputy soon. Tonight, if we can."

"No," Audra said. "We can't. If it goes wrong, if she gets hurt, then they'll crucify me. The press haven't said anything about Whiteside and Collins, I guess because they haven't been told what I said. As far as the public's concerned, Collins is just a sheriff's deputy doing her job. We hurt her, it'll only make things worse. There has to be another way."

"If you've got a better plan," Danny said, "I'm listening."

"The FBI agent. Mitchell. We go to her. You tell her everything you told me. She'll question Whiteside and Collins."

"You told her about them already," Danny said. "Has she questioned them so far?"

Audra looked away. "No, not yet. But she hasn't heard your story."

"There was an FBI agent attached to Sara's case too. Child Abduction Response Deployment, right?"

Audra nodded.

"My agent's name was Reilly. I told him all this right before I . . . Well, I don't know if he didn't believe me or just didn't want to deal with the fallout. Either way, he didn't do anything."

"But Mitchell will," Audra said. "I know it. She's a good person."

"Good people can make mistakes. They do it all the time."

"Let me try." She hunkered down in front of him, her hands clasped together, a gesture of pleading. "If I can get her to listen, will you talk to her?"

"That means putting myself at risk," Danny said.

"Of what?"

"Maybe I don't want the FBI or the cops looking too close at my case."

"Why? What did you do?"

He couldn't hold her gaze. "I won't talk to the cops or the feds. They won't help. Not without leverage."

"Leverage?"

"Outside pressure," Danny said. "If Mitchell hasn't acted on her own, then maybe a push from elsewhere will force her hand."

Audra stood and walked from one side of the room to the other, chewing a nail that looked like it hadn't much left to give.

"The press," she said. "I talk to the press. If Mitchell won't tell them what I said, then I will. Let the public know. Then she'll have to question them."

"It's risky," Danny said. "You hit out at the sheriff that way, then he'll hit back."

Audra stopped pacing. "I'll take that chance. They want a story? I'll give them a story."

CHAPTER 31

AUDRA SHOUTED, "HEY!"

Some of the reporters turned her way, most didn't.

"Hey! Over here!"

More saw her now, and they scrambled. Microphones, cameras, cell phones, anything that could take a picture or record a sound.

Audra stood on the top step outside the guesthouse door. She'd tried to tidy herself up, but she still looked a mess. So long as I don't look crazy, she'd thought as she checked a mirror in the hall. Mrs. Gerber had called to her as she walked to the door, said don't go out there, but Audra had ignored her. Now she stood waiting, watching the press people scurry toward her like pigs to a trough.

The first of them reached her, microphones outstretched, right under her nose. They shouted questions, but she didn't hear. She held her silence until all of them had gathered around, jostling with each other for the best angle. Still the shouting, one voice buried by the next.

"Quiet," Audra said.

They only grew louder.

"Shut up!" Loud enough to hurt her throat. "I have something to say."

Now they hushed, and the noise of the street seemed to swell around them. Across the road, Audra saw Sheriff Whiteside staring at her from his place on a bench outside the diner. Death in his eyes. The idea of turning around and going back inside fluttered through her mind, but she chased it away. Say it, she thought. Say it for Sean and Louise.

"I did not hurt my children," Audra said.

The clamor grew once more, and she raised her hands to quiet them.

"Sean and Louise were with me, a little hot and tired, but they were safe with me when I was pulled over just outside of town two days ago."

She pointed across the street. Whiteside's lips thinned.

"That man, Sheriff Whiteside, pulled me over. He told me my car was overloaded. Then he looked in the trunk and found a bag of marijuana. The bag wasn't mine. He planted it there so he could arrest me. My children were in my car while he searched and handcuffed me. He radioed Deputy Collins to come get Sean and Louise. I asked him where she was taking them, and all he said was, 'Somewhere safe.' Deputy Collins drove away with them in the back of her car. That was the last time I saw my children."

The microphones jockeyed in front of her mouth. A chorus of questions. Audra ignored them all.

"When Sheriff Whiteside brought me back to the jail, I asked for my kids. He said I had no children with me. He's been lying ever since, him and Deputy Collins. I've told this to everybody, the state police, the FBI, everyone, and nobody believes me. They didn't even tell you people, the press, what I said. But I'm telling you now. My children are out there somewhere, they're alive, and that man knows where they are."

She pointed at Whiteside once more, and he moved away from the front of the diner, along the sidewalk toward the station.

"Go ask him," Audra said. "See what he'll tell you."

Some of the reporters split off, headed in Whiteside's direction. He quickened his pace to a jog, looking nowhere but at the front entrance of the station.

"That's all I have to say."

She turned to the door, her back to the hail of questions. Inside, she barred the door behind her. She watched through the glass as the rest of the reporters set off toward Whiteside. Then she walked into the dim shadows of the hallway.

Mrs. Gerber waited in the doorway to the kitchen, almost hidden by the stairs, watching her.

"You just bought yourself a whole load of trouble," she said.

Audra didn't answer as she mounted the stairs and climbed.

"You know what I think of Ronnie Whiteside," Mrs. Gerber said, coming to the first step. "But Mary Collins. She's a nice girl. Are you sure about her?"

Audra paused on the turn and said, "Yes, I'm sure."

"You think you know a person. Do you still want that coffee and cake?"

"Yes, please," Audra said. "Can you make it for two? I have a guest."

"A guest? I don't allow visitors in the rooms. Who've you got up there?"

Audra thought about it for a moment before saying, "I'm not sure."

She made her way up to the second floor and back to her room. Danny waited there, still sitting where she'd left him.

"Well?" he asked.

"Well, I told them," Audra said. "We'll see if it shakes anything loose."

Danny got to his feet, his hand delving into the thigh pocket of his cargo pants. "I'm guessing they kept your phone. Here."

He tossed a cheap-looking cell onto the bed.

"It's prepaid," he said. "One number in the contacts list. Mine. You call me straightaway if anything happens. I'll keep my phone switched on. You do the same."

Audra lifted the cell, flipped it open. "Okay," she said. "Thank you."

"All right. I should get out of here now."

"Wait," Audra said, surprised at her own eagerness for this stranger to stay. She realized she'd been alone since her children were taken, and she didn't want to be alone again. Not yet, anyway. "The landlady, Mrs. Gerber, she's bringing up some coffee. And cake."

Danny shrugged and sat down. "Well, if there's cake . . ."

CHAPTER 32

ALL EYES TURNED TO WHITESIDE AS HE ENTERED THE STATION. The state cops, the FBI, all stared at him. Including Special Agent Mitchell, who marched toward him from the rear of the room.

"Well, I guess everyone heard that," he said. "Doesn't change anything. Woman's crazy, is all."

"It changes a lot," Mitchell said.

"You know she's talking nonsense, right? Maybe she believes it herself, but it's all bullshit. You can't take it seriously."

"I'm taking everything seriously." Mitchell folded her arms across her chest. "I have since I got here. And I'm not ruling anything out right now."

"Come on, then," he said, stepping in close. "Arrest me. Interrogate me. Hook me up to a goddamn polygraph machine. I'll take everything you got. Your people searched Collins' car, right?"

"That's correct," Mitchell said.

"And did they find a trace of those children ever being there? No? It was clean, wasn't it?"

"It was very clean," Mitchell said. "We found nothing but a few traces of bleach, like it had been scrubbed out."

"How about my cruiser?" Whiteside said, letting his voice harden. "You want to search that too? Or maybe my house? I got a cellar. You want to look in there?"

"That won't be necessary," Mitchell said, turning away. "For now."

"Release the pictures," he said.

Mitchell stopped. "What?"

"The T-shirt and the jeans. With the blood on them. Release those to the press, let them know they were found in her car. That'll put this to rest."

"I'll think about it," Mitchell said. "Is that all?"

"Yeah, that's all."

Whiteside scanned the room as Mitchell walked away, dared anyone to look at him now. They all made themselves busy with their maps and their laptop computers.

"Anyone got something they want to talk to me about?" he asked, his voice booming.

Not a one of them looked up.

"Didn't think so," he said.

He went to the side door, hit the push bar, and stepped out onto the ramp. A dry want at the back of his throat. Not for a drink. He craved one of Collins' cigarettes, imagined the heat of the smoke in his chest.

As if summoned by the thought, his cruiser pulled into the parking lot. Collins had been using it while the feds searched hers. She drove to the rear of the lot to find an empty space, the rest taken up by the state cops and the FBI vehicles. He descended the shallow ramp and walked in her direction, met her halfway.

"You hear the news?" he asked.

Collins looked over his shoulder, made sure no one else was in earshot. "Some of it. What do we do?"

"Nothing," he said. "The press still think she's crazy. They still want to see her burn. I might be able to encourage them a little."

"How?"

"Let me worry about that."

"Maybe . . ."

She stood there, her mouth opening and closing, an idea too fearful to reach her tongue.

"What?" Whiteside asked. "Just say it."

"Maybe there's a way out. Maybe it's not too late."

"What are you talking about?"

"We tell her she can have her kids back if she swears not to implicate us. We find them out wandering somewhere, we'll be heroes, so long as they keep their mouths shut. There's the half-million reward the father put up. It's not as much as we wanted, but it's not nothing."

He grabbed Collins' upper arm, squeezed hard. "Stop it. You think like that, you'll finish us both. Just hold your nerve. We do the exchange tomorrow, then it's over. All right?"

Her eyes brimmed as she nodded. "All right."

"Good," he said. "Now pull yourself together. One more day, that's all."

Whiteside turned to walk away, but Collins spoke again.

"The girl's sick," she said.

"Sick how?"

"She's got a fever, a rattle in her chest, sleeping a lot."

"What about the boy?"

"He's fine. It's just her."

"Shit," Whiteside said. He put his hands on his hips and stared at the hills as he thought. "You have medicine at your house, right? For your boy."

"Some," Collins said.

"Any antibiotics? Penicillin, amoxicillin? Anything like that?"

"Amoxicillin," Collins said. "I need to keep it on hand in case Mikey gets an infection."

"Okay, give her some of that. Bring it out this evening if you can. Give her a double dose to get her started."

"But it's Mikey's."

"Then get him some more." He looked around, lowered his voice. "Goddamn it, Mary, you gotta start thinking right. Don't fuck this up."

Whiteside walked back toward the station, willing his anger to be still.

CHAPTER 33

Private Forum 447356/34
Admin: RR; Members: DG, AD, FC, MR, JS
Thread Title: This Weekend; Thread Starter: RR

From: DG, Friday 6:02 p.m.
RR—Are we still going ahead? I don't know what anyone else thinks, but I'm getting a little nervous. We've never had media attention like this before.

From: MR, Friday 6:11 p.m.
I've been wondering the same thing. Should we cut our losses at this stage?

From: FC, Friday 6:14 p.m.
I've paid my half mill already. I assume we all have. I didn't throw down that kind of money just for the evening to be canceled over some news reports.

From: MR, Friday 6:18 p.m.
FC—There's a lot more at stake here than money. If you can't afford to lose half a mill, then you don't belong in this group.

From: FC, Friday 6:20 p.m.
MR—Fuck you. I can afford to lose more than you made last year and not even break a sweat. If you want to chicken out, go ahead.

From: MR, Friday 6:23 p.m.
FC—Easy to say, when you've got your father's safety net to catch your fall.

From: DG, Friday 6:27 p.m.
Gentlemen, please be civil. This isn't some Facebook comment thread, and there's no need to squabble. Let's just wait and see what RR has to say.

From: JS, Friday 6:46 p.m.
Any word, gentlemen? I must admit, I'm nervous too. It's all over the news.

From: DG, Friday 6:50 p.m.
Calm down, everyone. RR will let us know in good time.

From: RR, Friday 7:08 p.m.
Gentlemen, we proceed as planned. The seller has been in touch and made assurances that everything is under control.

Also, I have sourced some imported goods, so even if something goes wrong, we will have entertainment for the evening. We all prefer locally sourced goods, of course, but these will suffice if we can't acquire the intended items—and I have no reason to believe we won't.

FC & MR—bicker like that again and you're out.

See you all tomorrow.

CHAPTER 34

SEAN WAITED IN THE DARKNESS BENEATH THE STAIRS. A FEW seconds ago he had been lying with Louise, holding her close, her body burning against his chest as if she had a furnace inside. The front of his shirt still damp from her sweat, it now chilled him. Her breath rattled and wheezed.

He had risen from the mattress when he heard the buzz of the motorcycle approach. Now the footsteps above, crossing to the trapdoor. The rattle of the lock, the snap of the bolt, then light breaking in. He stepped back, let the shadows swallow him.

Collins trudged down the first few steps, stopped a third of the way from the top. Sean raised his hands.

"Sean? Where are you?"

He remained still and silent, his hands ready.

"I've got medicine for your sister," Collins said. "Come on out, now, let's get her well again."

Still and quiet.

"Sean, come out where I can see you. I don't want to get mad at you."

She took one step down. Then another.

"Come on, now. I'm dog tired and I haven't got the patience for this."

Now she descended farther, faster, and Sean watched her boots through the gaps between the steps. When her heels were at his eye level, he reached out and grabbed her ankles. Barely a touch, but it was enough.

There was a moment that seemed to stretch out for an age: her feet skimming the edges of the steps, her arms windmilling. Then she toppled forward, hit the stairs so hard he felt the force of it through the floor and the soles of his shoes. Collins rolled the rest of the way down, her shoulder and head glancing off the steps. She landed heavy on the floorboards, flat on her back, and he heard the air expelled from her lungs.

Move, he thought. Now.

Sean sprang from behind the stairs, around to the foot of them, and up, two steps at a time. A cry from below, rage and fear. He didn't look back, but as he neared the top, he felt Collins' weight on the steps below.

He reached the opening, out onto the cabin floor. His feet slipped from under him as he tried to halt, to turn back for the trapdoor. He scurried across to it, saw Collins charging up toward him. He reached for the door, hauled it back and over, threw it down with everything he had. Collins cried out again as it came down on her head, her hands scrabbling at the floor.

Sean ran for the door, leaped across the porch, onto the pine-needle carpet of the forest. Clean, cool air in his lungs, he passed the motorcycle and sprinted for the trees.

"Stop!"

He weaved between the pines, left and right, ready for a bullet to take him off his feet.

"Stop, you little—"

The voice had not drawn closer. Maybe he could outrun her. Maybe.

Then a tree root snagged his toe, and up was down, and he saw the ground fall away and rise again as he sailed weightless for a moment through the air. He rolled down the incline, shoulder then hip hitting the soft ground, end over end. Collins appeared in his vision as he came to rest. No air in the world, he tried to get his feet under him, but she hit him hard, body to body, putting him back down again.

Fight, he thought. Fight or you'll die.

He balled his hands into fists, threw them at her, felt them connect with the soft flesh of her breasts. She dropped her full weight on him and tried to grab his wrists. He snaked them out of her grasp, punched her sides, reached behind her, grabbed at fabric. Her hard flat palm slammed into his cheek, a white flash in his head, then black dots in his vision. She put a knee on his chest, pinning him in place.

"Jesus Christ, do you want me to kill you?" she shouted, her voice echoing through the trees. "Your sister too? Is that what you want?"

Sean blinked up at the sky. High above, an airplane left a trail against the deepening blue. Somewhere amid the fear, he wondered if someone might look down and see him trapped here. Then Collins leaned down, her nose almost touching his, and he couldn't see the plane anymore.

"I will do it," she said. "Don't you doubt that for a second."

She reached back, seeking something.

For a splinter of a second, Sean thought, Oh God, she'll know, she'll know and she'll kill me. Then she pressed the pistol's muzzle against his cheek and relief flooded through him. He almost giggled with the force of it.

She pressed harder. "I'll put a bullet in your fucking head, you hear me? You and your sister both. I'll do her first and make you watch." Collins lifted her knee from his chest, pushed up onto her feet. She aimed the pistol at his forehead. "Get up and walk."

Sean lay still for a moment, staring at the sky, looking for the plane. He found the trail, followed it until he saw the craft through the branches. Then he got to his feet, dusted the browned pine needles off his T-shirt and jeans.

Collins waved the pistol back in the direction of the cabin. "Move," she said.

Sean did as he was told, breathless, his head down as he walked.

"I don't think you'd do it," he said as they entered the clearing.

"Shut up," Collins said.

"I think the sheriff would," he said, risking a glance back at her. He saw the pistol still trained on him. "But you wouldn't. Because you have a kid my age."

"Shut your mouth and get inside."

A shove between his shoulder blades sent him stumbling across the porch and through the door. He walked to the trapdoor and the top of the steps. Louise still lay where they'd left her, eyes staring up at him from her sweating face.

Collins followed him halfway down before she stopped. He paused at the bottom to look back up at her. She indicated the paper bags on the floor.

"There's your food," she said. "And a bottle of antibiotics. Give your sister three now, and another three later tonight. She needs to get better if you want to leave here."

Sean got down on his knees, looked through the bags, set aside the sandwiches and fruit. There, a small bottle that rattled when he lifted it. Amoxicillin, it said.

"You try that shit again," Collins said, "then you'll see what I will or won't do."

She turned and climbed the steps, let the trapdoor slam shut, locked it.

"You left me," Louise said.

Startled, Sean turned his head to her. "What?"

"You ran away and left me," she said, her eyes hard and unforgiving.

"No, I didn't."

"Yes, you did," she said. "I saw."

Sean crawled across the floor to kneel beside the mattress. "I didn't run away," he said. "I just needed to get something."

"Get what?" she asked, lifting her head.

He reached inside the front of his jeans, found the metal with his fingertips. "This," he said. "Look."

"What is it?"

Before her eyes he opened the lock knife he'd taken from Deputy Collins' pocket, let her see the shining blade.

CHAPTER 35

AUDRA WATCHED THE NEWS REPORT, HER HAND OVER HER mouth.

The studio handed over to Rhonda Carlisle, Silver Water's main street darkening behind her.

"Another major development in Elder County this evening, following the earlier shocking statement given by Audra Kinney," Rhonda Carlisle said. "An anonymous source within the investigation into the whereabouts of Sean and Louise Kinney has leaked images of physical evidence taken from their mother's car, which was stopped outside this small desert town forty-eight hours ago."

The photographs of the stained T-shirt and torn jeans. Audra wanted to look away, but she couldn't.

"The source tells us these items were found hidden beneath the front passenger seat of Audra Kinney's station wagon by a team from the FBI's Phoenix field office. The source also tells us that traces of blood were found around the rear of the car, deepening the authorities' fears for the children's safety."

Back to the studio, and the male anchor addressed the reporter.

"Now, Rhonda, is it possible this leak is a direct response to the accusations against the Elder County Sheriff's Department that Audra Kinney made earlier today?"

The reporter again, her expression stern.

"It's certainly a remarkable coincidence, Derek. Of course it's only speculation, but a good guess might be that the investigation team wanted to undo the damage done by Audra Kinney's statement. Given the find of bloodied children's clothing, and what we know of this woman's emotional and mental health problems, along with her issues with addiction, it doesn't paint a very bright picture for her, or her son and daughter.

"And the source has gone further and told us that with this physical evidence in hand, the Arizona Department of Public Safety's Criminal Investigations Division has all it needs to arrest Audra Kinney for the suspected murder of her children. But, we're told, the FBI's Child Abduction Response Deployment team, who are heading up the search operation, have been holding the state police at bay in hopes of Mrs. Kinney giving up the location of her children, dead or alive. According to the source, the authorities' patience is at an end, and they are scheduled to execute a warrant for her arrest sometime in the next twenty-four hours. When that happens, this will officially no longer be a missing persons investigation: it will be a murder investigation."

Audra switched off the television and said, "Whiteside leaked the photos. It had to be him."

"I told you he'd hit back," Danny said. An empty cup and a plate of cake crumbs sat on the floor beside his chair. "If they were going to arrest you today, they'd have done it by now. My guess is they'll come for you in the morning. If we're going to move against Collins, we have to do it tonight."

"We can't," Audra said. "*I* can't. I'm not . . ."

She looked at him, looked away again.

"Like me?"

"That's not what I meant. I don't even know you."

Audra stood over the bed, looked once more at the map she'd borrowed from Mrs. Gerber.

The landlady had balked when she saw Danny in the corner, demanded to know who this new intruder was, and how had he gotten inside? It had been all Audra could do to calm her down and reassure her that everything was fine.

After some persuasion, Mrs. Gerber had fetched the map and pointed out the regions.

"If I was going to hide two children," she'd said, "I wouldn't do it in the low desert. I'd go north, where it's cooler, up high into the forest." She had tapped the paper with her fingertip. "That there's the

Mogollon Rim. It climbs fast up into the Colorado Plateau. One minute it's all prickly pears, next it's juniper, then before you know it, you're at seven thousand feet and it's pine trees for miles and miles. Nothing but forest between there and Flagstaff. If I wanted to lose somebody, that's where I'd do it."

Audra looked at it now, the sheer expanse of it, and shook her head.

Danny came to her side. "Even if I sneak you out of here, where would you start to look? We need to get Collins. That's the only way. You know I'm right."

"There's another option," Audra said. "You talk to Mitchell."

"I'm not going over that again. I can't—"

A knock on the door silenced him. He looked at Audra, and she at him.

"Who is it?" Audra called.

"Special Agent Mitchell. Detective Showalter is with me. Audra, can we have a word?"

Audra went to the door, put her eye to the peephole, saw the distorted forms of Mitchell and Showalter waiting in the dimness of the hall.

"Right now?" she asked.

"Yes, right now," Mitchell said, an edge to her voice.

Audra turned to Danny, pointed to the bathroom. He slipped inside, eased the door closed. Audra turned the key in the lock, pulled aside the chain, opened the door.

Mitchell and Showalter stepped through without waiting to be asked.

"I heard a voice," Mitchell said. "I thought maybe you had company."

"The TV," Audra said. "What do you want?"

Mitchell looked down at the map, still spread out on the bed. "Planning a trip?"

"I was wondering where Whiteside and Collins would have taken my children."

Showalter shook his head and rolled his eyes. Mitchell ignored him.

"And did you come to any conclusions?"

"North," Audra said. "Up into the forests. It's cooler there, plenty of places to hide."

Mitchell tilted her head. "Not east? Not back the way you came?"

Audra slumped down into the chair. "Please, I'm very tired. What did you come here for?"

"To tell you that was a damn stupid thing you did earlier."

"I don't care," Audra said. "I had to do something."

Mitchell sat on the edge of the bed, leaned forward, her hands together. "You want to do something? Try telling me where your children are."

Audra closed her eyes, leaned her head back. "Oh God, I can't do this again. If that's all you've got, then I'd rather you left."

Mitchell stood, crossed the space between them, hunkered down in front of her. "Look, I came here so we could talk informally, off the record. No cameras, no notebooks. Give you one more chance before the state police take action."

"Take action?"

"Audra, they don't need a body to charge you with murder. The clothing we found in your car is enough. The only reason you haven't been arrested for killing your children is because I wanted to give you a chance to tell the truth. To make things easier on yourself. Right now, I'm in charge of finding your children, but when this becomes a murder investigation, Showalter takes over. The Criminal Investigations Division decides when that happens, not me. I've held them off as long as I can, but I can't do it anymore. You made sure of that with your little stunt this afternoon. Now, for God's sake, tell me where Sean and Louise are."

"Jesus," Audra said. "How can you be so blind?"

"Tomorrow morning, ten o'clock," Mitchell said. "Fourteen hours. That's all you've got, Audra. After that, you're in the hands of the state cops, the Department of Criminal Investigations. Then I won't be here for you. You think this is tough? They will eat you alive."

Audra straightened in the chair. "Have you questioned Whiteside?"

"I've spoken with him, yes, but—"

"Have you questioned him?" Audra asked, her voice hardening. "As a suspect."

Mitchell shook her head. "No, I haven't."

"What about Collins?"

"No."

Audra looked her hard in the eye. "Then what good are you to me? I'd like you to leave now."

She didn't see Showalter move to her side, only felt his hand grip her hair and jerk her head back. She gasped and cried out at the pain. Her hands went to his fist, tried to pry his fingers away. He leaned in close and she smelled his cigarette breath, felt his spit on her skin as he spoke.

"Now listen to me, you crazy bitch. If it was my choice, I'd beat it out of you. I still might. You got until morning to tell us what you did to your kids. After that, you're all mine. And I don't play nice."

Mitchell got to her feet. "Detective Showalter, let her go."

He leaned in closer, tugged at Audra's hair. "Tomorrow morning. You hear me?"

"Goddamn it, Showalter, stop."

Audra cried out as he tightened his grip.

"Take your hands off her," Danny Lee said.

CHAPTER 36

DANNY HAD LISTENED AS LONG AS HE COULD. THE VOICES TOOK him back five years. The accusations, the willful disbelief. He had stood behind the bathroom door, clenching his fists, grinding his teeth, picturing Mya in that room, the same questions thrown at her. Then he heard the cry, the cop's bitter, hateful words.

When he stepped through the doorway, it had been with the intention of laying the cop out. But his mind had cleared when he saw it was indeed Audra there, not his long-dead wife.

As all three stared at him, he thought, what good can I do now? If I can't hurt them, what can I do?

"Who in the hell are you?" Special Agent Mitchell asked, her eyes wide.

"My name is Danny Lee," he said, stepping out of the bathroom doorway. He spoke to the big cop with a handful of Audra's hair, his rage bubbling beneath his voice. "Sir, I asked you to take your hands off her."

Showalter released his grip, pushed Audra's head like he was tossing away garbage.

"My friend," he said, "you better explain yourself pretty damn quick, before I kick your ass into next week."

He thought, what can I do?

Then he decided.

"Ma'am," Danny said to Mitchell, "can I speak with you?"

She put her hands on her hips. "What about?"

"I'd rather do it in private," Danny said, nodding toward Showalter.

"Wait a minute," Showalter growled.

Mitchell raised her hand to the detective, told him to be quiet.

"Tell me your name again, please?" she said.

"Danny Lee."

"Mr. Lee, I have no clue who you are or what you're doing here. In all honesty, your presence rather alarms me, and I have a good mind to ask Detective Showalter to arrest your ass for interfering with this investigation. So why should I give you my time?"

"Because you want to find those children," Danny said.

SPECIAL AGENT MITCHELL sat quiet and listened, her notebook open on the old dining table. She had declared the bedroom too crowded, so they had followed her downstairs. Mitchell had asked Showalter to wait out in the hall and he had protested, but Mitchell reminded him that, at least for tonight, she was still calling the shots.

Audra leaned with her back against the wall and watched Mitchell make notes as Danny talked. Mitchell did not interrupt, offered no views on anything he said. He tried to read her expression, but couldn't.

Danny sat on the far side of the table, across from Mitchell, and spoke in as flat a tone as he could manage, no emotion, even when he described finding his wife's body. As if he had expended all his tears long ago. Nothing left now but a hollow recital of facts.

When he finished, Mitchell remained still, her gaze on the notebook. The muscles in her jaw bunched. After a few moments she inhaled, exhaled, and got to her feet.

"Give me a minute," she said, lifting the notebook. She stepped out into the hall, closed the door behind her.

Audra left her place by the wall, came to the table, sat down. Danny shook his head as he looked at her.

"She won't go for it," he said.

"She might," Audra said. "Either way, we had to try."

Danny stood and went to the window overlooking the street. He eased the blinds apart and peered out. The street seemed so desolate now. So barren.

"The reporters have gone," he said. "Most of them, anyway."

"I think there's a motel in the next town," Audra said. "Don't worry, they'll be back in the morning. They won't miss their chance to feed again. You know. It happened to you."

"You're a monster, as far as they're concerned," Danny said, still watching the street. "Mya got it bad when it happened to us, but you got it worse."

"Why?" Audra asked.

He turned away from the window and looked at her. "You really don't know?"

She shook her head.

"Because your children are white. A little half-Chinese girl didn't matter so much to them."

"Christ," Audra said. She closed her eyes, covered her face with her hands. "If I don't get them back, I don't know if I'll survive it. What your wife did. How could I not do it too?"

"I think you're stronger than Mya was," Danny said. He crossed to the table, retook his seat. "You've been to some bad places, right?"

Audra removed her hands from over her eyes and said, "Right."

"You'll make it," he said.

All she could offer was a nod and a weak smile, but he saw the doubt in her. He offered her no further comfort. They both sat in silence until Mitchell returned.

The agent's face remained blank as she closed the door. She came to the table but did not sit down, placing her hands on the back of a chair, gripping it with her strong fingers.

"Mr. Lee, I was able to reach Special Agent Reilly. He confirmed that your child disappeared and your wife took her own life. I'm very sorry for your loss, Mr. Lee, but Special Agent Reilly told me he never believed your wife's version of events. He also told me you have quite a colorful past. Two stretches in prison for violent crime, a long list of arrests, including for murder."

"That was a long time ago," Danny said.

"So you're a reformed character, that's great, but it doesn't help me right now. Nor does it help Mrs. Kinney. Now, I'd like you to leave town tonight. If you don't, I'm going to have Detective Showalter arrest you for obstructing this investigation."

Audra stared up at Mitchell, balling her fists. Mitchell's hard glare almost made Audra look away. Almost.

Mitchell spoke to her now. "At ten a.m. tomorrow, a warrant will be served for your arrest in connection with the murder of your children, Sean and Louise Kinney. You've got tonight to think about it. I've been as kind and as patient with you as I can be, but once that warrant is issued, I can't help you anymore. Believe me, they will show you no mercy. They will tear you to pieces."

Audra stood, leaned across the table to Mitchell. "Just do one thing for me. Please."

"What?"

"Question Whiteside like you questioned me. Collins too. Put them on the spot. Put pressure on them, see if you can find a crack in their stories. Do it tonight."

"Please stop this," Mitchell said, pressing her fingertips to her forehead. "Just stop, for the love of God."

"Interview them," Audra said. "Then at least you can say you tried everything, that you did your job."

"Fuck you." Mitchell's eyes flashed. "I do my job, and I do it well. I've gotten more children back than any other agent on the CARD team. Seriously, fuck you. Why do think you have a right to question how I do my job?"

"Why?" Audra said. "Because you don't believe I hurt my children."

Mitchell stood in silence, her gaze burning on Audra's skin.

"Just question them," Audra said. "Please."

Mitchell shook her head and exhaled. "I'll see what I can do. But short of them leading me right to those kids, you will be arrested in the morning. And don't even think about absconding. There will be patrols all around this street to make sure you don't." She pointed at Danny. "I don't want to see you again."

Mitchell turned and left the room, slamming the door behind her.

"I think you pissed her off," Danny said.

"Good."

Danny got up from his seat and came to Audra's side. "Be ready to go at five a.m. I'll be waiting."

"Why?"

"Because no matter what Mitchell says to those cops, they aren't going to give up your kids. So tomorrow morning, we're going to get them."

Danny went to the door, left without speaking again.

CHAPTER 37

WHITESIDE CROSSED THE STREET FROM THE TOWN HALL WHERE the search effort was now being coordinated. The jangle of telephones still sounded in his ears, the lines set alight by that half-million-dollar reward. Outside, the town seemed ghostly empty now that the press had slipped away. He imagined them all in the motel over in Gutteridge, cheap as it was, getting some rest. Fatigue had begun to eat at the edges of his mind, and if he thought for a moment he would be able to sleep, he would go home right now and climb into bed. He might have tried, anyway, except Mitchell had called his cell and demanded he go back to the station.

He had called and texted Collins several times, but she had not replied since she left to go up to the cabin. The idea that something had gone wrong capered around his mind, but he did his best to ignore it. Worry wouldn't do him any good.

The station was quiet, the senior state cops having gone to their homes. The whole thing had a sense of winding down now, an acceptance that the children were gone, and that was that. He could see it in the cops' and the feds' faces.

All except Mitchell, who looked like she never gave up on anything.

She waited with that asshole Showalter down by the interview room. He nodded when she waved him over. Her lackey Abrahms sat at a desk, his laptop open in front of him. He watched Whiteside as he approached.

"What do you need?" Whiteside asked. "I was thinking about going home and getting some rest."

Mitchell opened the door to the interview room, let it swing open, room enough for him to step past her and through. Whiteside looked from the door to Mitchell to Showalter and back to her.

"What?"

"Just a few minutes of your time," Mitchell said. "You don't mind, do you?"

"You're going to interview me?" he said, pointing at the open door. "You serious?"

"A few questions, that's all."

Whiteside looked to Showalter, who shrugged, what are you gonna do?

"All right," Whiteside said, giving Mitchell a smile. "But let's make it quick. My bed's calling to me."

He sat at the table while Mitchell messed with the video camera, and he realized what Abrahms had been doing with the laptop.

"You going to send this down to the behavioral fella in Phoenix?"

"That's right," Mitchell said.

"And exactly what kind of behavior will he be looking for?"

Mitchell came to the table, sat down, arranged her notebook and pen. "Oh, nothing in particular. Just routine. You understand."

"Sure, I understand. Did your behavioral fella have anything to say about your interviews with Mrs. Kinney?"

"Yes, his report came back this afternoon."

"And?"

"Mrs. Kinney believes what she's saying."

Whiteside was about to argue, but Mitchell raised a hand.

"Please state your name and position, for the record."

Whiteside held her stare. "My name is Ronald Whiteside, Elder County Sheriff. Mrs. Kinney might believe this nonsense she's talking, but even setting aside the physical evidence found in her car, you and I both know Mrs. Kinney is batshit crazy."

"Mrs. Kinney's state of mind is open for debate, Sheriff, but she has been consistent in her version of events from the first time I questioned her."

Whiteside gave Showalter a wink. "So she's consistently crazy."

Showalter smirked.

"Let's take this seriously, Sheriff," Mitchell said.

"Oh, I'm taking it seriously, believe me. I've been taking it seriously since before you showed up, with your good suit and your camera. Now go on and ask whatever it is you need to ask, so I can get out of here."

Mitchell turned to a fresh page in her notebook.

"Where did you first encounter Mrs. Kinney?"

"In the parking lot at the general store out on the County Road, about five miles before the turn to Silver Water. I was sitting there in my cruiser, drinking coffee from my Thermos, when she pulled in. She got out of the car and looked all around. She noticed me, and that appeared to rattle her somewhat."

"How so?"

"She was trying real hard to look casual, if you know what I mean. Look, I told you all this two days ago."

"Not on camera. So you felt she looked nervous at your presence."

"Right. Like she didn't want to see a cop. So while she was in the store, I drove around the back, waited for her to come out and drive away. That way I could follow her and look for any problems with the car or how she was driving it. So happened the car was overloaded, so I pulled her in for that reason."

"And how was Mrs. Kinney when you approached her?"

"Skittish," Whiteside said. "Like a deer that knows you got your sight on it."

"And how was your manner?"

"Polite, casual, friendly. Like I always am."

He imagined the conversation, the woman in the driver's seat, her hands on the wheel.

"At that time, did you notice the booster seat in the rear of the car?"

He pictured it, empty.

"Yes, I did."

"Didn't you think it strange to see the booster seat, but no child?"

"Not really," Whiteside said. "Plenty of times a parent goes out without their kids, they don't take the seats out of the car."

"In a car with New York plates," Mitchell said. "You thought it was normal for someone to drive all the way from New York State with a child's booster seat in the back, but no child."

"Not right at that second, but later, yes, I—"

"Did you ask Mrs. Kinney about the seat? Or the child or children that weren't there?"

He shook his head. "No, I didn't. No one mentioned children until after I put her in the cell back there. That's when she asked me where they were."

"And what was your response?"

Whiteside tried to read her. Nothing. He wondered what cards she held.

"I said, 'What children?' She started to get worked up at that point, so I let her be for a while, hoping she'd calm down. When I came back later, we talked, and I explained there were no children in her car when I pulled her over. That's when she assaulted me, as you saw on the CCTV footage. After that, I started inquiring with the authorities about these children. And that's about when you invited yourself along."

"Where was Deputy Collins at this time?"

"Out on patrol. She does a circuit of the town and the surrounding roads. Basic traffic stuff. Then she went home, as far as I know. She lives with her mother and her little boy out on Ridge Road. Will you be questioning Collins also?"

"I haven't been able to reach her," Mitchell said. "Any idea how I might get hold of her?"

He looked at his wristwatch. "She's off duty by now. Friday night. She's relaxing with a beer or a glass of wine, if she's got any sense. Could be she switched off her cell."

Mitchell turned a page. "Let's talk about Mrs. Kinney's version of events."

"Jesus," he said. "While we're at it, let's talk about how the moon landings were faked. Or how 9/11 was an inside job."

Mitchell didn't drop a beat. "Mrs. Kinney is adamant that when you pulled her over, her children Sean and Louise were in the backseat. She says you spoke with them, including admonishing the boy to get back into the car. She also states that you radioed for Deputy Collins to come get the children, to keep them safe while you dealt with their mother. You helped Deputy Collins get the children into the back of her car and, once she drove away, that was the last she saw of them."

Whiteside waited for more, but got only Mitchell's needle stare.

When it was clear she would offer no more, he said, "Yeah, that's her story. Doesn't matter how many times you tell it, doesn't make it true. According to this woman's husband, she's been unstable for years. God knows what kind of fantasies she has in that head of hers. It's nonsense, all of it. Me and Collins stole her children. I mean, what in the hell for? Did you ever hear such a thing?"

Mitchell smiled a cold smile. "Actually, I have. Just this evening."

He looked from Mitchell to Showalter, who shrugged, then back to Mitchell.

"What?" he said. "Quit fucking with me, Mitchell."

Her smile sharpened. "I was told an interesting tale earlier. About a man whose wife drove off with their little girl. The wife got stopped by a small-town cop and arrested on some trumped-up charge. When the wife asked after the welfare of her little girl, the cop said, 'What little girl? You were alone when I stopped you.' Sound familiar?"

He pictured the man in the diner this afternoon, the man who ordered another sandwich to go, the man who said he knew what Whiteside had done.

"So someone else thought up the same story. So what? Let me guess, was this story told by a Chinese gentleman?"

"An Asian-American man, yes, that's right. What might also sound familiar is that the assumption of guilt fell on the mother. Everyone was convinced she had harmed her child somewhere between leaving home and being stopped by the police officer."

"This is a big country," Whiteside said. "There must be hundreds of thousands of traffic stops every day. And how many missing children? And out of all those missing children—you should know this—out of those children, how many times does it turn out that a parent hurt them? So you got a similar story from another whack job. One crazy attracts another crazy. Bet you've seen that before too."

Mitchell did not drop that goddamn smile, like she held all the secrets of the world behind her teeth. Whiteside concentrated all his effort on keeping his face blank, mild annoyance at the intrusion, nothing more.

"There were some interesting details, though," she said.

Whiteside wanted to slap the smile from her face. "Such as?" he asked.

"You've heard of the Dark Web, yes?"

"I think so," he said, shrugging. "It's like the back streets of the Internet. They share kiddie porn there, at least that's what I've heard."

"Among other things," Mitchell said. "Child pornography, snuff films, illegal software, hacking tools, anything one might want to discuss in secret with like-minded others. Any sort of illegal activity, really. People arrange the sale of drugs and weapons, even organize contract killings. And in one dirty little corner, so I'm told, a group of very wealthy men uses corrupt law-enforcement officers to procure children."

Whiteside's mouth dried, his tongue clinging to the roof of his mouth. A cold bead of sweat took a slow course down his back. But he kept his face blank, not a blink, not a twitch. If he allowed a tell, no matter how slight, he might as well put his pistol to his head right here and now. He rolled spit around his mouth, freed his tongue, and said, "I wouldn't know anything about that. Sounds like a nasty business."

"It is," Mitchell said. "I don't suppose you'd volunteer to hand over all computers, tablets, and smartphones to my colleague, Special Agent Abrahms, for inspection?"

Another drop of sweat. And a twitch. Below his left eye, he felt it like an angel's touch. And Mitchell saw it too, her eyes flicking toward it and away again.

"You suppose right," he said. "You want to search anything of mine, you show me a warrant. Now, I think I've had about enough of this conversation. I need some sleep, and I'm going home to get it. You want to question me further, you put me under arrest and do it with a lawyer present."

He got to his feet, kicked the chair away, walked to the door, and said, "Goodnight to you both."

Out in the office, the glow of the laptop's display reflected on Abrahms' boyish face. He wore earphones, scribbled on a notepad. Whiteside resisted the urge to slap the pen out of his hand and tear up the notes. Instead, he marched to the men's room, kicked the door open, slammed it closed behind him.

Inside, he passed the urinal and entered the single stall, locked himself in.

"Fuck," he said. "Fucking goddamn shit motherfucker."

Tremors erupted from his core, out to his arms and legs, his hands quivering. He put a knuckle between his teeth and bit down hard, seeking the clarity it would bring, but none came. His lungs expanded and contracted, air ripping in and out of him, as if some giant hand pumped his chest. A constellation of black stars in his vision, his head seeming to float somewhere above his shoulders. His lungs going harder, faster, his heart running to keep up.

Panic attack.

I'm having a panic attack, he thought.

He dropped down onto the toilet seat, hands on either side of the stall to keep himself upright.

"Jesus," he said. "Jesus Christ."

He bent over, put his head between his knees. Breathe, he told himself. Breathe. Inhale through the nose, one-two-three-four, hold, one-two-three-four-five-six-seven, out through the mouth, one-two-three-four-five-six-seven-eight. Over and over, in, hold, out.

Eventually, the world leveled off enough that he could lift his head away from the odor of ancient urine and excrement. Another minute or two and he could breathe almost normally. One more, and he could get back to his feet.

Whiteside dug in his pocket for his cell. He hesitated, knowing he shouldn't use his main phone, he should use the burner, but there was no time. For the fifth time that evening, he called Collins. He listened to the dial tone, certain she wouldn't answer.

"Hello?"

He stifled a gasp of startlement.

"Hello? Ronnie?"

"Mary, listen to me. Don't come back to the station. Don't go home. Meet me in thirty minutes. You know where."

"Ronnie, what's—"

Whiteside hung up, shoved the phone back into his pocket. He flushed the toilet, exited the stall, washed his hands. Then he strode through the office without looking at Mitchell, Showalter, or Abrahms, out to his car.

CHAPTER 38

ANNY WOKE IN PURE DARKNESS, THE NAUSEATING SENSATION of falling, disoriented. A few moments passed before he remembered where he was: the upstairs storeroom of the soft-furnishings place he'd scouted earlier in the day.

Once he'd left Audra at the guesthouse, he'd gone straight to his car and driven out of Silver Water, climbed up out of the basin, into the hills. There, he'd pulled over, waited for the sky to turn from dark blue to black.

He'd watched the orange band on the horizon as it was devoured by the mountains, thought about the beauty of the country. Danny had not ventured out of San Francisco often in his life. Mya had talked about traveling when Sara was older. Explore America, maybe even Europe. That dream had turned to dust, along with his wife.

Once darkness had smothered the land, he headed back to town, switching off his headlights as he worked through the lowly houses on the outskirts, crossed the bridge, and turned into the alley at the top of Main Street. He left the car there, out of view of the street, and worked his way down the rear of the properties until he found the soft-furnishings place. He was inside within two minutes; the store wasn't alarmed. Upstairs, he found a box full of uncovered cushions. He emptied them onto the floor, formed them into a nest, and set his phone's alarm for three a.m.

Now awake and alert, he checked his watch: two forty-six. But what had woken him?

He listened.

There: movement, a footstep. A rustling. Leather on linoleum, fabric on fabric.

Danny reached for the small cluster of belongings he'd left by the nest, his shoes, wallet, phone. The Smith & Wesson Model 60 and the ammunition remained hidden in the rental car, in the trunk, beneath the spare wheel, along with the cable ties, wire cutters, tape, knife, and other items he'd bought at the hardware store in Phoenix.

Noise on the stairs. Two pairs of feet. One heavier than the other.

He knew then who it was, and he felt relief that he'd left the pistol behind. If he'd had it here, it would have provided all the excuse they needed to shoot him down. He got to his feet, stuffed his possessions into his pockets, backed toward the wall, put his hands up.

Shuffling and whispers on the other side of the door that led to the stairway. A sliver of light moved around the doorframe.

"I hear you," Danny said. "Come on in. I'm not armed."

Silence for a moment, then the door burst inward, the flashlight beam blinding him. He put his right hand out to shield his eyes.

A click, and the overhead fluorescent light stuttered into life.

Whiteside and Collins faced him, both dressed in civilian clothes. Collins aimed a Glock at his chest while Whiteside switched off the flashlight.

"Just passing through, huh?" Whiteside said.

"Thought I'd stick around another day," Danny said, his hands still raised. "How'd you find me?"

"Wasn't hard. I knew you wouldn't leave town like you were told, there's plenty of empty properties, so I just checked for any sign of a B&E. And here you are."

"Here I am," Danny said.

"You should've gone to the motel over in Gutteridge," Whiteside said. "It's not much, but Jesus, it's better than this."

"I'm easy to please."

"Yeah, and you got a smart mouth on you too. Now, this presents me with a dilemma. Do I arrest you for vagrancy, breaking-and-entering, or both?"

"Or I could just be on my way," Danny said. "No harm done."

"No harm done?" Whiteside laughed. "Boy, you crack me up, you really do. You done plenty of harm. You're unarmed, you say."

"Yeah," Danny said, smiling. "Pity, right?"

Whiteside returned the smile. "Well, it might have simplified matters. You don't mind if I check, though, do you? Just put your hands on your head and take a couple of steps forward."

Danny did as he was told and stood quiet and still while Whiteside patted him down, went through his pockets. The sheriff examined what he found, leafing through the contents of the wallet, studying the cards, counting the cash. He pulled the driver's license out, read the details, before slipping it back inside.

Whiteside handed the wallet and phone over. Danny lowered his hands, took them, and put them back into his pockets.

He saw Whiteside's fist coming, but too late to block it.

The blow caught Danny on the left side of his jaw, rocked his head back and to the right. His legs disappeared from under him as the room tilted. He hit the floor shoulder first. Although every instinct told him to get up, fight back, he made himself stay down. As his mind and vision steadied, he put a hand to his cheek, tested his jaw. No break, maybe a tooth loosened, that's all. He'd had worse.

"Stand up," Whiteside said.

Danny spat on the floor, saw blood on the linoleum. "I'm okay here," he said.

"Get up, goddamn it."

Whiteside drove his boot into Danny's flank, below the ribs. Danny's diaphragm convulsed, expelled the air from his lungs, denied him breath to fill them again. He tried to get onto his hands and knees, crawl away, but Whiteside kicked again, this time connecting with his thigh. Danny rolled onto his side, held his hands up, enough.

"Get on your feet," the sheriff said. "You got ten seconds before I kick every one of your ribs in."

Danny got his knees under him, then doubled over with a coughing fit until his sight blurred. Whiteside's hard hand gripped him under the arm, hauled him upright.

"All right," Whiteside said, stepping away. "Mr. Lee, I would appreciate it very much if you would put your shoes on and accompany Deputy Collins and me outside."

"Am I under arrest?"

Whiteside pulled a revolver from the back of his waistband. He cocked the hammer, leveled the muzzle at Danny's stomach.

"No," he said, "you are not under arrest."

CHAPTER 39

SEAN'S HANDS BLED AND HIS SHOULDERS ACHED. HE'D BEEN working at the wood all night, driving the blade in, stabbing, digging, twisting, chips and splinters falling away. By inserting the blade between the edge of the trapdoor and its frame and running it along the length, he'd been able to find where the bolt was located. The door was composed of nine boards screwed from the other side to a Z-shaped frame. He had considered trying to pry the frame away from the boards, but he knew the blade would break long before he even loosened it. Instead, he concentrated on the area around the bolt. The board it was attached to was no more than a half inch thick, and the wood was old. Not rotten, but not as strong as it had once been. Even so, it was slow and hard work, and blood trickled down his forearms.

Sean had paused a while ago to rest and give Louise the second dose of antibiotics. The first had already seemed to have an effect, her forehead cooler to the touch, her shivering abated. Now she sat upright on the mattress, watching her brother at the top of the steps.

"You nearly done?" she said, her voice hoarse.

"No," he said.

After a rattling cough, she asked, "When will you be done?"

"I don't know," he said. "Not for a while yet."

"But when?"

"In a while," he said, raising his voice.

"When we get out, are we going to find Mommy?"

"Yeah."

"Where will she be?"

"I don't know."

"Then where do we go?"

"I don't know. We just run, as far away as we can."

"But where?"

"I don't know. Look, just lie down and get some sleep. I'll tell you when it's done."

She did as he suggested, lay down on the mattress, her hands clasped beneath her cheek for a pillow. Sean felt a tug of regret for getting snippy with her. He dismissed it and went back to work.

A memory crept in from a faraway place in his mind: a lecture from his father, one of the few times Patrick Kinney had tried to communicate with his son. About the importance of hard work. Nothing good in life could be gained without effort. Hard work was how he accounted for his wealth. But Sean suspected it was more to do with his grandmother's money.

So far he had chipped the wood away from two of the screws that secured the lock to the door. He guessed there were four. All he had to do was weaken the wood around the screws, push up on the door as hard as he could, and the lock would tear away. It had taken a good many hours to locate the first screw, but from that he'd been able to figure out the position of the second. Now he was having trouble finding the third.

Sean tried a spot closer to the edge. He stabbed upward, burying the blade's tip maybe a quarter inch. Then he rocked it back and forth in line with the grain, then against it, widening the cut. Another stab, more rocking and twisting, and a piece the size of a thumbnail fell away. One more and . . .

There. The hardness inside, something unyielding. The screw. Now he had to circle it, strip and chip away the wood, leaving the screw nothing to cling to.

He couldn't help but grin, relish the savage pleasure of it.

A few minutes later he had worked about two-thirds of the way around the screw. Already he could imagine the splintering, cracking sound the lock would make as it tore away, how the air would feel when he and Louise were out there in the trees. How wonderful it would be. Encouraged, he dug harder and deeper, twisted the knife further.

Then the blade snapped.

He'd been applying his weight to the knife, putting his shoulders behind it. Then it was gone and he was pushing against air, falling forward, the handle still gripped in his bloodied fingers. He let it go, reached out for the rail, grabbed hold, cried out as splinters bit into the already raw flesh. His body turned around that point, his legs carrying his momentum, and his shoulder taking the worst of it.

Sean hung there, one hand on the rail, his back against the steps, watching the knife handle bounce down the steps to the floor. He looked up, saw the blade still wedged in the wood. His feet found a step and he straightened, examined his palm and the splinters in the heel.

"Shit," he said, picking the biggest of them away.

"You said a curse," Louise said.

"Yeah, and I'm gonna say some more."

He looked back up at the blade, down at the handle, knew that their one chance had broken. He rested his forearm on his knees, lowered his head. Then he wept, too tired to care that Louise could see.

CHAPTER 40

THEY HAD DRIVEN FOR ALMOST AN HOUR, DANNY AT THE WHEEL of his rental car, Whiteside directly behind him. Occasionally Danny felt the muzzle of the pistol through the seat back. In the rearview mirror, he could see the single headlight of the motorcycle, Collins following them.

The car bounced and juddered along the track. They had left the road behind long ago, now using the unsurfaced trails that ranchers used for their ATVs and pickups. It occurred to Danny that this was about as far from civilization as he had ever been.

There was only one reason to bring him out here. They probably wouldn't even attempt to bury him. Just leave him and the car in the desert, let the scavengers pick at his remains until someone chanced upon the scene, months from now, maybe years. He thought of Sara and wondered if she would be the same when he saw her again, frozen at the age she was taken, or would she have grown? If anyone had asked, Danny would have denied believing in such things, but deep down he felt it, the thread that attached him to his wife and child.

He thought of Audra Kinney and her children, knew they were alive out there somewhere. And he wondered if there was any hope for them, or were they already lost?

"Slow down," Whiteside said.

Danny lifted his foot from the accelerator, eased it onto the brake. From twenty down to ten, to five, to a crawl.

"Turn off here, to the left."

The car jerked and thumped down a shallow slope as Danny

steered it between the cacti. Ahead, the lights caught the shapes of rocky outcrops.

"There," Whiteside said. "Between those. Now stop. Leave the engine running."

Danny applied the handbrake, put both hands on the wheel. He watched Collins draw up beside the car. She shut the bike's engine off, kicked out the stand, and dismounted. She hung the helmet from the handlebars. For the first time Danny noticed the second helmet fixed to the pillion seat, and he knew how they planned to get back to town.

Collins drew her Glock from its holster, aimed at Danny's head through the glass. She reached out and opened the door.

"Out," she said.

He did as he was told, took his time about it, smooth and easy movements. Collins couldn't hide the tremors in her hand as she motioned with the pistol for him to move in front of the car. The rear door opened and Whiteside climbed out. He moved around to join the others, the three of them glowing in the headlights.

"I guess you understand what's happening here," Whiteside said.

"Yeah," Danny said.

"Then get down on your knees."

"No," Danny said.

Whiteside took a step closer. "What?"

"I haven't kneeled to any man since my father died," Danny said, "and I won't kneel to you, motherfucker."

He saw Collins move from the corner of his eye, felt her foot catch him behind his left knee, buckling it. Grit dug into his kneecap.

"Just answer me one thing," Danny said.

"Sorry, friend, you don't get any last words."

"Why are you doing this? You know what those children are going to suffer. You think the money's going to keep the nightmares out of your head?"

"I served in the Gulf," Whiteside said. "I saw more horrible shit than you can imagine. I haven't had a good night's sleep since I left the military, so I don't believe this will leave me any worse off. As for why, it's pretty simple. I am sick and fucking tired of being poor. I'm fifty-five years old and I have nothing. Not a goddamn thing. That a good enough reason for you?"

Danny squinted through the glare of the headlights, seeking to meet Whiteside's gaze.

"My daughter's name was Sara," he said. "She liked dancing and reading. She wanted to be a gymnast or a dog trainer, she could never make up her mind. She was six years old when they took her. I try not to think about what they did to her. But I can't help it. It killed my wife. It killed me too; I just didn't lie down."

"Go on and do it," Whiteside said to Collins.

She put the Glock to Danny's temple. He turned his head so he could see the fear on her face. The terror. The rise and fall of her shoulders, the quickness of her eyes.

"Their names are Sean and Louise. He's ten years old. She's six. Same age as my little girl was. You know what they're going to do to them."

"Shut up," Collins said.

"Pull the trigger," Whiteside said.

"You got any kids?" Danny asked. He saw the flicker in her expression. "You do, don't you? Two? Three?"

"Shut up."

Whiteside took another step. "Goddamn it, Collins."

"Maybe just the one," Danny said. "One, right? Boy or girl?"

Collins slammed the Glock into the back of Danny's head. A starburst back there, a brilliant flash behind his eyes. He fell forward, got his hands down, pushed himself up again.

"You doing this for your kid? So long as your child doesn't suffer, right? But Sean and Louise, they're going to suffer. Every dollar you spend cost those children their—"

Another blow, another luminous starburst, and this time Danny collapsed to the ground, sand and grit scouring his cheek. A sickly swell of pain inside his skull, like a balloon expanding. Don't pass out, he told himself. Don't. He got his hands under his chest, pushed himself up once more.

"For Christ's sake, just do it," Whiteside said. "Or do I have to?"

Danny ignored him, turned once more to Collins. Her eyes wide, her breath ragged, her teeth bared.

"Are you really willing to make those children, Sean and Louise, suffer and die for money?" Danny nodded toward Whiteside. "He can live with it. But you're not like him. Are you? Can you face—"

She swung once more, but this time Danny was ready.

He ducked to the side, seized her wrist with his left hand, used her momentum, let her fall into him. His right hand enclosed hers, pulled her arm out and up, found her trigger finger, squeezed one shot, then another. Both cracked the air over Whiteside's shoulder. No chance of a hit, but it was enough to make Whiteside drop to the ground.

Danny wrested the pistol from Collins' hand, pressed the hot muzzle to her temple as Whiteside sprawled in the dirt. Collins struggled, but Danny pressed the Glock harder into her temple.

"Stop," he said. "Be still."

She did so, and Danny got his soles on the ground, his back against the car's grille. He pushed up with his legs, bringing Collins with him. Whiteside got to his knees, but Danny let another shot ring over his head.

"Stay down," he said. "Toss the weapon."

Whiteside licked his lips, flexed his fingers.

"Don't do it," Danny said. "I'll take your head off. Toss it."

Whiteside remained still for a few moments, hate in his eyes. Then he threw the revolver away, out into the dark pools beyond the reach of the car's headlights.

"Put your hands on your head," Danny said. Then into Collins' ear, "Take the keys for the bike out of your pocket. Throw them that way."

He pointed into the black with the Glock's muzzle. Collins did as instructed. He heard a faint jangle out in the shadows.

"Let's go," he said.

He backed around the driver's side of the car, paused to open the driver's door, pressed the muzzle against the back of Collins' skull to hold her there while he opened the rear door.

"On my word, get in and close the door," Danny said. "Now."

They each lowered themselves in, Collins in the front, Danny in the back, as Whiteside watched them with fury in his eyes. The doors slammed in unison.

"Okay," Danny said as Whiteside stared back at him in the glow of the car's headlights. "Now take me back to Silver Water."

As Collins reversed, he heard Whiteside scream over the sound of the engine.

CHAPTER 41

AUDRA DREAMED OF HER CHILDHOOD HOME. AN OLD HOUSE on the outskirts of a town not far from Albany. The big yard with the apple tree at the bottom. The rooms she was afraid to enter because her father had said no, don't go in there. To enter those places would make him angry, would make his fists swing, and his belt.

She dreamed of her bedroom at the top of the house, the way the light swept in, and how if she lay on the bed and looked to the window, she would see only sky. As if the house floated high above the earth, and she pretended she was Dorothy soaring up and away to a land of wonders.

The bedside alarm clock pulled her from the dream, and she fell onto the bed as if from a great height, her body bouncing on the mattress. As she gathered her senses, she wondered what time she had fallen asleep. Sometime after midnight, lying here in her clothes, she had been staring at the ceiling, wondering what Sean and Louise were doing.

She hoped they were asleep.

She hoped they weren't afraid.

She hoped they were safe.

When she'd set the alarm for 4:30 a.m., she'd had no confidence of ever slipping into the dark, yet she had, and she was glad of it. She sat upright, climbed out of the bed, and crossed barefoot to the bathroom. There she used the toilet, washed her face and body with cold water from the hand basin. She regarded herself in the mirror, saw new lines around her eyes and mouth, new grays in her hair. Without thinking, she touched her reflection, fingertips tracing the shape of her face.

A sudden and new emotion came upon her: mourning. Mourning for herself, the girl she had been, the years lost to a marriage that leached the soul from her, leaving a hollow woman behind. Too late to get those years back, not too late for the time ahead. But only with her children. No point without them. No point to anything.

Back in the bedroom, she pulled on a clean shirt and buttoned it, ill-fitting as it was. Clean socks, the running shoes that were one size too big. She slipped out of the room, closed the door as softly as she could, not wishing to wake Mrs. Gerber. The stairs creaked beneath her feet, and she winced at every step. Down into the hall, back toward the kitchen.

Audra opened the door, stepped through, and saw Mrs. Gerber at the table, a mug of coffee in front of her, a half-smoked cigarette suspended over a clean ashtray. They stared at each other for a moment, each caught in an act they didn't want the other to witness.

"I only take one a day," Mrs. Gerber said. "Maybe two if I'm worried."

Audra nodded and moved toward the back door.

"Are you running away?" Mrs. Gerber asked.

"No," Audra said. "I'm going to find my children."

Mrs. Gerber gave her a hard, narrow-eyed look.

"I didn't hurt them," Audra said. "Whatever happens, please remember that."

Mrs. Gerber reached into the pocket of her dressing gown, removed a set of keys. She slid them across the table toward Audra.

"You'll need those for the door and the padlock on the gate." She nodded to the coat that hung on the peg by the door. "You took them from my pocket. I'll find them in the alley in a short while."

Audra reached for them, pushed the screen aside. She looked back over her shoulder and said, "Thank you."

As she turned the key in the lock, Mrs. Gerber spoke once more.

"I killed my husband," she said.

Audra stopped, turned around.

"Almost fifteen years ago," Mrs. Gerber said. "He came home drunk one night and I waited for him at the top of the stairs. I didn't even push. Not really. I just reached my hand out, put it where his center of gravity should be. I still remember the look on his face. The shock. And it's funny, see, because I feel more guilt about smoking a cigarette than I do about watching him break his stupid neck." She took another long drag on the cigarette and said, "I hope you find them."

Audra watched her for a moment, then nodded. Mrs. Gerber did the same, and Audra let herself out.

A mild breeze swept across the yard, cooling her skin. She made her way down to the gate, undid the padlock, stepped through into the alley. She opened her hand, let the keys drop onto the baked earth.

Audra looked in both directions, saw no sign of Danny. She reached into her pocket, took out the cell phone he'd given her the day before. As she looked up the one number in the contacts list, the phone vibrated in her hand. She pressed answer and brought it to her ear.

"Danny?"

"Yeah."

"Where are you?"

"A couple of streets away, behind the guesthouse. There's a state patrol car doing a circuit of Main Street; it's half assed, but still, we can't risk being seen. Head south along the alley, toward the river end. There's another alley branching off to your left about twenty yards along. Take that into the next street, cross over, and through the alley that's facing you. I'm on the other side. But be careful. Don't let anyone see you."

Audra hung up, stowed the phone, and made her way along the alley. She found the left turn just as he'd said, and she cut through toward the street on the other side. A voice stopped her a few feet from the alley's mouth.

"Make," a man said. "Goddamn it, make."

Audra flattened herself against the wall and listened.

"All right, suit yourself, but if you shit on the floor again, I'm gonna put a cork in your ass."

She watched as a small middle-aged man passed the alley, a squat mongrel dog on a leash trailing behind. The man slipped out of view, but the dog stopped, planted its feet on the sidewalk. It stared into the alley, its hindquarters quivering. It let out a high yip and the leash jerked, the man telling the dog to come on, goddamn it.

Audra counted to ten before moving to the street. She saw the man and the dog making their way along the sidewalk, the dog glancing back at her, the man tugging it along. Across the street, the next alley, and a dark shape that might have been a car. She jogged toward it, her head down, her step as quiet as she could manage.

When she reached the other side, she saw Danny in the shadows, leaning against a dust-covered Chevrolet. Her lungs strained for breath by the time she got close. She stopped a few feet away, saw the blood matted in his hair, the swelling of his lip.

"Jesus, what happened?" she asked.

Danny smiled, winced, brought his fingertips to his lip. "I had a talk with Sheriff Whiteside. Here, I got something for you."

He reached behind his back, to his waistband, pulled out a pistol. She took a step back when he extended it to her, grip first.

"God, no, I don't want that," she said.

"Take it," he said. "We have to be armed."

"But I don't know how to use it."

"It's a Glock," he said. "There's no safety. You just point it and pull the trigger. Easy. Take it."

Audra came closer. She reached for the gun, felt the cold grip fill her hand. Danny pressed the barrel with his fingertips, guided it away so it aimed at the ground.

"Just keep your finger away from the trigger," he said. "Don't aim it at anything unless you're ready to shoot. You got it?"

"I guess so," she said. "Are we really going to do this? Kidnap Collins?"

Danny looked at her sideways. "Oh, didn't I say?"

He reached for the rear door handle, opened it wide, and stepped back.

"Oh, shit," Audra said.

Deputy Collins lay across the rear footwells, her ankles bound with cable ties to the metalwork beneath the passenger seat, her wrists tied behind her back, a strip of tape across her mouth. She stared wide-eyed up at Audra.

"They're in a cabin to the north," Danny said. "Up in the forest, on the Colorado Plateau, just like your landlady said. A couple hours' drive."

Audra felt heat in her eyes, a thickening in her throat. She took Danny in her arms, pressed her lips hard to his cheek, withdrew when he hissed at the pain it caused.

"Thank you," she said.

"We haven't got them yet," he said. "Let's move. Whiteside is still out there. We need to be long gone before he makes it back."

DANNY DRIVING, Audra in the passenger seat, they took a dirt track out of town, heading east, then turning north. The sun breached the mountains ahead, heat building, and Danny turned up the car's AC. He had hauled Collins upright, wedged her into the corner between the seat back and the door, her hands still bound behind her. She had let out a low groan when he stripped the tape from her mouth, leaving a red rectangle around her lips. She directed them to this back road, a route once used to get to the mine that had closed years ago. Furrows had been gouged out of the dusty earth by the wheels of great machines, the ghosts of their tracks still visible in the early light.

After twenty minutes of coarse dirt tracks, they joined a narrow surfaced road that twisted through the hills, followed by long, straight climbs that caused pressure in Audra's ears. Soon the sun scorched the world around, and she wished for the sunglasses she'd left on the passenger seat of her own car. She lowered the visor, cupped her hand around her eyes.

Then a memory of four days ago entered her mind. A random thought, but it appeared there clear and hard. She acted on it, placed the backs of her fingers against the windshield. A second or two later, she had to withdraw them, the skin red from the heat. She remembered telling Sean to try it. He had done so, said ow, and giggled as he pulled his hand away.

Audra turned her head to gaze out of the passenger window, tried to hide the quiver in her breathing as she held back tears.

"For what it's worth," Collins said, "I'm sorry."

Audra wiped at her eyes and said, "Go to hell."

CHAPTER 42

ANOTHER HOUR PASSED BEFORE ANYONE SPOKE AGAIN.
The road had climbed and climbed, twisting up into the hills like an unspooled ribbon. They passed one other vehicle, a pickup truck, the driver old and grizzled. He lifted his forefinger from the wheel in greeting as he passed. The long stretches were punctuated by strings of switchbacks as they ascended—the Mogollon Rim, Audra recalled—and the temperature dropped until Danny shut off the AC.

They reached a plateau, and the road straightened. All around, pines as far as Audra could see. Sometimes the land fell away to one side or the other, and the forests stretched to the horizon. Beautiful and terrible, she thought, hundreds of miles of nothing but trees.

My children are out here on their own, she thought. But I'm coming for them.

A question appeared in her mind, from nowhere, and she felt desperate for the answer.

"How much?" she said.

Danny turned to look at her.

Audra turned in the seat, looked back at Collins.

"I said, how much?"

Collins kept her gaze to the window. "Half a million," she said. "Ronnie's share was more. I don't know how much in total."

"Half a million dollars," Audra echoed. "What would you have done with it?"

"Got my boy the care he needs." Collins' eyes glistened. "He has a heart condition. The drugs cost so much, and my insurance doesn't cover even half of them. My mother mortgaged her house a second time, and that's almost gone. Every time he takes a bad turn, he has to go to the hospital, and they take their cut. I got nothing left. Nothing. I just wanted my boy to be well. That's all."

Audra studied her, the trails of her tears. "And you were willing to sacrifice two other children to make that happen."

"That's right." Collins turned her eyes away from the glass, matched Audra's stare. "I mean, they're not *my* children."

The car felt colder than before, and Audra wrapped her arms around herself.

"Up here, maybe a hundred yards," Collins said. "There's an exit onto a dirt road. Take it."

Danny slowed and made the turn, a cattle grid rattling beneath the wheels. The ground was softer here, more forgiving than the low desert, a bed of pine needles to cushion the worst of it.

"Follow this trail for like fifteen, twenty minutes," Collins said. "Then we have to get out and walk."

They made the rest of the drive in silence until Collins told Danny to stop.

Audra climbed out, stretched her limbs, shivered at the chill in the air. She had to remind herself it was still early morning, the car's touchscreen saying it was not yet seven-thirty. Danny came around the car and opened the rear door.

"Get the Glock," he said.

Audra reached in through the passenger door, retrieved the pistol from the glove compartment. Cold and heavy in her hand, it sent another wave of chills through her.

"Keep it on her," Danny said. "If she tries anything, shoot her in the leg or the arm. Don't kill her."

"I'll try not to," Audra said, raising the pistol, aiming past Danny at Collins' thigh as he used a pair of wire cutters to snip the cable ties.

Danny stepped away and Collins climbed out. She took two steps before falling, landing hard on her shoulder, unable to break her fall with her wrists still tied at the small of her back.

"Shit," she said.

"Come on," Danny said as he reached down to help her up. "Walk around a little. Get your blood moving."

They gave her a minute or two to recover before Audra said, "Which way?"

Collins looked beyond the car and said, "That way. About a ten-, fifteen-minute walk."

"Let's go," Audra said. "You lead."

Collins left the trail and made her way through the trees. Audra and Danny followed. They made slow progress, and Audra pushed Collins between the shoulder blades to hurry her along. Collins stumbled, but didn't fall. She looked back at Audra.

"If you undid my hands I could walk faster," she said. "I can't keep my balance like this."

Audra looked to Danny. He shrugged.

"I won't do anything," Collins said. "You guys still got the guns."

"All right," Audra said, leveling the Glock at Collins' shoulder.

Danny took the wire cutters from his pocket and approached. He snipped the cable tie and let it fall away. Collins rubbed her wrists, stretched her arms, rolled her shoulders.

"Now move," Audra said.

A little of the chill left the air as they walked, causing perspiration to spread on her back. Birds called high among the trees and creatures stirred below, rustling in the shadows. Audra kept her gaze ahead, past Collins, looking for any sign of the cabin.

And there it was, through the pines.

Audra froze. There it was, her children inside.

She ran. Arms churning, feet pounding the forest floor, past Danny, past Collins, she ran like she hadn't run in years, since school, when she ran for the pure joy of it. Danny called after her, but she ignored him.

"Sean!" Her voice echoed through the trees. "Louise!"

Audra didn't slow as she burst into the clearing, as she mounted the porch, as she shoved the open door aside. Her feet skidded on the wooden floor as she tried to halt, and her balance deserted her. She landed on her hip, didn't pause, got onto her hands and knees, still holding the Glock. She crawled to the open trapdoor, calling their names, calling . . .

Open?

She saw the splintered trapdoor that rested back on its chains. She saw the lock torn loose from the wood, still hanging from the loop on the floor. She looked down into the basement and saw it empty.

Knowing they wouldn't hear her, Audra called her children's names once more.

CHAPTER 43

SEAN AND LOUISE KEPT WALKING. LOUISE LAGGED BEHIND, and Sean had given up cajoling her into hurrying. He had realized some time ago they were lost, so there seemed no point rushing. But they had to move, no matter what.

"I want some water," Louise called from ten feet behind.

"You already had some," Sean said. "I told you, we have to make it last. I don't know how long we'll be out here. Might be days. We need to conserve our supplies."

Sean carried those supplies in a plastic bag: two twelve-ounce bottles of water, four candy bars, two apples, and a banana. He had wrapped the handles around his wrist because his palm still stung and bled. The bag seemed extraordinarily heavy for all it contained, his shoulder aching at the effort. His lungs also. No matter how deep he breathed, there never seemed to be enough air. The altitude, he supposed, and clearly Louise felt it too.

He didn't know how long they'd been walking, but he guessed it was at least an hour. The trail that led back to the road hadn't been that far away from the cabin, so he knew they had gone the wrong way. He cursed himself for it now. He'd been in too much of a hurry to get away to pay attention to the direction of their flight. Even if there'd been a sense of the land rising or falling as they walked, he might have been able to find a way down to lower ground, but the forest remained level, no matter how far they trekked. Maybe they could stop soon, share one of the candy bars and the banana. But not yet.

The thing Sean wanted more than anything else in the world, other than to see his mother, was to lie down on the bed of pine needles and go to sleep. He hadn't slept the night before, and his hands still bled from the effort. The knife's handle had lain on the bottom step for an immeasurable time while he stared at it, angry at the blade for breaking, furious at himself for thinking it wouldn't. Eventually he had descended the stairs and picked up the handle, turned it in his hands as he studied it.

It was only then that he noticed the blade had not in fact snapped. Rather, the handle had come apart, the halves separating so that the blade came away. He worked the halves with his thumbs, noted how they flexed. Then he sat down on the bottom step, stared at the handle some more. By now, Louise had fallen asleep, and she snored on the mattress. Proper sleep, not the fever-drowse of the last day or so.

He looked back up to the trapdoor, and the blade still lodged by the third screw. A blade and a handle was all he needed, wasn't it? He simply needed a way to put them together again. At the top of the stairs, he examined the blade itself. He slipped off his T-shirt, wrapped it around his right hand, and reached for the metal. A push and a pull, and it came loose.

The blade's thick root slotted into the handle easily, so the two halves simply needed to be tightened around it. Something to tie it with. He looked at his feet and saw the laces of his shoes. Less than a minute later he was ready to tie the knife back together. But he paused for a moment. There was a better way, wasn't there?

Yes. Yes, there was.

He turned the handle sideways so that it formed an inverted T with the blade. The picture formed in his mind: the pieces bound together with his lace, maybe a little more material from his shirt to cushion his hand. It didn't take long to put together, once he'd made up his mind.

Sean set back to work, the new tool held in his fist, the blade protruding from between his fingers, most of it wrapped in cotton, only an inch or so of the tip exposed. Now he could expend less effort and dig away more wood. Even so, it took hours, but he didn't mind. Especially when he heard that glorious crack as he pushed up on the door.

At that moment he had known for certain everything was going to be all right.

Now he wasn't so sure.

He stopped, turned in a circle, looking for a break in the trees. A clearing, a building, a road. Anything at all. There was nothing else to do but walk and hope.

"Can we stop?" Louise asked.

"No," he said, his voice harder than he'd intended. "Keep up."

He reminded himself that she was still sick. The worst of the fever had gone, but it had left her weak and tired. He would give her some more antibiotics when they stopped.

"Is this the wilderness?" Louise asked.

"I guess so," Sean said.

"Don't people die in the wilderness?"

"Maybe," he said. "Sometimes."

"Are we going to die?"

"No," Sean said. "We're not."

They kept walking.

CHAPTER 44

UDRA AIMED THE GLOCK AT COLLINS' FOREHEAD. "WHERE ARE they?"

Collins stood in the clearing, her hands raised. "I left them here last night. I don't—"

"Where are my children?"

Audra stepped off the porch, advanced toward her, the pistol steady.

"I swear to God," Collins said, "I locked the door last night. They were here, I promise you, they—"

Audra's left hand lashed out, slapped Collins hard. She staggered back at the force of the blow, a red bloom on her cheek.

"What kind of animal are you?" Audra said.

Collins put her hands up once more, and once more Audra struck her. And again, this time catching her nose, drawing blood. Danny stepped back, watched with an impassive expression.

"Get on your knees," Audra said.

Collins' eyes widened. "What?"

"On your knees," Audra said, a calmness washing over her. "Right now."

Collins lowered herself to her knees, her hands up, palms facing Audra. "Whatever you're thinking about doing, please don't."

"Shut up," Audra said. "Look away."

"Please," Collins said.

Audra curled her finger around the Glock's trigger, put the muzzle against Collins' temple.

"Please don't," Collins said.

Audra looked at Danny.

"You do what you need to do," he said.

"Oh Christ, oh Jesus," Collins whispered, her hands trembling. She brought them together. "Oh God, forgive me for my sins."

A dark stain spread from the crotch of her jeans.

"Please, Jesus, forgive me. Look after my boy, Lord, please, and my mother. Please, God, have mercy on me."

Audra watched her pray, imagined the bullet tearing through this woman's head, her existence spread over the forest floor.

"Goddamn it," she said, and lifted the Glock's muzzle away from Collins' head. Then she brought it down again, slammed the butt into her skull. Audra felt the force of it up through her wrist, her arm, into her shoulder.

Collins collapsed forward, her eyelids flickering, a rivulet of dark red snaking past her ear to her jaw. She muttered something incomprehensible into the pine needles.

Danny looked at Audra from the other side of the clearing. "What now?" he asked.

Audra turned in a circle, studying the faint currents of mist between the trees. "We look for my children."

"Out here?" Danny came to her side. "They could be anywhere by now."

"Then how do we find them?"

Danny pointed at Collins, still half conscious on the ground. "We take her back to town. Hand her over to Mitchell. They can organize a search, now we know where to concentrate it."

"That's two hours back the way we came," Audra said. "God knows how long to get Mitchell and the state cops to move."

She turned in a circle once more, wondering which way they might have gone. If they knew where it was, surely they would have headed for the trail and followed it to the road? She strained her eyes, looking for something, anything.

Audra stopped. What was that? Something had snagged her eye. She turned back again, slowly, seeking it out, whatever it was. Look, look, look.

There.

A glimpse of pink against the brown carpet of needles. She lost it again as the breeze moved the lower branches of the trees, obscuring the pinpoint of color. Without a word, she set off at a run, into the trees, ducking the low branches, skipping over the roots.

Was it? Could it be?

"Audra, wait," Danny called.

She ignored him, kept running until she came to the spot. And there he was: Gogo. Pine needles clinging to his worn fur, half burying him. Audra stopped, breathless and dizzy, got down on her knees, reached for the old stuffed rabbit. The raggedy old thing, she'd wanted to throw it in the garbage so many times, but Louise wouldn't let her.

Audra brought Gogo to her nose and mouth, inhaled, let Louise's scent fill her head.

"Oh God," she said, feeling the heat in her eyes. "Oh, sweetheart, I'm coming for you."

She turned her head, saw Danny picking his way through the trees toward her.

"They went this way," she said. "We can follow them."

A noise from back in the clearing, an animal groan. Danny spun on his heels, Audra peered past him. She saw Collins stumble for the trees on the other side, her arms out for balance, wavering from side to side.

"Shit," Danny said, making after her, drawing a revolver from his waistband.

"Leave her," Audra said.

Danny slowed, but didn't stop. "The keys are in the car. She gets it, she'll leave us stranded out here."

"It doesn't matter," Audra said. "Let her go."

Danny halted, looked back to Audra.

"Look," she said. "It's Gogo. She dropped him. They went this way."

He started to walk back to her. "But how long ago?"

"Don't you see?" Audra asked, running her fingers over Gogo's fur, feeling fresh tears on her cheeks. "He's dry. Everything else is covered in dew. Gogo's dry. It means it wasn't long ago. If we follow them, we can find them."

Danny came to her, hunkered down, brushed Gogo's fur with his fingertips.

"Then I guess we'd better move," he said.

CHAPTER 45

SEAN FELT LIKE HIS LEGS COULD CARRY HIM NO FARTHER. HIS feet ached, and he could feel the moist heat of blisters inside his socks. It had become a constant struggle to keep Louise moving. It seemed every twenty yards she would demand to rest, sitting down on the pine needles, whether he told her to or not. Twice he had shouted at her, another time he had hauled her up by her arm, and each time she had cried hacking, bitter sobs.

"I don't want to be mean," he'd said, "but we have to keep walking."

And so they had journeyed for at least another hour, maybe more, the ground sometimes rising, sometimes falling. Sean had no sense of which direction they were headed, and for the life of him he couldn't remember if the sun traveled east to west or the other way around. All he could do was make a point of keeping the sun at his right shoulder, knowing at least it was one constant direction.

"I'm not walking anymore," Louise called from behind.

Sean turned to see her flop down on the ground once more. He trudged back and sat down beside her.

"All right," he said. "Five minutes, that's all. Then we need to go."

He pulled a water bottle from the bag, unscrewed the cap, and offered it to her. She took it and swallowed, before handing it back. He took a mouthful, washed it around his teeth and tongue, then stowed the bottle away.

"I'm not walking anymore today," Louise said. She ran her fingers through the browned pine needles, making small tracks.

"We have to," Sean said.

"No, we don't. We can make a camp and walk some more to-morrow."

"How can we make a camp?" he asked. "We don't have a tent."

"You can make a shelter out of branches," she said. "I saw it on TV."

"I don't know how to do that. It'll get cold out here tonight."

"Then we can make a fire."

"I don't know how to do that, either. You know, we're way up high here, like in the mountains. There might be bears. And mountain lions. Maybe wolves, I don't know."

"Shut up," Louise said, pouting.

"It's true," he said.

"No, it's not. How come I didn't see any?"

"Because they mostly come out at night. That's why we have to keep moving till we find help. We don't want to be out here when the bears and the wolves wake up."

"You're telling lies, and I'm going to tell Mom when she comes to get us."

Sean reached out, took her hand, even though it stung his raw palm. They'd held hands a lot over the last few days. He couldn't remember the last time they'd held hands. Probably not since she was a toddler.

"Listen to me carefully," he said. "You remember you asked me earlier, were we going to die out here in the wilderness? I said no, right?"

Louise nodded, sniffed, wiped her nose on her forearm.

"I was lying then," Sean said. "Truth is, we might. If we don't keep moving, if we don't find help, then we might die out here. Maybe not tonight, but tomorrow, or the next day. We'll die and we'll never see Mom again."

Louise began to cry, her face red, shoulders hitching.

"I'm not saying it just to be mean," he said. "I just need you to understand why we have to keep walking. So we can find help, some-one who can call Mom, or even take us to her. You want to see Mom again, don't you?"

Louise sniffed and said, "Yeah."

"Then we need to keep walking. You ready?"

She wiped her hand across her eyes and said, "Yeah."

"All right, then. Let's go."

Sean got to his feet, helped Louise to hers. He went to move off, but she tugged at his hand. When he turned back to her, she wrapped her arms around his middle, pressed her face into his chest.

"I love you," she said.

He embraced her and said, "I love you too."

They set off, walked hand in hand through the trees, the sun still at Sean's right shoulder. Somewhere along the way, they began to sing. Nursery rhymes, songs he hadn't sung since kindergarten, and he belted them out now, hearing his own voice echoing through the forest. Old MacDonald had a farm, ee-aye-ee-aye-o, Bingo was his name-o, and more. Sean went light-headed, not enough air for singing this high up, but he didn't care. He sang, anyway, as loud as he could.

He lost track of time as they journeyed on, so he had no idea of the hour when the trees thinned and he saw clear air up ahead.

"What's that?" Louise asked.

"Dunno," he said, quickening his step, pulling his sister behind him. He would have run if he could. Moments later, they stepped out of the trees, Sean expecting to see another clearing. But this was something entirely different.

They stood at the top of a shallow slope, weeds and grass leading down to a flat surface that went on and on. Like a frying pan, sloping sides and a flat bottom, but it wasn't round. It was more like a vague oval, and it stretched as far to his left and right as he could see. Directly in front he could see the other side of the basin, and yet more trees. Between here and there, an expanse of bald cracked earth, like some alien landscape from a space story.

"What is it?" Louise asked.

"I think it used to be a lake," Sean said. "But it's all dried up."

"Where did all the water go?"

"Dunno," he said. "Evaporated, I guess."

"I know what that is," Louise said, sounding pleased with herself. "It's when the sun sucks up all the water, then it turns to rain someplace else."

"That's right," he said. "I guess that's what happened."

A movement caught Sean's eye, off in the distance, above the trees. A great bird circling over the pines. He shielded his eyes with his hand, peered at the wide wings that barely moved as it glided in a wide arc. It seemed so far away, yet it was so big. Its body and wings a deep dark brown, its head pure white, along with its delta-shaped tail.

He pointed. "You know what that is?"

"What?"

"It's a bald eagle," he said. "I'm pretty sure it is."

"It's big," she said.

"Yeah. You know how lucky we are? They're rare. Most people never ever see one out in the wild. Look, it's going to land."

They both watched as it glided to the top of one of the tallest pines, Sean guessed at least a mile away, maybe more. The eagle slowed itself, its wings drawn up, its feet extended. The pine swayed under the weight of it, side to side.

Above the tree, high in the air, the faintest ribbon of gray, no more than a wisp.

Sean shielded his eyes, squinted, tried to focus.

Was it? Yes. Yes, it was.

"Smoke," Sean said, and a giddy laugh escaped him.

"What?"

"There's smoke. Somebody made a fire. Somebody's there."

He tightened his grip on Louise's hand, started down the slope to the dry lakebed, the ghostly finger of smoke fixed in his sight.

CHAPTER 46

T HEY MARCHED ACROSS THE STREET, SHOWALTER LEADING, A uniformed patrolman by his side. He carried the warrant in his hand. Mitchell followed, Whiteside beside her, his brain feeling like it was about to burst out through his ears. His eyes felt gritty with fatigue, and he was conscious of the jitteriness of his movements.

"Jesus, you look like shit," Showalter had said when Whiteside had arrived at the station twenty minutes before. He'd barely had time to change into his uniform and hadn't shaved. A splash of cold water on his face did no good at all.

Whiteside had been tempted to say something, maybe slap the stupid cop, but he held it in check. He knew he wasn't in his right mind and liable to make rash decisions. And he couldn't afford mistakes right now.

It had taken hours to find the key to Collins' motorcycle. He'd walked in circles, taking baby steps, shining his flashlight into the grit and the scrub, wary of finding a snake instead of the key. A rattler or a coral could make a bad situation a hell of a lot worse. It wasn't until the sun came up above the mountains that he finally saw the glint of metal in a place he had checked at least a dozen times previously. He had giggled when he found it, and he had clamped his hand over his mouth, hearing the madness in his own laughter.

He had to hold it together. Just had to.

But he could feel himself coming undone. He knew it would only take someone to pull at the right thread and he would unravel.

Hold it together, he thought.

The money was surely gone now, there was no helping that. But he was still a free man, and he meant to keep it that way. He just had to take care of a few things. The first was the woman. Once Showalter served the warrant and got her back into custody, Whiteside simply needed to find a way to get her on her own. Then he would get a strip of bed sheet, a belt, maybe even the leg of her pants, and put it around her neck, string her up to something. People killed themselves in their cells all the time. She could do the same.

But they had to arrest her first.

Showalter knocked on the front door of the guesthouse. The pale shape of Mrs. Gerber already waited on the other side of the glass, like a ghost haunting the hallway. She opened it a crack and peered out.

"Ma'am," Showalter said, "I have a warrant here for the arrest of Audra Kinney. This warrant allows me to enter these premises and—"

"She's not here," Mrs. Gerber said.

"Excuse me?"

"I came down for my breakfast this morning and found the back door open, and the gate out of the yard. I went out there and found my keys lying in the alley. Then I went back in and checked that lady's room, and she was gone. Just left everything and went."

Mitchell turned to look at Whiteside, a look of suppressed rage on her face.

Showalter waved the warrant at Mrs. Gerber. "Ma'am, you understand me and my colleagues are going to come in and search the premises, anyway, right?"

Mrs. Gerber stood back and opened the door wide. "You go on and do whatever you need to."

Showalter and the patrolman disappeared inside. Mitchell remained on the porch, hands on her hips, shaking her head. "You have any ideas as to where Mrs. Kinney might have gone?" she asked.

"Well," Mrs. Gerber said, "if you ask me, I'd say she's most likely gone to look for her children. Seems no one else is much concerned about doing it, so I suppose she might as well."

Mitchell bristled. "Mrs. Gerber, is there something you want to tell me?"

"No, nothing that comes to mind," she said, shaking her head. "Except that I know crazy when I see it, and I know a lie when I hear it. And, Sheriff Whiteside, you're not welcome on my property. Please step off my porch and onto the sidewalk."

The door closed and Whiteside turned, walked down the steps and across the street. He heard Mitchell's footsteps behind him, jogging to catch up.

"Leave me alone," he said.

"Sheriff, we need to—"

Whiteside spun around, pointed a finger at her face. "Either arrest me or leave me the fuck alone."

He left Mitchell there and made for the station, and the parking lot on the other side. Cracking, cracking, cracking, everything coming apart. The whole damn world turning to splinters and dust. He shook his head as if trying to get rid of a bothersome fly.

"Coming apart," he said aloud, before he could catch himself.

Halfway to the lot, his cell phone vibrated in his pocket, and he cried out. He grabbed for it, looked at the display: his own home number. He stopped walking. Cold sweat prickled on his forehead. He thumbed the green button.

"Who is this?"

"It's me," Collins said.

Whiteside turned in a circle, looking for Mitchell. He couldn't see her.

"What are you doing at my house?"

"I couldn't think of anywhere else to go. I can't go home. I can't go to the station."

"All right," he said. "Just wait there, stay out of sight. I'll be there soon."

He ran to the cruiser, climbed in, started the engine. The tires squealed on the pavement as he pulled out of the lot.

WHITESIDE STEERED the cruiser through the gate into his yard. Beneath the carport he saw the shape of a vehicle covered by one of his old tarpaulins. Lee's rental, he guessed. He pulled up to the bumper, walked around to the rear of his house. The screen door stood ajar. He edged up to it, put his foot on the single step, saw that the back door had been forced. It creaked as he pushed it aside and entered his kitchen.

"Where are you?" he called.

Collins stepped into the doorway from the hall. Her cheek was grazed and bruised, a trail of drying blood from a wound on her scalp that still glistened. He grabbed a towel by the sink and tossed it to her. The scent of stale urine and sweat wafted from her.

"Christ, you're bleeding all over my house," he said.

She pressed the towel to the wound. "I'm sorry, I didn't know what to do."

"What happened?"

Tears erupted from Collins' eyes. "He made me drive to town. He tied me up in the backseat and went and got Audra Kinney. Then they made me take them out to the cabin."

Whiteside felt a swelling behind his eyes, pressure in his jaw. If he hadn't put a hand on the kitchen table, he might have fallen. "You took them there?"

"I had no choice."

"You took them there?" His voice ripped at his throat.

Collins dropped the towel on a chair and took a step back into the hall. He followed her, his fists balled at his sides.

"Wait, listen. They were gone. We got there, and the trapdoor was open, and the children were gone. I don't know where they went. I would have been killed if I hadn't got away. But listen, I've been thinking it through. We have no alternative now. We have to turn ourselves in."

"Don't," he said.

"What choice do we have?" she asked as she backed farther along the hall, her voice keening.

He followed her. "Stop talking, Mary."

"There's no other way," she said.

"Shut your mouth," he said.

"We're done, whatever happens now, we're going to be caught. At least if I hand myself in, I might get some—"

He felt her nose crunch beneath his fist, felt the pain of it coursing up his arm from his hand before he knew he'd thrown the punch.

Collins went down hard. The back of her head connected with the tiled floor. She blinked at the ceiling for a few moments. Then she coughed, spat blood into the air as it coursed from her nose over her lips and cheeks.

"Fuck," Whiteside said. "Fuck me."

He pressed his palms to his temples as if to keep his mind in place, as if it might crack and crumble if he didn't hold on tight enough.

"Jesus," he said, his voice high and whining.

Collins heaved herself onto her side, then onto her stomach. She tried to get her knees under her, tried to crawl away.

Whiteside knelt down, reached for her. She slapped at his arms, but he gathered her up, held her close.

"I'm sorry," he said. "Christ, I'm sorry. I didn't mean to do that."

She coughed again, spattering his sleeves with red. Her body jerked and twisted as she tried to pull away.

"I'm so sorry," he said.

Her chin fit neatly into the crook of his elbow as he wrapped his right arm tight around her neck. His left arm curled around the top of her head. He squeezed.

"So sorry," he said.

Her body bucked, her legs kicked, hands grabbing at his arms and shoulders, nails seeking his face.

"I'm sorry."

Then she became very still, and he kissed the top of her head as his tears rolled down from his cheeks to soak into her hair.

CHAPTER 47

"**D**ID YOU LOVE HIM?" DANNY ASKED.

"I thought I did," Audra said. "And I thought he loved me, at first. I wanted it to be true. I told myself things would get better. That he'd change, but he didn't."

They each sat with their backs against either side of a tree trunk. A few minutes' rest from the relentless trek through the forest. Coming up on two hours, according to Danny's watch. Audra had grown hoarse from calling her children's names, hearing nothing back but the echo of her own voice. With the air as thin as it was up here, maybe she shouldn't have wasted her breath on shouting, but it had seemed the only sane thing to do.

With no cell signal out here, they had no choice but to keep moving. The compass app on Danny's phone had meant they could keep track of their direction. Even so, the risk of getting lost out here was great. The farther they strayed from the cabin where Sean and Louise had been held, the deeper the danger of never finding the way back. Audra had agreed to give it another hour or so, and if they didn't find anything, they'd retrace their steps, get back to the road, and hope to spot a passing car.

"Tell me about your wife," Audra said.

"Mya," Danny said. "She was a miracle. Saved my life. Without her, I'd be in prison or dead. Her and my little girl were everything I had. And those bastards took them away from me. When I find them . . ."

He didn't need to finish the thought.

"I hope you do," Audra said.

"I've spent five years thinking about it," Danny said. "How I shouldn't have let Mya go that morning. I should have begged her to stay. But I was too proud, too damn stubborn. And now they're gone and I can't ever get them back."

They fell into silence, the trees whispering all around, laced with birdsong.

Audra heard Danny sniff. She turned her head, saw his head bowed. She reached for his hand, took it in hers.

"We'll put it right," she said. "Whatever we have to do, we'll do it."

His fingers squeezed hers.

CHAPTER 48

THE DRY LAKEBED WAS WIDER THAN SEAN THOUGHT. IT SEEMED to take an age to cross it, the ground hard like rock beneath their feet. The sun had risen above the trees, and his skin prickled with the strength of it, the heat cutting through the mountain air's chill.

By the time they reached the other side, the ribbon of smoke had thickened, become darker. Sean kept hold of Louise's hand as they ascended the slope on the other side and re-entered the trees. Cold again, the sun blocked by the branches.

Sean peered up through the pines, felt a moment of panic when he couldn't find the smoke. He stopped, released Louise's hand, and turned in a circle.

"What's wrong?" she asked.

"I've lost it," he said.

"Lost what?"

"The smoke. We need to follow the smoke, but I can't find it."

He turned in a circle, his eyes to the shards of sky he could make out through the canopy. Think, he commanded. Where's the dry lake? He faced that direction. Now where was the eagle? He stretched out his arm as if it was a needle on a compass, rotated until he felt sure his fingers pointed in the right direction. Then he looked up, stared hard.

There. Thank God, there it was, the pale smear of gray in the sky.

"Come on," he said, taking Louise's hand again.

They picked their way through the trees, Sean keeping his attention on the smoke, for fear of losing it again. No matter how fast they walked, however long, the smoke seemed to come no closer. A phantom against the blue, a mirage to trick them deeper into the forest.

"Can we stop?" Louise asked after a while.

"No," Sean said. "We're almost there."

"You said that ages ago, and we're not. Can we stop and have a candy bar?"

"No," Sean said, quickening his pace, his hand tightening on Louise's. "Just a little farther, I promise."

Then he looked to the sky once more and stopped, causing Louise to stumble into him.

No smoke. He'd lost it again. Panic threatened to crack open in him. They were too far now from the dry lake to use that as a waypoint. Sean wasn't even sure whether he'd be able to find it again if they turned back.

"Shit," he said.

"You said a curse," Louise said.

"I know. Be quiet a second."

Look, look, look. He stared at the sky until his eyes ached. He dared not turn in case he lost their direction entirely. He focused and unfocused, searching for even the faintest wisp. Nothing. His gaze dropped to the ground, ready to give up, but something caught him. Something flickery orange. He looked up again, through the trees.

There it was again. Like a glowing eye blinking in the distance. A fire, he was sure of it.

Sean dropped the bag of supplies, grabbed Louise's hand, and ran, dragging her after. She shouted in protest, but he kept going, as fast as he could run while keeping her with him. Soon a clearing was in sight, a break of light through the trees.

"See it?" he asked between ragged breaths.

"No," Louise said. "Slow down!"

"Look," he said. "It's a fire."

He could see it now, a cluster of flames over the rim of a metal drum. The clearing coming closer as he ran faster and faster, the blisters on his feet forgotten. Now, in the spaces between the trees, he saw a small cabin. A pickup truck, dull red against the green.

They burst from the treeline into the clearing, and Sean halted. Louise carried on until his grip on her hand stopped her. The barrel stood in front of the cabin, a metal grille placed over the top, flames licking up through it. No one in view.

A peal of barking startled them both, and Louise came close to Sean. Around the side of the cabin came a dog, a scruffy mongrel with a shaggy black coat and bright amber eyes. The dog advanced toward them, its teeth bared. Sean pushed Louise behind him, his arms out to shield her.

"What's the matter, Constance?"

An old man dressed in weathered khaki gear walked around from the rear of the cabin, his arms full of scraps of cardboard and paper. He paused when he saw Sean and Louise at the edge of the clearing.

"Quiet, Constance."

The dog kept barking.

"I said, quiet, Constance, goddamn it."

Constance's barks lowered to a deep growl in her chest. She continued to stare at the visitors.

"Go to bed," the old man said. "Constance, go to bed, right now. I reckon these two are a little small to be coming to rob us."

Constance trotted to the cabin's porch, glancing back at Sean and Louise, and nestled down into a dog bed. The old man walked to the barrel, dropped the armful of cardboard and paper, and used a pair of tongs to remove the grille. He scooped up the garbage and dropped it into the barrel. Fresh flames and embers rippled up, and more smoke. He returned the grille to its place before turning to Sean and Louise.

"So, what are you kids doing all the way out here in the asshole of beyond?"

Sean took a step forward. The dog lifted its head and barked. The man told her to shut up, goddamn it. He turned back to Sean and said, "Speak up, boy."

"Sir, we're lost. We need help."

The old man looked from Sean to Louise and back again.

"That right? Well, then I guess you'd better come inside," he said.

CHAPTER 49

WHITESIDE STUFFED THE FEW HUNDRED DOLLARS HE HAD left into his bag. He stepped over Collins' body and left the bag by the back door. A few clothes, the little money he had. It wasn't much to show for his life.

Thoughts like that had been landing heavy on him for the last hour as he toured the house, gathering up whatever he needed to take with him. That after fifty-five years, there was nothing to show for himself. Each time the idea resurfaced, he stopped whatever he was doing and rode the wave of grief and sorrow, trying not to cry like a baby.

He had no idea where he would run to. Down to the border was the obvious choice, but once he'd crossed into Mexico, what then? Three hundred dollars and some change wouldn't get him far. But what else was left now?

His last task was to destroy any trace of his conversations on the Dark Web. His ancient laptop sat on the kitchen table. He didn't know much about these things, but he knew if the feds got hold of the computer, they would surely have everything they needed on him.

Aside from the dead body on his hall floor?

A ridiculous laugh bubbled up from his belly, and he brought a hand to his mouth. Too much of this, he thought. Madness breaking through and surfacing before he could catch it. No more. Now was not the time.

He reached for the laptop, turned it upside down, and examined the bottom. A rectangular cover fastened by a plastic catch contained the hard drive. He thumbed the catch and the cover came away. He pried the hard drive loose, detached the ribbon cable, then dropped it to the floor. His toolbox lay on the cupboard floor. He opened it, took out the claw hammer, and crouched down by the hard drive. Half a dozen sharp blows and he thought the drive was about as broken as it could be. He left the pieces on the floor and went out to the hall, stepping over Collins' corpse once more.

Whiteside stopped, looked down at her.

What to do? He could simply leave her there, knowing that Mitchell and her people would come looking for him at some point and find Collins instead. Or he could try to hide her. Maybe move her to the trunk of the rental car that was parked outside.

And what good would that do? Maybe none, but he felt it needed doing, anyway.

As he bent down to get hold of Collins' ankles, his cell phone vibrated in his pocket, causing him to cry out. He grabbed for it and looked at the display, didn't recognize the number. His thumb went to the green. He put the phone to his ear and said nothing.

After a few moments a man's voice said, "Hello?"

"Who is this?" Whiteside asked.

"Is that Ronnie?"

"Yes. Who is this?"

"Hey, Ronnie, how are you? This is Bobby McCall, up in Janus."

Sheriff Bobby McCall, pushing seventy, had served Janus County for more than forty years. He had two more deputies than Whiteside had, and a better budget.

Whiteside cleared his throat, steadied himself.

"Hey, Bobby, what can I do for you?"

"Well, I just got a call over the radio from an even older fart than me, John Tandy, up in the forest here. He has a place out in the middle of nowhere, not far from Lake Modesty, or what used to be Lake Modesty before the drought. Crazy old son of a bitch, he was a survivalist before they even had a name for that. He lives out there with his guns and knives, never leaves the place except to get supplies once a month or so. Anyway, John just called me on the radio—he's got no phone out there—and he says two kids just showed up on his front step."

Whiteside swallowed, felt a dizzy wave rush through his head. "Two kids?" he asked.

"Yessir, a boy and a girl. He says they just walked out of the trees and asked for help. Of course I thought of the trouble you're having down there in Silver Water and called the station. Couldn't get through, so I tried your cell phone. I hope you don't mind."

Whiteside leaned his forehead against the wall. "Not at all. The kids' father put out a reward and the phone lines have been jammed ever since. You did the right thing. Thank you."

"You're welcome, but the thing is, like I said, John Tandy is about as crazy an old bastard as you'll ever meet. Not two months ago he radioed to tell me there was government people, NSA or Secret Service or whatever, spying on him through the trees. A month before that, he told me there was UFOs flying over the lake, except they weren't really UFOs, they were experimental aircraft the government was testing. So, I have to say, there's a good chance old John somehow heard about the mess down there in Elder, about the two missing kids, and he's just imagined them appearing on his property. In fact, I'd say it's probable. He offered to drive them down to me, but I thought I'd check with you first, see how you wanted to play this."

"Don't let him move them," Whiteside said, too fast, too hard. He took a breath. "It's just the FBI are running this show. There's this woman Mitchell."

"Is that the black lady I saw on TV?"

"Yeah, that's her. She's a real hard-ass, needs to be in charge all the time. You know the type. She'll want to organize a team to go up there. If she finds out I let you go past her on this, she'll tear me a new one. Best to just let her handle it."

"I don't know," McCall said. "Like I said, John Tandy's a survivalist, and his cabin's full of guns from floor to ceiling. He sees feds rolling up, he's liable to come out shooting."

"Tell you what," Whiteside said, "why don't I tell Mitchell and her team to stop by your office on the way, take you with them. That way you can smooth things over with this Tandy fella."

Silence as McCall thought it over for a moment.

"Well, I guess that'd be all right," he said. "Like I told you, it's more than likely it'll be a waste of everybody's time. We'll get out there and old John Tandy'll say those kids just left ten minutes ago. But if that's the way you want to do it. You got a number I can reach her on?"

"Don't worry, I'll pass it on," Whiteside said. "Save you the trouble. You got some GPS coordinates for this place?"

"Yeah, you got a pen to hand?"

"Sure do. Go ahead."

Whiteside scribbled the numbers on the back of his hand, thanked McCall, and hung up. Then he steadied himself against the wall as a torrent of giggles rose in him. He laughed so long and so hard that his knees weakened and his head went light. When he thought he could stand it no longer, he slapped himself hard across the cheek, once, twice, three times. Clarity came back in a brutal wave.

He straightened and said, "All right. You know what to do."

Collins' body no longer mattered. They would find her soon enough, no matter what he did with her. There was a more urgent task that needed tending to.

Whiteside left the house through the front door and went to the passenger side of his cruiser. Inside, he opened the glove compartment, reached up, and found the phone. He waited while it powered up, then opened the web browser. Within a minute, he had logged in to the forum.

One new direct message:

From: RedHelper
Subject: Re: Items for sale
Message:
Dear AZMan,
Exchange will take place today at 4:00 p.m. at the aforementioned location. Once exchange has taken place, monies will be deposited to your nominated account. Please confirm.

Once again, I remind you of the importance of discretion. Security is our paramount concern.

Best wishes,
RedHelper

Whiteside hit reply:

To: RedHelper
Subject: Re: Items for sale
Message:
Dear RedHelper,
I confirm exchange today at 4:00 p.m. as discussed.
Regards,
AZMan

Whiteside sent the message, powered off the phone, then secured it beneath the dash once more. He went back to the house, fetched his bag, then returned to the car. A few minutes later, he had the coordinates McCall had given him programmed into the GPS on his main phone and was steering the cruiser out of his yard.

One hour fifty-four minutes, the route calculator said.

Less than two hours, and he'd have them back.

A few hours after that and he'd be heading south to the border, three million dollars richer.

CHAPTER 50

Private Forum 447356/34
Admin: RR; Members: DG, AD, FC, MR, JS
Thread Title: This Weekend; Thread Starter: RR

From: RR, Saturday 10:57 a.m.
Gentlemen, it's a go. Seller has confirmed handover of the goods for this afternoon, which my assistant will take care of. My driver will pick up at the airport in two groups, at 5:00 p.m. and 6:00 p.m. respectively.

And don't forget, we also have three more imported items, so plenty to go around.

Looking forward to seeing you all, my friends, and to a lovely evening.

From: DG, Saturday 11:05 a.m.
Leaving for the airport now, hope to get some sleep on the flight. I'm looking forward to seeing you all, but even more than that, I'm eager to meet the goods.

From: FC, Saturday 11:13 a.m.
Likewise. See you all soon.

From: MR, Saturday 11:14 a.m.
On my way. It's going to be a wonderful evening.

From: AD, Saturday 11:20 a.m.
I'm so glad it's all worked out. See you all there!

From: JS, Saturday 11:27 a.m.

Excellent. And thank you once again, everyone, for allowing me to join this group. I can't tell you how good it is to find like-minded people. So many times I've felt isolated and alone with this thing inside me, but not anymore.

And RR—thank you for procuring these goods. We've all seen the photos on the news, and you were quite right, they are beautiful.

CHAPTER 51

DANNY STOPPED AND LEANED HIS HAND AGAINST A TREE, HIS chest heaving. He pulled his phone from his pocket, checked the compass. As far as he could tell, they'd followed the direction they thought the children had taken in more or less a straight line. He was no Boy Scout, didn't know the first thing about tracking, but it seemed they'd given it a good shot. They'd found nothing, but they'd tried.

"We should go back now," he said, knowing she would argue.

"No," Audra said. "They're children. They can't have gone that far. We can't give up."

"It's not a question of how far they got," he said. He pushed off from the tree, came face to face with her. "They have no way to navigate. They could have veered off in any direction. Besides, it's not giving up. We go back the way we came, find the road, try to get to a town. Then we can get hold of Mitchell, tell her what's happened, and they can organize a search party. They'll have search planes, dogs, all of that. They know how to look for someone out here. We don't."

Her eyes brimmed, and she wiped the back of her hand across them. "But we're so close. They're here, I know it."

Danny took her in his arms. "The farther we go, the more time we lose. We can't just keep wandering out here. For all we know, somebody might have found them already. We need to find a town, or get to somewhere with a cell signal, then we need to call Mitchell."

"Another hour," she said. "Thirty minutes."

"No, Audra, we have to—"

Her eyes widened, and she clamped her hand over his mouth.

"Listen," she said.

He did so, heard nothing. Taking her hand away from his mouth, he inhaled, ready to protest, but she sealed his lips with her palm once more.

"Listen."

Now he heard. A rumble in the near distance. Metallic rattles. The sound of an engine rising and falling with the gears.

"This way," Audra said. "Run."

She took off through the trees, and Danny followed. Though his lungs, legs, and lower back ached, he kept pace with her, just a few yards behind. Up ahead he saw the thinning of the trees, a change in the light. A road or a trail there. The engine noise swelling.

The track—that was all it was, he could see now—rose from right to left, climbing higher into the forest. Down the slope, Danny caught a glimpse of white. A car climbing as its engine revved hard.

"Come on," Audra called, breathless, nearing the treeline.

The car came closer, and Danny saw the gold insignia, the dark-blue lettering. The blue and red lights on top.

"No," he said. "Get down."

If Audra heard, she didn't let it show. She kept her arms churning, her feet hammering on the ground. Danny dug deep and found a shred of extra speed. He cried out at the effort, reached for the back of her shirt, grabbed the tail with his fingers. She went down on her knees, and he landed hard beside her.

"What are you—"

"Wait," he said. "Look."

The car passed in front of them, the lettering clear: ELDER COUNTY SHERIFF'S DEPARTMENT. The driver with the big hands and bigger shoulders.

"Whiteside," Audra said.

"Yeah," Danny said between gulps of breath.

"Why is he here?"

"I don't know," Danny said. "But it's no coincidence."

"We have to go after him."

"Yeah, but keep to the trees. Let's go."

They followed the trail, keeping it to the right, even as the engine noise faded into the distance. They maintained a steady jog until they heard gunfire.

Then they ran.

CHAPTER 52

SEAN SAT OPPOSITE THE OLD MAN, HIS HANDS ON THE TABLE. Tiredness dragged at his eyelids, filled his head with cotton. Louise lay on a couch covered in animal furs, sound asleep, little snorts and wheezes coming from her. Occasionally she gave hard coughs that rattled in her chest.

The walls of the cabin were lined with guns suspended from hooks. Rifles, shotguns, pistols, a couple of bows, quivers of arrows, even a crossbow. Sean couldn't count how many. The old man had said his name was John Tandy. He had made the call using a radio hooked up to a car battery. The place had a low smell, as if the air hadn't moved in years.

"You doing all right, kid?" Tandy asked. He scratched his stubbled cheek. "You want a smoke?"

"No thank you, sir," Sean said.

"You want a drink?"

Sean hadn't realized until that moment how thirsty he was. The idea of some water, maybe even a soda, made him move his tongue around his teeth. "Yes, please," he said.

Tandy rose from the table, went to a box by the fireplace, and fetched two glass bottles. He brought them back to the table, popped the caps of both on the edge, then set one in front of Sean.

Beer, Sean realized.

"Sorry it ain't cold," Tandy said. "Ain't got no fridge. I'd fix you something to eat, but Sheriff McCall should be here any minute. Do me a favor when he gets here, though, would you?"

"What?" Sean asked.

"Don't tell him I had a fire going. Ain't supposed to, on account of how dry it is up here. Might burn the whole damn forest down."

"I won't tell."

Tandy winked. "Good boy."

Sean looked at the bottle. Tandy fetched a tobacco pouch from his pocket, pulled a pack of papers from it, and proceeded to roll himself a cigarette.

"Drink up," he said. "Do you good."

Sean reached for the bottle, put it to his lips, took a small mouthful. He tried not to grimace, but he couldn't help it.

"What's the matter?" Tandy asked, lighting his cigarette. "They don't got beer where you come from?"

"Not for kids," Sean said.

Tandy let out a single bark of a laugh along with a billow of smoke. "My daddy gave me my first beer when I was five, and my first cigarette when I was six. Momma never thanked him for it, mind, but I didn't complain."

Sean took another swallow. This one wasn't so bad.

"Do you live alone?" he asked.

"Yep," Tandy said. "Ever since Momma died. That was, oh, twenty years ago now. She's buried out in the yard with my daddy. Your folks still around?"

"Yes. But they got separated. We live with our mom."

"You get on with your daddy okay?"

Sean shook his head. "He doesn't really care about us."

"Sounds about right," Tandy said, taking another drag. "See, men, for the most part—except for you and me—are generally assholes. That's why I keep myself to myself."

Sean looked around the room once more. "You like guns."

"I guess you could say that. And I intend to keep them till the day I die. Any government man comes around here looking to take them, well, he's going to have a fight on his hands."

Sean took another swig of beer, not minding the taste at all now. "Government man?"

"The feds," Tandy said. He leaned across the table, spoke in an angry whisper. "They're everywhere, those bastards. Always watching me. They think I don't know it, but I do. Any one of them shows his face, he'll get two barrels of buckshot up his ass, let me tell you."

Sean giggled, though he wasn't sure why he found it funny.

"Look down there," Tandy said, pointing to the floor.

Sean saw the trapdoor there, and he didn't want to laugh anymore.

"My daddy dug that out with his bare hands, lined it with concrete, back when they thought the bomb was going to fall any day. I still keep it supplied. Enough canned food to last me a couple of years at least. The feds come around here, they'll get shot to hell, then I'll hole up in there. The government man won't get John Tandy, no way, no how."

Outside, Constance growled.

Tandy turned in his seat to look out the window.

Constance's growl turned to a steady bark.

"Sounds like Sheriff McCall finally decided to show hisself," Tandy said.

He got up from the table, went to the door, and opened it. Sean heard the engine now, rumbling as it climbed the track up to the clearing. He went to Tandy's side to see it approach. The white cruiser emerged from the shadows of the trees.

"Wait now," Tandy said. "That ain't McCall."

Sean's stomach went cold. The cruiser slowed to a halt, the engine running. Sean peered at the windshield, but he couldn't make out the driver. Tandy didn't look away from the car as he spoke.

"Son, reach over there and fetch me that rifle, there's a good boy."

Sean went to the corner, lifted the gun, felt the weight of it. An assault rifle, he thought, like the kind he'd seen in movies. He brought it back. Tandy took it from him and held it loose by his side. Sean slipped behind him, peeked around to see the cruiser.

"Step on out of the car," Tandy called. "Let me get a look at you."

A few moments passed before the driver's door opened. Constance sprang forward, hysterical barks ripping from deep inside her.

"Constance, wait," Tandy said.

The dog froze, growling.

Sheriff Whiteside climbed out, and Sean's bladder suddenly cried for release.

"No," he said.

Tandy glanced back and asked, "What's wrong?"

"Not him," Sean said. "Don't let him take us."

Tandy raised the rifle, aimed it at Whiteside's chest.

"Just hold it there, friend," he said. "I radioed Sheriff McCall, and you ain't him. State your business."

"I'm Sheriff Ronald Whiteside from Silver Water, Elder County. You may have seen it on the news. Those children have been missing for four days now, and I'm here to take them back to their mother. Maybe you could do me a favor and call off your dog."

"I ain't got no television set, so I don't much keep up with the news. Either way, the boy here tells me he doesn't want to go with you. So I guess you wasted a trip. Best just turn around now and head back where you came from."

Whiteside kept the car door between him and Tandy. "Afraid I can't do that. These children belong with their mother, and I promised her I would bring them back safe and sound. Now, let's not have any trouble."

Tandy smiled and said, "Well, friend, trouble's what you've got. Seeing as you ain't shaved in a couple of days, and you got blood on your shirt, I'd say you're up to no good. Now, you got about ten seconds to get back in your vehicle and drive away before I tell Constance to go for your throat."

The old man glanced back at Sean and spoke in a low voice. "Take your sister down into the cellar, bolt the door behind you."

Sean looked at the trapdoor. "No," he said.

"Do it right now, boy. Go!"

Sean ran to the couch, where Louise had stirred. She rubbed her eyes and asked, "What's happening?"

"We have to hide," he said, grabbing her hand and pulling her from the couch. He dragged her over to the trapdoor, let go of her hand, and took hold of the handle. The door hardly budged, no matter how hard he pulled. "Help me," he said.

Louise wrapped her hands around his, and they both hauled at the door. Now it lifted, and Sean held it long enough to see the ladder inside.

"Get down there," he said.

"No," Louise said.

"Just do it."

She mounted the top rung of the ladder and descended, her arms and legs shaking. Once she'd cleared the bottom rung, he lowered himself in, struggling to hold the door open with his shoulder while he descended. He heard Tandy say something, some final warning, before the door sealed shut. Sean felt around in the dark for the bolt, found it, slid it home.

He dropped down the last few feet as the first shots rang out overhead.

CHAPTER 53

WHITESIDE DREW HIS SERVICE PISTOL, A GLOCK 19. HE HELD it behind the door, out of the old man's sight. He didn't doubt that Tandy would plug him with the AR-15 before he could aim, let alone fire.

"Tell you what," Whiteside said. "Why don't you lower the rifle and go radio Sheriff McCall. He'll tell you he called me and told me to come up here."

"I don't think I will," Tandy said. "I don't know if you're keeping count, but those ten seconds are up, and then some. I'll give you just one more chance to be on your way. You going to take it?"

Whiteside readied himself. "I guess not," he said.

"Well, then." Tandy nodded and spat on his porch. "Constance, go get him."

The dog launched forward as if its hind legs were coiled springs. Whiteside ducked inside the car, pulled the door over, but his left foot trailed behind. The dog seized the heel of his boot, mostly grabbing the rubber sole, but a few of its teeth pierced the leather. Whiteside howled as he tried to pull his foot away, but the dog growled and shook its head from side to side, refusing to give up its prize.

Whiteside swung the door fully open, leveled the pistol at the dog's back, fired two rounds that pierced the animal between the shoulders. Through the ringing in his ears, he heard it whine, but it held on, even as its legs gave way. He kicked at its snout with his right foot, and as the dog's eyes dimmed, it finally released him.

He went to climb out of the cruiser, but a shot cut the air above his head. He dropped down low, using the door as a shield, and another round shattered the driver's window. Glass fragments showered down over his head and shoulders.

Whiteside counted off, one, two, three, picturing in his mind where Tandy stood in the doorway, the distance between them. Then up, pistol aimed through the broken window, front and rear sights aligned, and squeezed the trigger three times.

The third shot caught Tandy's right shoulder and the old man fell back into the house. Whiteside heard the thump and clatter of his body hitting the floor, followed by the rifle. Then a string of curses.

Whiteside stood upright and stepped around the car door, his Glock raised and aimed toward the cabin's dim interior. Inside, the curses had faded to low groans. Whiteside took slow, careful steps toward the cabin, veering to the left, out of sight of the doorway.

He saw a movement low to the floor inside and by reflex ducked to the side. The muzzle flash illuminated the interior for a fraction of a second, Tandy's wide eyes and bared teeth visible in the gloom. The shot went wild, the bullet shredding pine branches at the other side of the clearing.

Whiteside made a crouching run for the porch, moving out of sight of the doorway. He reached the cabin, flattened himself against the wall, beside the window, and listened.

"Goddamn you, son of a . . . son of . . ."

He edged up to the window, peered inside long enough to see Tandy use his left arm to swing the rifle around to the glass. Whiteside dropped low as the window exploded outward. He crawled forward, toward the doorway, his knees complaining at the pressure.

When he neared the edge of the doorframe, he reached around, aimed blind into the cabin and fired low to the floor three times. Silence for a few moments, only the echoes of the shots rumbling through the trees, then he heard an agonized howl. Keeping down, he crawled forward, glanced inside.

Tandy lay flat on his back, the rifle lying loose at his side. One bullet had entered through the sole of his left shoe, the second was buried in his groin, the third in his upper thigh. Yet still he breathed, a high desperate whine.

Whiteside hauled himself upright, keeping his eyes and his aim on Tandy. He stepped inside, approached the old man, and kicked the rifle away from his reach.

"Where are they?" Whiteside asked as he walked around to Tandy's right side.

"Go fuck yourself," Tandy said, his voice a weak crackle.

Whiteside placed a boot on the old man's wounded shoulder, put his weight on it. Tandy screamed.

"Where are they?"

Tandy laughed and wheezed. "You still here?" he said. "I thought I told you to go fuck yourself."

Whiteside looked around the cabin's dim interior. One open door leading to a bedroom, no sign of anyone in there. Nothing in here to hide behind.

Then he noticed the handle set into the floor.

"Never mind," he said. "I think I found them."

Whiteside held the Glock's muzzle an inch from Tandy's forehead. He didn't give the old man time to curse him again.

CHAPTER 54

AUDRA RAN AS HARD AS HER EXHAUSTED BODY WOULD ALLOW, her feet slamming into the dirt and pine needles, the cover of the treeline abandoned. Danny ran a few paces behind, his breath as sharp and even as hers was ragged. Off to the east she could make out an open expanse, the dry bed of a lake spirited away by the drought. Wherever the gunfire came from, she knew it had to be at the end of this trail.

How many shots had there been? She couldn't tell. They had come in clusters, two distinct sounds, one a hard snap, the other a boom that rolled through the trees. The last shot she'd heard had a terrible finality about it, like settled business.

The trail seemed to climb forever, and Audra's lungs felt as if they would burst from her chest. Her thighs weakened as they screamed for oxygen, and her stride faltered. She stumbled, her arms cartwheeling as her momentum carried her forward, but Danny's hand grabbed her upper arm, kept her upright, kept her moving.

"There," he said, the word snatched between breaths.

He pointed to a smaller trail that branched off, a clearing with a cabin and cars visible through the trees. Audra allowed him to guide her that way, and somehow, from somewhere, she found a reserve of energy that propelled her forward.

As they reached the clearing, Audra started to call her children's names, her mouth open wide, but Danny silenced her with his palm across her lips. He took her arm, forced her to stop.

He pointed to his eyes, then his ears. Look. Listen.

They both moved to the treeline, keeping low and watchful. Whiteside's cruiser stood facing the front of the cabin, its trunk open. A dog lay in blood and glass fragments by the driver's door. Lazy smoke curled from the remains of a fire in a barrel to the side of the property. The cabin's front door stood ajar, one of the windows shattered.

Danny went ahead, crouching as he advanced, keeping the cruiser between him and the cabin. Audra followed, keeping low. She reached for the pistol she had stowed in her waistband. Danny paused by the open driver's door, peered through the space where the window had been. Glass crunched under Audra's feet as she joined him.

"Look," he whispered. "In the doorway."

Audra peered into the gloom and saw a man's feet, and she knew it was the body of whoever lived here. Then she heard a low grunt from inside, followed by muttered curses. She looked at Danny, and he nodded, yes, he heard it too. He pointed to the right end of the building, the one with the window intact, then gestured to the ground, telling her to stay low.

Danny moved to the rear of the cruiser, around the back and along the passenger side, Audra close behind. He watched the doorway for a few moments before setting off at a crouching run to the cabin. He stopped short of the porch, then stepped onto it, one foot at a time, slow as he could move.

More curses and grunts from inside.

Danny waved at Audra to come to him. She took a breath, then ran, her head down. She reached the porch, looked at the wooden boards, and wondered how she would cross them without a thunderous creak. Danny beckoned her once more, and she crossed the porch in two light strides, barely a sound.

"Come on," the voice inside growled.

Audra heard a loud, hard cracking sound followed by a metallic rattle. Then a rhythmic crunching, accompanied by chesty grunts. She eased up and looked through the window. A bedroom, a simple metal-framed single bed at the center, a bare minimum of furniture. Danny inched toward the door, the whisper of his movement masked by the noise from within, Audra at his back.

When they reached the door, Danny eased himself upright, and

Audra stepped around him, copying his stance, the Glock raised and ready.

Inside, on his knees, Sheriff Ronald Whiteside, his shirt spattered with blood, pried at a trapdoor with a crowbar, sweat beading on his forehead, his teeth gritted. He did not notice them, his world centered on the task of opening the door, which he had almost accomplished.

One last crack, and whatever held it closed from within gave way. Whiteside gave a triumphant roar, swapped the crowbar to his left hand, grabbed the handle, and hauled the door open.

"Whiteside," Danny said.

The sheriff's eyes widened as he swiveled to the sound of his name. His right hand grabbed for the pistol on the floor. Danny squeezed off a shot, but Whiteside dropped down to his belly as the bullet cut a hole in the wall.

The pistol in his grasp, he rolled to the side, into the mouth of the basement, and disappeared.

CHAPTER 55

WHITESIDE TUMBLED DOWN INTO THE DARK. BY INSTINCT, HIS left hand released the crowbar and reached out, his fingers slapping against a rung of the ladder, grabbing the next. As the crowbar clanged on the floor, his weight wrenched at his shoulder. His fingers lost their grip and the hard floor slammed into his back. He cried out at the pain.

Above, footsteps running across the floor, then Lee appeared at the edge. Whiteside raised his Glock and fired twice up into the light, and Lee was gone. He rolled onto his side, into the shadows, then up onto his knees.

"Christ," he said, the sibilant hissing through his teeth.

Pain shrieked from his back, threatened to blot out all else, but he willed it to be quiet. He had no use for it now. Suppressing another cry, he forced himself up onto his feet. He backed away from the square of dim light the open trapdoor projected onto the rough concrete floor.

His heel caught the crowbar on the floor and he stumbled back. Something loose and heavy bumped and rolled around the rear of his head. He reached up for it, found a flashlight suspended from a beam in the ceiling. Holding on to it, he turned a circle in the darkness, his eyes scanning the shades of black. He pressed the power switch and a sharp beam cut through the dimness, throwing wild shadows around the basement as the flashlight swayed on its cord.

His gaze swept across the rows of canned food, the piled blankets and clothes, the chemical toilet. There, behind a stack of boxes at the rear of the room, the boy and the girl. Whiteside staggered toward them, the Glock aimed at the girl's chest.

He grabbed for both of them. The boy struggled, but Whiteside slapped him hard across the head. He dragged the boy by the collar out onto the open floor, then reached for the girl and did the same. His free arm swept around them as they squealed, gathered them close. He aimed the Glock up at the trapdoor.

"Mom!" the boy shouted.

"Shut up," Whiteside said. "Be quiet or I'll kill you all."

The woman's head appeared in the opening, peering down at them. The boy shouted for her again.

"Listen to me," Whiteside called. "You and your friend get out of here or I'll take your children's heads off."

Her face slipped away from the opening, and for the briefest of moments Whiteside thought she had heeded his warning. Then her feet dropped down and found the ladder.

From above, "Audra, no."

She climbed down, unarmed. Whiteside leveled the pistol at her as she descended. When she reached the bottom, she turned to face him, her eyes blazing as the flashlight beam danced between them. Lee's face appeared above once more.

"Audra, what—"

"Stay there," she said. "If he tries to leave this basement, shoot him dead."

"Audra, listen to—"

"Just do it," she said, taking a step closer.

"You best back off," Whiteside said. "I'm taking these children, and that's all there is to it."

"No," Audra said, stepping forward. "You won't take them from me again."

Whiteside backed away, bringing the boy and girl with him, his left arm still wrapped around them both.

"Goddamn it," he said, his voice resonating between the concrete walls, "stop right there."

"Sean, Louise," she said, "you're going to be all right."

"Shut up," he said, stabbing the pistol's muzzle in her direction. "I'm taking them with me. Don't make me hurt them. I killed Collins. I killed the old man. You better believe I will kill again, if you push me."

She moved closer yet and said, "Let my children go."

Whiteside felt a hysterical laugh rise up to his throat, but he swallowed it.

"Listen to me," he said. "There's a man will pay me a million dollars a child. Three million for a pair. Now, you can plead and you can beg and you can threaten all you want. But there ain't a word you can say that's worth more than three million dollars. Is there?"

Audra stooped down and reached for the crowbar on the floor. It scraped on the concrete as she lifted it and straightened. She held it loose at her side.

"One last time," she said. "Let my children go."

Whiteside looked at the crowbar in her hand. "What are you going to do with that?" he asked.

She looked him hard in the eye and a finger of cold fear touched his heart.

Then Audra swept the crowbar up and across, slamming it into the flashlight. It careened across the basement, its bulb flickering out as it went.

CHAPTER 56

AUDRA SAW THE BRILLIANT MUZZLE FLASH AS SHE THREW herself to the floor, felt the pressure of the discharge in her ears. Through the whine she heard small feet sprint away into the dark and then a hoarse, angry cry.

She got to her knees, kept low as she advanced into the black.

Another muzzle flash, this time aiming in the direction the footsteps had run. She held her breath through the sound of pulverized concrete crumbling to the floor until she heard the footsteps again, running to the far end of the room.

Whiteside fired again, and she felt the bullet zip past her head. She dropped down onto her stomach, remained still as cans fell and rattled, liquid glugging out of a container. The sheriff screamed in rage, his voice rising to a piercing shriek.

Audra crept forward on her belly, her eyes locked on the point of the last muzzle flash, the crowbar held off the floor for fear of giving herself away.

"Goddamn you," Whiteside shouted. "Goddamn you to hell."

The voice above her head, she fixed its position. Another few inches, coarse concrete scraping her elbows and knees.

"Goddamn you," he said again, his voice withered down to a high keening.

Audra got to her knees, swung the crowbar, putting her shoulders behind it. The metal connected with bone, and Whiteside screamed. She heard his body slam into the floor and she rose, the crowbar over her head, ready to bring it down on any part of him it could find.

She saw the flash once more, beneath her now, and felt something hot tug at her shoulder. Before her mind could register the pain, she swung the crowbar hard, felt something break as it struck. A rattle as the pistol skimmed across the concrete, a clang as she lost her grip on the crowbar, and another cry of pain.

Audra roared, an animal fury erupting from the heart of her. She straddled him and raised her fists, brought them down, raised them, brought them down, again and again, each blow sending shocks up through her wrists and elbows and shoulders. She heard the pounding of flesh, and it sounded like music, and she laughed and laughed until she had no air left in her lungs.

Someone cried, stop, stop, please stop, but the voice was far away in the darkness, a pathetic whimpering that meant nothing to her.

A flash of lightning filled the room, a brilliant flickering, and she saw Whiteside below her, his arms raised up to protect his face. Then a slapping and rattling sound, more flashes, making it appear as if Whiteside danced under her, all jerking movements and slashes of red.

"Mom," Sean said.

She froze, her bloody fists above her head, and turned to her son's voice.

There, across the room, the flashlight in his hands, his sister by his side. He shook the flashlight, smacked it against his palm, trying to keep the bulb alive.

"Mom, stop," he said.

Behind them came Danny, the revolver aimed at Whiteside.

Audra dropped her hands. She crawled off Whiteside's body, toward her children, onto her knees, stretched her arms out wide. They came to her, the hot damp skin of their faces pressing into hers, her arms swallowing them up, their bodies joining together.

She wept as the flickering light danced around them.

CHAPTER 57

THE SUN HAD CLIMBED HIGH ABOVE THE TREES AND WASHED the clearing with warm light. She felt the heat on her skin and relished it. Of all the things that should have been important to Audra at that moment, the sun in the sky should have been the least. But still, there it was.

Whiteside sat on the porch, his bleeding head bowed, his swollen right arm cradled in his lap, his left bound to it at the wrists by his own handcuffs. He had screamed at the pain as Danny had forced his broken arm into place. Now he trembled, sweat mixing with the blood from his nose and lips, forming pale-red streams down his chin.

Sean stood watching him. He'd asked if he could have a pistol to hold on Whiteside, to guard him. For a moment, Audra had doubted if her boy would have the nerve to aim a weapon at another person. Then she saw a new coldness in his eyes and she knew different. The realization had caused an ache in her heart that still echoed through her. Even so, she told him no. Whiteside wasn't going anywhere.

Danny had found an old first-aid kit in the cabin's basement and now he tended to the wound on Audra's shoulder as Louise lay curled in her lap. Just a graze, he said, but it hurt like hell when he sprayed it with antiseptic. He packed the wound with gauze and pressed tape over the area to seal it in.

"You'll be fine," he said. "It'll need to be stitched when we get back to civilization, but you'll survive till then."

Danny went to stand up, but Audra said, "Hey."

He crouched down next to her again.

"Thank you," she said. "I owe you . . . everything."

He reached to her, brushed his fingers against her cheek. "Just take care of them. That'll be enough."

As Danny got to his feet, Audra beckoned to her son. Sean came to the porch and nestled in next to his mother. It caused a flare of pain for Audra to lift her arm and put it around him, but she did it, anyway. She kissed the top of his head as he leaned into her.

Danny approached Whiteside, put one foot on the porch next to him, bent down to speak.

"Where and when was the exchange?" he asked.

"Fuck you," Whiteside said.

Danny punched his devastated arm, and Whiteside squealed.

Louise buried her face in Audra's bosom, but Sean watched. Audra pulled him in tight, guided his face away with her hand.

Danny took a knife from the sheath hooked to his belt, the one he'd taken from the old man's cabin wall. He held it before Whiteside's eyes, sunlight glinting on the metal. Then he grabbed the sheriff's left ear, readied the blade.

"Tell me," he said, "or I'll show you why they call me Knife Boy."

"Four o'clock," Whiteside said through his teeth. "Halfway between Las Vegas and here. At a closed-down shopping mall off I-40."

Danny released Whiteside's ear and said, "That's what, two hours away?"

"About that."

Danny looked at his watch, went quiet for a moment, then said, "It's two, maybe two and a half hours back to Silver Water. We should go. Hand this piece of shit over to Mitchell."

"No," Audra said.

Danny looked at her, confused. "What?"

"The exchange is two hours northwest of here at four p.m."

"So he says."

"What time is it now?" she asked.

Danny looked at his watch again. "One-forty."

"I can handle Whiteside," Audra said. She looked at the battered and rusted truck parked beside the cabin, then back at Danny. "Just help me get him into the cruiser and I'll take him back. There'll be a cage between him and us. He can't hurt us anymore. You take the pickup and go to the exchange. Find those men. Then you ask them the question you asked the others, those cops who took your little girl."

Danny held her stare for a moment, then turned his eyes away. "I already know the answer."

"No, you don't," Audra said. "Not for sure."

He exhaled, a quivering sigh. "Maybe I don't want to know. Maybe I've got used to the idea of never finding those men."

"I don't think that's true," Audra said. "You won't have peace until you know."

"And if I ask them, and they don't give me the right answer . . ."

He returned his gaze to hers and she realized he sought her permission, as if it could ever be hers to give.

"Then you do what you have to do," she said.

CHAPTER 58

DANNY WATCHED THE BLACK SUV ENTER THE EMPTY PARKING lot through the grime on the pickup truck's windshield. He checked his wristwatch: five minutes to four. He had arrived almost fifteen minutes before that. The old pickup had rattled and wheezed so much along the way that he'd feared it might not survive the journey. It didn't matter now. If things went as he planned, he wouldn't need the truck again.

The parking lot sprawled for hundreds of yards in all directions, its asphalt bleached pale gray by the sun. Half a mile from the interstate, it should have been jammed full of cars, shoppers coming and going with their money and their bags. Instead, the mall buildings huddled together like abandoned children. A property deal gone bad, no doubt a victim of the economic crash. Someone lost his shirt over this, Danny thought.

The SUV crawled across the parking lot toward his position. With its tinted windows, he couldn't make out the occupants. Even with the dirt on the pickup's glass, they would see him long before he saw them. He had arranged a pile of blankets on the passenger seat to give the impression someone might be huddled there. The assault rifle he had taken from the dead man's floor lay within his reach.

Would he die today?

Danny thought he might. And he didn't mind. So long as he did what needed doing. So long as he found out what he needed to know. So long as they paid.

The SUV stopped, facing the pickup, ten yards away. Danny waited and watched. So did the occupants of the SUV. He reached across to the passenger seat, pulled the rifle across his lap, the grip snug in his palm, his finger against the trigger guard. Going by his watch, a full minute passed before anything happened.

At last, the driver's door of the SUV opened. More seconds passed before a large man with a shaved head and a black suit eased his bulk out of the car. Leaving the door open, he took slow steps toward the pickup. Danny counted them as he approached, judging the time it might take the other man to run back to the SUV if he fled. The big man stopped halfway between the vehicles, his open hands by his sides, his weight on both feet.

Danny wound down the driver's window. The man tilted his head, squinting as he listened to the creak of the lowering glass. Another few seconds of silence. The man glanced back over his shoulder at the SUV, returned his gaze to the pickup.

Danny thought: Now.

He threw the door wide open, slipped out of the truck, hoisted the rifle up, and aimed it through the open window. The big man's eyes widened and he made a panicked grab for the holster beneath his suit jacket.

"Don't," Danny called.

Maybe the man didn't hear. Maybe he thought he could draw and aim fast enough. It didn't matter either way, because the burst of rifle fire put him on his back, his pistol clattering across the asphalt.

Danny didn't hesitate. He stepped around the open door and marched toward the SUV, ignoring the desperate gurgles and gasps of the man he had put down. As he neared the SUV, he heard a woman's breathless voice.

"Oh God," she said, "please God, no, no, no, oh God, no, oh God . . ."

He slowed as he neared the still-open driver's door. Peering inside, he saw the woman, her body stretched over the cup holders and armrest, the pants pocket of her navy-blue business suit snagged on the gearstick, her hands on the steering wheel as she tried to drag herself across. Around forty, long red hair tied back to tame the curls. She blinked up at Danny.

"Please don't kill me," she said.

Danny looked into the rear of the car, saw no one else. "Where were you going to take them?" he asked.

"Las Vegas," the woman said. "There's a party. A house in Summerlin."

She told him the name, the owner of the house, the ringleader, and Danny pictured the face. An Internet billionaire, known for his philanthropy as well as his money.

"Five years ago," Danny said. "Do you remember a little girl? Six years old. Black hair, dark eyes."

The woman shook her head as she let go of the steering wheel. "I don't know," she said. "There've been so many."

Danny pressed the rifle's muzzle against the top of her head. She closed her eyes tight.

"I don't remember, I'm sorry, please don't, please, please don't . . ."

"Take me there," he said.

She opened her eyes, steadied her breathing, and asked, "Will you let me live?"

"We'll see," Danny said.

CHAPTER 59

A UDRA DROVE, THE WIND THROUGH THE SHATTERED WINDOW blowing her sweat-soaked hair back, cooling her forehead. Sean and Louise huddled together in the passenger seat, both of them sound asleep. Whiteside in the rear, the metal cage between him and them. In the mirror, she saw him slumped against the door, his eyes hooded, his mouth slack. Bloody sputum trailed from his lips.

She had taken Whiteside's phone and used its GPS to find her way back to Elder County. Two hours she'd been driving, another twenty minutes to go. The wound on her shoulder burned and itched every time she moved, but she didn't care. All she wanted in the world now was to crawl into a bed with her children and sleep with them in her arms.

Another few minutes and she saw the sign for Silver Water. Audra slowed the car, pulled in, and applied the hand brake. Up ahead, on the other side of the exit, was the spot where Whiteside had stopped her just three days ago.

"Collins was right."

His voice startled her. She looked up to the mirror, saw him staring back, his eyes glistening.

"About what?" she asked.

"I should've killed you," he said.

"But you didn't. Even if you had, you would have wound up back here, anyway. Even if you got all that money, it would've cursed you. You know that, don't you?"

He looked away from the mirror, then back again. "Will you do one thing for me?" he asked.

"What?"

Whiteside exhaled, a watery sigh. A tear rolled down his bloody cheek.

"Kill me," he said. "Just put a bullet in my head and dump me out here."

Now Audra looked away, turned her gaze to the rolling desert, the distant mountains, the ocean of blue above.

"I know you want to," he said.

She looked back to the mirror, locked eyes with him. "Yeah, I want to. But I'm not going to. Don't worry, you'll get your due."

Audra turned the key in the ignition, put the car into drive, and set off once more. She made the turn into the exit, climbed the winding road, remembering being in the back of this same vehicle, behind that same cage, no idea of what lay ahead of her. A deep sorrow took hold of her as she crested the rise and began the descent into the basin on the other side.

The same switchbacks, the same clusters of houses, the same desperate poverty as just a few days ago, but all different now. She knew that nothing would be the same again, not for her, not for her children.

Whiteside sniffed and whimpered in the rear of the car as she approached the bridge across what was left of the river, crossed it, and entered Silver Water. He banged his head on the glass once, twice, three times, leaving a smear of blood there.

Audra eased the cruiser along Main Street to the far end, where state police cars stood outside the sheriff's station and the town hall. Press trucks parked along the street, reporters milling around, bored expressions on their faces. She stopped the car in the middle of the street and shut off the engine. Then she put her hand on the center of the wheel, pressed down on the horn, held it there until the cops and the reporters raised their heads. She opened the driver's door, let it swing out as far as its hinges would allow.

One of the state cops saw Audra, said, "Jesus Christ, it's her."

She hauled herself out, fighting her own exhaustion. The same cop saw the Glock in her hand, drew his own pistol.

"Drop the weapon!"

The other cops came running, all of them drawing guns. A dozen of them, maybe more. A chorus of shouts, get down on the ground, drop the weapon. Audra raised her hands above her head, kept the Glock in her right, her finger away from the trigger. But she wasn't ready to give it up. Not yet.

The reporters scrambled, cameras pointing. The cops moved in, tightening the circle. The chorus got louder. On the ground. Drop the weapon. They would have shot her dead, if not for the cameras, Audra was sure. She should have been terrified, but an oily calm had settled on her as soon as she'd stopped the car. Even a dozen pistols aimed at her, ready to take her head off, couldn't shake the cool peace at the center of her.

Another voice rose over the others, and Audra recognized it: Special Agent Mitchell.

"Hold your fire! Don't shoot! Do not shoot!"

She pushed her way between the cops, breathless, her eyes wide.

"Audra, give me the weapon."

"Not yet," Audra said as she stepped back to the rear door, her hands still raised. With her left she reached for the handle, pulled the door open. Whiteside spilled out, shoulder first, not quite hitting the ground. Audra grabbed his collar, hauled him the rest of the way. He cried out in pain as he tumbled onto the asphalt.

Mitchell shook her head. "Jesus, Audra, what did you do?"

"This man took my children," Audra said, raising her left hand once more. She walked to the front of the car, slow steady steps.

The cops lined their sights on her, some shouting again.

"Hold your fire," Mitchell called.

Audra rounded the front of the cruiser to the passenger side and opened the door. Sean had stirred, but Louise still dozed.

Mitchell moved to the side of the car, stared inside. "Oh my God," she said. She spun around, shouted at the cops. "Lower your weapons. Lower them right now."

One at a time, slowly, the cops did as they were told. Mitchell turned back to Audra, extended her hand.

"Give me the gun," she said. "Please."

Audra didn't hesitate. She lowered her hands and passed the pistol over. Mitchell popped the magazine, emptied the chamber.

Audra hunkered down by the open passenger door. She reached in, stroked Sean's hair, touched Louise's cheek. Louise's eyes flickered open.

"Mommy," she said. "Are we home?"

"Not yet, honey," Audra said. "But soon. Come on."

She reached in, took Louise in her arms, and lifted her out. Sean followed. With Louise's arms around her neck, legs around her waist, Sean's hand in hers, Audra walked through the cops and the reporters. She ignored the wide eyes and open mouths, the shouted questions.

Down the street, the guesthouse door stood open, Mrs. Gerber waiting there, her hands over her mouth, tears in her eyes.

Mitchell came running behind. "Audra, where are you going?"

Audra looked back over her shoulder without slowing her step.

"To put my children to bed," she said.

CHAPTER 60

W HEN THEY REACHED THE HOSPITAL IN SCOTTSDALE, THE nurses had tried to separate them, put them in different rooms. Audra had refused, clung tight to Sean and Louise. It was Mitchell who stepped in, insisted that the hospital provide a private room for the three of them. The best they could do was a side ward with two beds.

One now lay empty, Audra and her children huddled together in the other. They'd given Louise another dose of antibiotics, and now she lay with her head on Audra's left breast, snoring softly. Sean rested on the other side, watching the television up on the wall.

Audra had grown tired of the news cycle. The same shaky footage of her circling the car, Whiteside falling from it, the children in the passenger seat. The reporters had exhausted their hyperbole, and the story had taken on the sense of winding down, that it was ready to be told in past tense.

The only new footage in the last hour or so had been Patrick helping his mother into a black town car outside a hotel, telling the reporters no comment as they crowded around.

When it was all settled, Audra would have a comment for them. When the press came scrounging for her story, she would tell them every rotten thing her husband and his mother had done. Let their rich and powerful friends see them for who they really were. She relished the idea, but it was for another time.

Audra reached for the remote control, was about to switch the TV off when the anchor's tone changed. He studied a sheet of paper that someone had placed in front of him.

"Leaving events in Silver Water for a few moments," he said, his words faltering as he read, "we have a breaking report of multiple deaths in a mass shooting at a luxury home in the Las Vegas suburb of Summerlin. The name of the homeowner has not yet been made public, but we're told he is a very prominent, very wealthy public figure in the tech industry. Details are sketchy, but it appears one or more gunmen entered the secluded property sometime between six and seven p.m. and opened fire on the occupants. The number of casualties is unclear at the moment, as is the fate of the shooter, or shooters. What we do know is that all the victims were adults, and the lives of three young children were spared. More on this breaking story as we get it."

The anchor moved on to a political rally in Washington, D.C., protestors marching along a city street, waving placards and chanting. Audra switched the television off.

"Was that Danny?" Sean asked.

"I don't know," Audra said.

"I hope he . . ."

Sean couldn't finish the thought, the idea too big for him.

"Me too," Audra said.

She kissed Sean's head, took in the smell of him, still pure despite the hot shower he'd had earlier.

Mitchell had accompanied Audra inside the guesthouse, let her put the kids down for a sleep while they talked out in the corridor. Whiteside had been arrested on the spot; they'd been looking for him since Collins' body had been found at his home that afternoon. Now he was somewhere in the same hospital, having his arm set and his other wounds tended to. Audra had made Mitchell swear not to let him take his own life. Make sure he stood trial for what he'd done. He would be placed on suicide watch, Mitchell had assured her.

The days ahead would be difficult; Mitchell had warned Audra of that, even though she didn't have to. The questions would be unending, the authorities and the press lining up to squeeze every drop of information from her. But for now the world was quiet. She savored the peace while she could.

"Will we still go to San Diego?" Sean asked.

"I don't think so," Audra said.

"Will we go back to New York?"

"Do you want to? Your father's there."

Sean thought about it for a moment, then said, "No, I don't want to go back there."

"Me neither," Audra said.

"So where will we go?"

He turned his head to look up at her and she saw the man behind his eyes.

"I don't know," Audra said. "But we'll figure it out. Together."

Acknowledgments

Many and various people helped me beat this novel into shape, and I owe them all my gratitude:

My agents Nat Sobel, Judith Weber, and all at Sobel Weber Associates who have worked so hard for me and given me such tremendous support, along with the ever-excellent Caspian Dennis at Abner Stein.

Nathan Roberson, Molly Stern, and all at Crown; Geoff Mulligan, Faye Brewster, Liz Foley, and all at Harvill Secker and Vintage Books; thank you for taking a chance on my novel.

Three individuals provided invaluable assistance in researching this book, and I owe each of them several beers: my old friend and excellent author Henry Chang, who helped me bring Danny Lee to life; John Doherty of Northern Arizona University, who took me on a road trip around the state, the details of which are threaded through these pages; LAPD Detective Jim McSorley, who kept me right on the legal stuff. Any errors or liberties taken with reality are entirely my doing.

A special thanks to my many friends in the crime-fiction community whose friendship and support keep me afloat.

And my family, without whom this book would not exist.

About the Author

HAYLEN BECK is a pseudonym for award-winning crime author Stuart Neville, whose string of Irish-set thrillers has garnered critical acclaim around the world.